**“Is this Buckleber**



Dalia felt a smile comin
hold it back. “Sure is.”

“Whoa! What is he now, twenty? He looks amazing! What’s your secret, huh, buddy?”

Tony’s voice sounded all high and sweet, like it had that day in the barn with the kittens. He’d always been almost goofily affectionate with animals.

“Remember when I rode him?” Tony asked.

Their eyes locked across Buck’s back. In an instant, the years fell away and they were eighteen again, Tony in yet another graphic T-shirt with the state of Texas on it, Dalia pulling him to his feet and brushing the dust off him, both of them stumbling and laughing and falling into each other’s arms.

She couldn’t hold back the smile anymore...but she turned her head to hide it.

Dear Reader,

Memory is a funny thing. It can be vague and hazy, barely more than an impression, or as strong and vivid as the real thing. Either way, memory doesn't always line up with the way things really happened. Maybe we didn't know the whole story and filled in the blanks with whatever made sense to us. And if there's no one around to set us straight, our faulty memories just get stronger over time.

Which brings us back to Limestone Springs, and to Tony and Dalia. Long before they helped Dalia's friend Lauren find her way out of heartbreak to the love she needed in *Hill Country Secret*, they had their own story—a shared history, carved into the very boards of the old ranch house at La Escarpa. Dalia hardly has a single memory of home that Tony isn't mixed up in somehow. But something drove them apart, the way hurricane-force winds shattered Dalia's home—and Dalia's memory of what happened has taken on a life of its own.

But in Limestone Springs, friends and neighbors help each other out. Storms may come, but broken things get rebuilt. And in the end, the truth shines bright.

Enjoy your stay.

*Kit*

# HEARTWARMING

# *Coming Home to Texas*

---

*Kit Hawthorne*

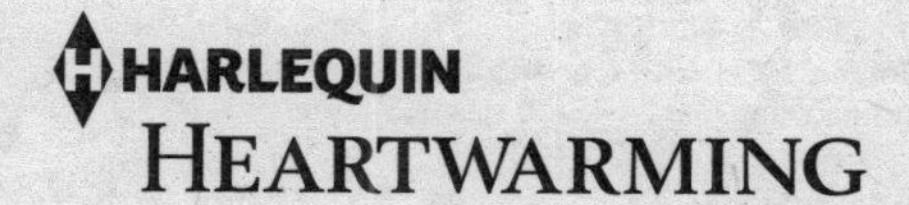

ISBN-13: 978-1-335-17977-7

Recycling programs for this product may not exist in your area.

Coming Home to Texas



This edition published by arrangement with Harlequin Books S.A.

For questions and comments about the quality of this book, please contact us at CustomerService@Harlequin.com.

Harlequin Enterprises ULC
22 Adelaide St. West, 40th Floor
Toronto, Ontario M5H 4E3, Canada
www.Harlequin.com

**Printed in U.S.A.**

**Kit Hawthorne** makes her home in south-central Texas on her husband's ancestral farm, where seven generations of his family have lived, worked and loved. When not writing, she can be found reading, drawing, sewing, quilting, reupholstering furniture, playing Irish pennywhistle, refinishing old wood, cooking huge amounts of food for the pressure canner, or wrangling various dogs, cats, goats and people.

**Books by Kit Hawthorne**

**Harlequin Heartwarming**

***Truly Texas***

*Hill Country Secret*

To my husband, Greg, who has been patiently explaining football to me for close to thirty years now. You taught me that all that running around on the field actually means something, that every game has its complexities of character, backstory, motive, conflict, resolution—basically all the components of a good story. Like most things, football is a lot more interesting when I have you to talk it over with.

**Acknowledgments**

Many thanks to all those who answered my technical questions for this story: Dr. Mark Berry, Isaac Dehoyos, Grace Midkiff, Greg Midkiff and Wes Short. I'm grateful for your generosity with your wisdom and time.

## *CHAPTER ONE*

The red-checked kitchen curtains hung askew, waterlogged and specked with dirt. Indoors and outdoors were all mixed together, with glass shards and china fragments scattered over what was left of the porch, and tree leaves covering the kitchen counters. The rafters didn't look quite ready to fall down, but daylight shone through where the metal roof had peeled back like the lid off a sardine can. The little kitchen table where Dalia and Marcos used to jostle each other for space while doing homework was smashed to kindling beneath the porch swing, which had been driven straight through the window by hurricane-force winds—and the porch swing itself wasn't looking too good. A calico barn cat perched on its remains, licking herself.

This was Dalia's first good look by daylight. She'd arrived last night, three days after the storm, and she'd been hoping against hope that the damage would turn out to be not so bad after all, but no. Her mother's kitchen, the emotional center of her childhood home, lay in ruins.

So did Dalia's routine, for that matter. She longed for her own controlled, streamlined environment, where everything was where it belonged and she knew just what to expect. The loss of that felt like a physical ache, or caffeine withdrawal.

Her mom hobbled over on her crutches. "Can you believe this mess? I never in my life heard a wind like that one. It was like a freight train inside a tornado."

She didn't have to sound so gleeful about it, Dalia thought resentfully. She *liked* having such an exciting story to tell, and a captive audience to tell it to. Dalia had heard it all before, over the phone and in person.

"What are you even doing up, Mom? It's not safe for you to be walking around here. This place is a disaster area."

"I know! Isn't it awful? The cleanup alone is going to take days. There's so much to do, I don't even know where to begin—and with the FFF just two weeks away."

Ah, yes—the firefighter fundraiser. Dalia had been getting an earful about that, as well.

"Why not cancel the FFF this year?"

Her mom looked at her as if she'd said, *Why not stop breathing oxygen this year?*

"Or, you know, put it off," Dalia added quickly.

"We can't. There's a reason we do it on that exact weekend in September. August is the Persimmon Festival, and everyone needs a few weeks to recover from *that*, and anyway, the FFF has to be in the fall for the pumpkin patch and corn maze to make any sense. But October is the county fair and Oktoberfest, and then Halloween, and the next thing you know it's November and you're right in the thick of the holidays. No, we can't change the date."

"Well, then let someone else host it for a change."

"But we've hosted the firefighter fundraiser at La Escarpa for five years in a row! It's never even been held anyplace else."

"All the more reason for someone else to take a turn."

Her mom shook her head. "We're the ones who're set up for it. It's not like we can move the corn maze or the football field. We have the big cleared space for the tent, and most of the tables and things are stored in our tool barn."

Dalia poked a lump of soggy insulation with the toe of her boot. "I understand that, Mom, but something's got to give. If you can't do it, you can't do it—that's all. It's not your fault. It's just how things are. You can't help it that your house got wrecked by a storm."

"Lots of people suffered storm damage. And the firefighters helped us all through it. They went right out into the teeth of it to rescue people—and now it's our turn to support them. They *need* this fundraiser. They're all volunteers, and their expenses aren't covered by taxes. Most of their operating funds for the year come from what we raise at this one event."

Dalia sighed. Her mom was right, of course. If the roles were reversed, Dalia would be making the same arguments. But her stomach sank as she saw the weeks of her visit to Texas unfurling longer and longer in her mind.

It wasn't the work itself that was the problem. Dalia didn't mind hard work. She'd gladly rebuild the kitchen herself if she had the carpentry skills… But she didn't. All she could do in this case was facilitate things—run the household, take care of her mother, keep on top of the builders. The whole process was going to involve a lot of coffee and tea, a lot of poring over magazine pictures and catalog pages, debating the merits of various designs and materials and finishes in excruciating detail, then debating them all over again the next day. A lot of nodding, and shaking her head, and making sympathetic noises, and not tearing her hair out.

*Eliana should be here instead of me. She* likes *this stuff.*

But Eliana couldn't exactly drop out of college for a semester to come hold their mom's hand for the rebuild. Marcos was away serving his country, so he had an even better excuse. And as Marcos had been quick to point out, Dalia hadn't been home in literally years—since her dad's funeral, in fact. She was due.

Well, one thing at a time. "When does the builder get here?"

Dalia's mom shot her a quick look. "Um, about that—"

Then her mom's phone rang, and she actually answered it—answered it *instantly*, without grumbling about how the person should have texted instead, or even checking if she knew the number. She just swiped to answer and said, "Hello!" in that same bright, cheerful voice.

"Oh, hi, Carol!...Yes, she got in last night...Flew in to Austin and drove out in a rental car...She's here for as long as I need her. She's going to telecommute to her work in Philadelphia."

Her mom said this like telecommuting was some futuristic marvel and Dalia was a good daughter, caring for her mother with joy in her heart and a song on her lips and not being at all grumpy or impatient or longing for peace and quiet and her own space.

The conversation rolled along. There didn't seem to be any point to the call; they were just...*talking*. It was weird. Dalia had exactly one friend she cared enough about to keep up with. They texted off and on and had scheduled Skype sessions. But she'd witnessed half a dozen of these shooting-the-breeze phone conversations between her mom and her mom's friends since last night alone.

They were talking over the storm now. "I know it!" her mom was saying. "When that wind came through, it sounded just like a freight train inside a tornado!"

Gah! Dalia couldn't listen to it one more time; she just couldn't. She had to get away now before she lost her last marble.

She picked her way through the gap in the wall where the kitchen door had been, onto the porch and down the steps to the sandstone walkway.

The Texas sky was perfectly clear, acting all innocent, like it had never hurled a late-summer hailstorm at Dalia's ancestral home. She breathed in the cool morning air and kept walking, out the gate and onto the caliche drive. The sound of her mom's voice faded to the point where Dalia couldn't make out the words anymore.

Then she heard the crunch of tires on gravel, and here came a truck around the bend. The driver's door had a decal with some sort of graphic that looked like a house. The builder!

*Finally. Now we can get down to business. Make some plans. Set some deadlines.*

The truck was an old stepside with a tomatoey orange-red paint job that looked original. A good sign. Anyone who drove a truck like that had respect for the past. He wouldn't try to push any tacky period-inappropriate stuff onto the house.

The truck pulled smoothly into the spot by the stand of cedar trees where visitors always parked. The driver got out. There was something familiar about his shape.

He shut the door, and Dalia saw the lettering on the decal: Reyes Boys Construction.

She barely had time to think, *Wait, what?* before the passenger door opened and out stepped another figure, even more familiar.

Her heart gave a painful throb before her mind fully understood what was happening.

*Oh, no. No. It can't be.*

But it was.

Anyone would have thought an old has-been washed-up jock like Tony would have lost his looks in the years since he flunked out of college and broke Dalia's heart. That would only have been fair.

But no. The clean V shape of his torso,

his crisp jawline, his outrageously full head of glossy black hair—it was all the same. If anything, he looked better than ever, with the physical maturity of his midtwenties giving solidity and dignity to what had always been a spectacular shape. He'd been magnificent enough back in the day, but evidently he hadn't peaked until now.

From their late teens on, Dalia was always surprised by how *big* he was—six foot four, broad and powerful. It just didn't seem right for a man's shoulders to go out that far. She could still remember the physical shock she'd felt the first time she'd put her arms around him. There was so *much* of him.

He stopped in his tracks and looked at her with his head to one side, like he kinda-sorta recognized her but couldn't quite place her. Wow. Talk about adding insult to injury.

While he stood there puzzling her out, Alex came over with arms wide open. He always had been a hugger.

"Dalia! I didn't know you were in town."

He looked enough like Tony for it to be unnerving—an inch or two shorter, and less massive, but with the same basic proportions, the same jawline, the same smile.

"Hi, Alex! Yeah, I just flew in last night," she heard herself saying.

"Yeah? How long you here for?"

"Um, I don't know yet. I'll be helping my mom while her ankle heals. Overseeing the work on the house and all."

"You're here for the duration, then."

Tony joined them. Dalia's heart pounded. Up close he looked better than ever. Had she actually thought Alex resembled him? Ha! Alex was a pale imitation—Tony Lite. Tony was the real thing.

He seemed taller, somehow. Was it possible he'd grown? He towered over Dalia, and she was not a short woman.

"Hey, Dalia. How you been? You look good."

He could have taken the words out of a manual of things to say to an ex, and he said them exactly right, all soft and smooth. His charm, like the rest of him, hadn't suffered with the passage of time.

"Hello," she managed.

A very different *hello*, high and trilling, rang out behind her. And here came her mom, booking it across the rubble-strewn porch on her crutches, headed for the steps.

Dalia was too horrified to speak. The surgery was just two days ago. There were pins and things sticking out of the incisions.

"Whoa, hold on there, Mrs. Ramirez!" Tony called out. "Don't come to us. We'll come to you."

But it was Alex who led the way, looking over his shoulder now and then to tell his brother, "Ground's kinda rough," and, "Watch out for these porch steps." Alex always did have a fussy-old-woman streak.

They made it to the porch. Tony found a wooden porch chair in decent shape and brushed off the seat.

"Here you go, Mrs. Ramirez. Do you need to elevate your foot? How are you? Looks like you got busted up almost as bad as the house did! How did it happen?"

Dalia suppressed a scream as her mom started the story from the beginning.

"Well! I was unloading the dishwasher that morning, waiting for my coffee to brew, when all of a sudden the sky went black, and the wind rumbled over the roof, just like when a cold front comes in, you know. Then the alert went off on my phone. Severe storm! Thunder and lightning! Golfball-sized hail! I'd already let my chickens out to forage, and they were scattered all over the orchard. So I grabbed a chunk of watermelon out of the fridge and ran out the door calling, 'Here, chick chick chick!' I've got them trained pretty well, and they all came running up the ramp and into the coop. I tossed the watermelon inside, shut the door and started back to the house, but somehow I missed the steps. I fell off the coop porch and came down hard on my foot."

Dalia shuddered, trying not to think how much worse the accident could have been. It was bad enough as it was.

Tony winced. "Oh, no! That coop's up pretty high. That's not a minor fall."

"No, it's not! The fracture I got is called a trimedial malleolus, and it's a doozy. I had to have surgery all over my ankle. I've got screws and a metal plate in there, and a little cage to hold everything together."

She sounded proud, but Dalia knew the pain must have been horrible. She'd done her own research into trimedial malleolus fractures after the accident. The injury involved breaks to three different parts of the ankle, as well as ligament damage. Not a minor thing at any time, and worse at her mother's age.

"Wow!" Tony said. "How'd you ever make it back to the house?"

"I didn't! I couldn't even get up. I tried to crawl, but I hadn't made it three feet before the hail started coming down. Ended up scooching under the chicken coop and waiting it out there, watching the hailstones bounce off the grass. But I didn't lose a single chicken!"

"That's the spirit! You're one tough lady, Mrs. Ramirez."

"Oh, well, I didn't have much choice. Anyway, as it turned out, I'd have been a lot worse off if I *had* made it back to the kitchen. You boys are the heroes, going out into it all to help people. Did you know the chief made it over here in twelve minutes? He took care of me until the ambulance arrived. Good thing I had my phone on me to call."

A lightbulb went off in Dalia's head at the words *you boys*. Dang it. Tony was a volunteer firefighter. Of course he was. Which meant he would be here at La Escarpa for the FFF in two weeks. She was going to have a full day of Tony, from the early-morning exhibition football game to the bonfire at night.

Tony and Dalia's mom went on talking in a casual, breezy way about the storm and what it had done to various people and places. There didn't seem to be much point in rehashing all this now; it wasn't like there was anything new to relate. But it did give Dalia an opportunity to get in a few good looks at Tony—the first she'd had in years.

Dark brown eyes. Black crescent eyebrows. Squarish face with a full jaw and a chin like a superhero. Every feature in his face was ridiculously strong, but his expression was open and friendly.

He had the thickest, glossiest, springiest hair she'd ever seen on a human being—longish at the top, velvety short at the back and sides. The artistic sideburns were new. So was the sculpted Van Dyke beard, perfectly formed in graceful curves and points.

He laughed at something her mom said. He always laughed like that, head thrown back, eyes shut, mouth wide open to show all his strong white beautiful teeth. Dalia knew all Tony's expressions. The tilted-head, furrowed-brow combo. The unbelievably tender smile. The going-in-for-a-kiss stare.

Whatever reservations her mother might have had about Tony when he and Dalia first got together in high school, she sure was charmed by him now. It was freaking Dalia out—but at the same time it was kind of inevitable. Tony charmed *everyone*. Everyone loved him. How could they not? Look at that smile, those eyes, that rapt attentive expression. It looked so real. Almost real enough to fool Dalia.

Tony took a long look at the wreckage, then pulled up a stool and took a seat. "Well, Mrs. Ramirez, looks like we're going to be doing a ground-up rebuild."

"Oh, I know it. I ought to be more broken up about it than I am, but to be honest I'm kind of glad for the excuse. I've never really liked the layout of this kitchen, and it's too small. Now I can start fresh."

"I'm happy to hear you say that! I've got some ideas for a new floor plan for the southeast wing of the house. I realize we're limited by the footprint of the original, like we can't go knocking down stone walls, but there's a lot we can do within those limits."

Alex spoke up. "The main structure was built when? Eighteen-fifties?"

"That's right," Dalia's mom said. "Before that, the family lived in the old cabin, which later got incorporated into the bunkhouse. The good news is, the stone portion of the house is still in great shape."

"I don't doubt it," said Tony. "Those German stonemasons really knew their stuff."

"Yes, they did. The old kitchen used to be in a detached building off the south corner. It got incorporated into the house around the turn of the century, along with a new dining room. Then in the seventies my in-laws added the new kitchen addition and converted the old kitchen into a master suite. That's why that side of the house has such a cobbled-together look. And obviously the new construction wasn't as sturdy as the original structure."

Tony stroked his new beard thoughtfully. "I don't know what your budget is, but have you considered doing the rebuild in stone?"

"Oh, I don't know about that. I'd rather go with wood siding again than have new stonework that doesn't match the old."

"No, I don't blame you. But the stonemason we work with is very good, and very experienced at matching old stonework. I can send you some pictures of his work. Just something to think about."

Dalia's suspicion levels rose. Why was Tony trying to upsell her mother?

"How much damage did the storm do to the master suite?" Tony asked.

"Not much. The kitchen bore the brunt. There's some water damage on the closet wall, but nothing structural."

Tony gazed into the kitchen. "What if… What if we added a walk-in pantry along the back wall of the dining room, with access from the kitchen, and then a built-in dining room hutch in front of that? You'd have to sacrifice some square footage in the dining room, but we could gain some of it back with a bay window. That would add some visual interest to the facade, as well as helping with the transition between the old stonework and the new, if you decide to go that route. Plus with the pantry and hutch there, you'd get to recess your entry to the master bedroom with a little hallway, instead of having it open directly onto the dining room, which I've always thought was a little awkward, no offense."

"Oh, none taken!" Dalia's mom said. "I've always thought the same thing."

"Then from the bay window, we extend that front exterior wall even with the rest of the facade. Same thing with the side wall—just bring it back in line with the master suite. That'll add significant square footage to the kitchen. Then we'll extend the porch around that end so it wraps around on three sides. What do you think?"

Dalia seethed. The nerve of him! Who did he think he was, with his bay windows and his recessed entries? How could he be so disrespectful of the old floor plan? So what if the master bedroom opened directly onto the dining room? It had been that way for *forty years*. If it was good enough for her grandparents, it was good enough to keep.

Her mother practically squealed in delight. "It's perfect! I love it!"

Dalia suppressed a groan. *Way to negotiate, Mom.*

Tony didn't stop there. Why should he? He proposed other improvements—a reconfiguration of the master bath and closet, a new laundry room, even an outdoor grill and entertainment area in the space between the back wings of the house. And all the while her mom kept nodding rapidly and saying, "Mmm-hmm. Mmm-hmm. Mmm-hmm. I can see that."

And Dalia didn't know how to stop it.

There would have been no problem if she'd been on her own. She'd have shut down Tony's sales spiel fast enough to rattle his teeth. But she wasn't the one in charge of the interview. She didn't know how to break in without making her mother look like a silly, gullible woman who couldn't be trusted to handle her own affairs.

Tony was on a roll. He was talking with great enthusiasm about exposing the old stone in the dining room wall when Alex came back and nearly got clobbered by one of his brother's sweeping arm movements. Alex ducked just in time.

"Oops, sorry," Tony said.

Alex just said, "No problem, my bad. I've got all the measurements I need to draw some preliminary plans."

*His* bad? How was it his bad? How was it his responsibility to avoid being clobbered, and not Tony's responsibility to watch where he swung his gigantic arms?

Why did people like Tony always get away with hurting others?

*Because someone is always there to enable him, that's why.*

Well, he wouldn't get away with it this time. Dalia would see to that. Not today, not in front of her mother, but somehow she would catch him in his own tangled web and put him in his place.

She got up and walked over to the side porch. Out in the orchard, the chickens foraged contentedly in the shade of their completely undamaged-by-the-storm coop.

A hollow clomping of boots sounded along the porch floorboards behind her—slow, deliberate, long-legged steps. Her heart raced, and her stomach flipped. What was the matter with her? How could he still make her react this way after all these years, when she knew better?

But it wasn't Tony. It was Alex, and only Alex, who joined her at the porch rail. She found that she had been holding her breath and let it out slowly. From relief, or disappointment?

"Have you been out to check that old bunkhouse since the storm?" Alex asked. "I saw it as we drove up. Looks like it took a beating, too. Windows are broken, and the front door got ripped clean off the hinges."

"Oh, that's the least of our concerns right now," said Dalia. She couldn't handle another project being added to the rebuild.

"Do you want us to take a look? The damage might not be *that* bad. A little work now might save further expense and trouble down the line."

"No. Bunkhouse repairs are not in the budget."

She had no authority to say such a thing, but she didn't care. She was not going to let Tony tack any more jobs onto what already promised to be a monstrous bid. She'd see the bunkhouse turned into a tack barn first.

Alex looked longingly in the direction of the bunkhouse. "Too bad. Such a nice old building. Be a shame for it to fall into ruin."

"Yeah, well, a lot of things are a shame, but they happen, anyway."

Alex smiled and shrugged in an embarrassed sort of way, like he was apologizing for something. Dalia walked away. She didn't want to hear him make excuses for his brother, and she sure didn't want his pity.

She'd almost reached what had been the front wall of the kitchen when Tony came around the corner, and suddenly they were facing each other across the remains of the old porch swing.

They both froze. Tony's smile stiffened, then faded away.

How many hours had the two of them logged in that swing? Talking, making out, rocking quietly together. Her head on his chest, or his in her lap. Was he remembering, too? How could he not be?

He crouched down and started randomly moving bits of wreckage around. He had his head bowed now, but she could see a dark flush rising up his neck. Huh. So he did have some vestige of a sense of shame.

In his nervous and pointless shuffling of debris, he lifted a piece of black roofing paper from a section of siding. Underneath lay a board with letters carved into it by a childish hand.

*Tony loves Dalia.*

The sight of it gave her actual physical

pain. It was like something had reached inside her chest cavity and squeezed.

Tony didn't look up or say anything. He laid the roofing paper gently back over the board, like he was covering something dead.

## *CHAPTER TWO*

TONY GOT INTO Alex's truck and shut the door. All the final goodbyes—his own voice, his brother's and Mrs. Ramirez's—rang in his ears, and his last leftover smile was straining his facial muscles to the snapping point.

His hands shook.

He knew it would be rough going to Dalia's childhood home, dealing with her mom, acting like he was okay with it. Just going to La Escarpa once a year for the FFF was hard, and that was with music and games and plenty of other people around. But then suddenly there was Dalia herself, in the flesh, and because the earth did *not* open up and swallow him whole, he had to smile and talk and make it through.

Now reaction was setting in, like a post-adrenaline crash. He thought he might throw up.

Alex opened the driver's-side door. Just a few more seconds and they'd be driving away.

Then Mrs. Ramirez called out, "Wait!"

*Oh, come on, now. Seriously?*

He heard Alex walking back toward the house, but he stayed put, like a prey animal holding still in the grass. He stared at his clenched fists on his knees and waited… and remembered.

It was Dalia's scent that first clued him in. He'd recognized her shape at first sight, sure, but she'd been backlit by the morning sun, just a tall, slim silhouette, and he didn't trust his eyes. Then he caught a whiff of that juniper berry body lotion, and he knew. His gut clenched and his knees nearly buckled. It was amazing he'd managed to stay on his feet at all.

She had on a racerback tank and boot-cut jeans. No jewelry, no detectable makeup. She always dressed so simply compared with other women, like she didn't need a lot of ornamentation. Elegant, that's what she was. Like a diamond on black velvet. A full moon in a clear sky. A single rose.

Tony's time with her was a memory of pure joy. All kinds of wonderful things had seemed possible then. It was like there'd been a shadow over the world before, but he hadn't known it until she'd pulled it back, and suddenly everything was bright with colors he never knew existed—or like one of those dreams where he could fly, only this time it was real. The future was this rich, full, shining, glorious thing. Dalia loved him, and they would be together forever.

And then it all came crashing down.

Alex got into the truck and put something in Tony's lap.

"Eggs," he said. "A dozen and a half. Some of them are those little blue and green and pink ones that come from those Easter Egger chickens. I'll make us some *migas* for breakfast tomorrow."

Tony turned on him. "Did you know Dalia was in town?"

Her name felt weird in his mouth, strange and familiar at the same time. It was the first time he'd said it out loud in years.

Alex gave him an incredulous look. "Whoa. How can you even ask me that? You think I wouldn't've told you if I'd known? You think I'd let you walk into all that without a heads-up? What kind of brother do you think I am?"

"Sorry."

Alex started the ignition and backed up the truck. "You okay?"

"I guess."

"She looked good, huh?"

"Are you kidding me? She looked amazing."

Alex shifted into Drive and looked Tony right in the eye.

"You should tell her the truth."

Tony shook his head. "Nah. What's the point? That ship has sailed—and capsized, and burned, and sunk to the bottom of the ocean. Nothing'll ever change that."

"Yeah, well, maybe it doesn't have to be about changing anything. Maybe just tell her because it's the right thing to do."

"No! I'm not telling her—and don't you do it, either."

"Wow. Seriously? You think you have to tell me that? You actually think I would go behind your back?"

Tony looked out the window. "No."

Her hair was still long. He'd wondered a lot over the years about her hair, whether she'd cut it all off, or colored it, or started straightening it like some women did. But it looked exactly the same, flowing down her back in those deep dark natural waves. Back in elementary school she used to wear it in a single thick braid. It reached all the way to her waist.

How many times between kindergarten and junior high had he tugged that braid? Never enough to hurt; he'd just wanted her to turn around and look at him. She was so serious, so collected, even as a kid. It made Tony clown around twice as much, trying to get her to react. A smile from her was worth more than a laugh from anyone else. But whenever she did smile, she always turned away, hiding her face like it was a secret.

But she sure hadn't smiled today. She'd gone full-on death glare while he was talking to her mom. It was like all those other times when he'd charmed a whole room, everybody but her, and she'd just stared at him without a hint of a smile, and he didn't know what it meant.

"I'm not glaring," she'd told him, back in the early days when they'd first gotten together and had to go over every memory of their shared history up to that point. "That's just my face. Just because I don't wear a goofy smile all the time doesn't mean I'm mad."

So which was it this time? Did she hate him? Or did he even mean enough to her for that? Maybe she didn't have any emotion left for him. She was a citified big shot, and he was a has-been that never was. If anything, she was congratulating herself on her escape, on not getting tied down to a deadweight flash-in-the-pan like Tony.

The truth was as plain as her handwriting on that big box at the university post office—black ink, all caps, neatly spaced. Tony's name and address in one corner. Dalia's address in the other, in smaller print, without her name. Like she'd taken herself right out of the situation, which he supposed she had. He knew what was in the box, as sure as if he could see through the cardboard. His letter jacket, his ring. Their ticket stubs from *Iron Man 2*. The silver cross he'd given her for Christmas. The buckle he'd won riding a bull at that little rodeo just after he'd turned eighteen. Every card he ever sent, every note he ever scribbled out in English class senior year, every letter he wrote her from his dorm room desk.

It hurt. Not a sharp pain, but a dull ache—it might fade over time but would never, never go away. He'd known all along that this day would come, that he couldn't keep her, that he wasn't enough. And in the end, he'd pushed her away for her own good. The whole thing was his doing. But that didn't make it hurt any less.

## *CHAPTER THREE*

*Of course the particulars will vary, depending on the nature and extent of your rebuild, but roughly speaking, you can expect to spend three to four months on construction alone—not counting the planning, design and permit stages, which can easily double that. The process is a long one, and you're basically in a temporary marriage with your contractors. Take steps to keep the relationship a healthy one, providing an occasional pot of coffee or breakfast bagels, or buying lunch for the crew. Friendly gestures like this will keep everyone on a good footing and the project going smoothly.*

Dalia sat back in her desk chair, stunned, staring at the article on her laptop screen. She felt like she'd been doused with ice water. Three to four *months*, if not *twice* that? Coffee and *bagels*? It wasn't enough she had to endure Tony's company for months on end; she had to make *nice*?

"Really?" she'd said to her mother yesterday as Alex and Tony drove away. "Tony? That's who you hired to do the work?"

Her mom shrugged. "He's good. He and his brother do beautiful work. And they're polite, clean, wholesome people that you don't mind having in the house."

*Wholesome, ha! The things I could tell you...* But she didn't. She hadn't told her family the real reason for the breakup back when it happened, and she wasn't about to start now. She hadn't needed Marcos or their dad going all vengeful on Tony, defending her honor. She'd simply said that she'd finally realized Tony was too selfish and immature to make the relationship work, and that it had been an error in judgment on her part to ever think otherwise. She'd been amazingly matter-of-fact about the whole thing. And they'd taken her explanation at face value.

How could her mom possibly guess, all these years later, how much Tony haunted her? Almost every one of Dalia's childhood memories was connected to him, along with every street, house and business in the city limits, and every road, tree, hill and fence post in the county. The first time she'd come home after the breakup, she'd had an actual panic attack in the feed store parking lot.

After that, she'd stayed away. She'd made the trip exactly one more time, for her father's funeral. And that was it…until now.

"You acted like you wanted to adopt him," Dalia said. "What was that all about? I thought you didn't like him."

"Who, me? Oh, no. That was all your dad. He had a grudge against that whole family."

"Why?"

"Probably because I dated Carlos in high school."

"*What?* You went out with The Player? Are you kidding me? You never told me that."

"Didn't I?"

"No, you did not. I'm sure of it. Believe me, I would remember if you told me you had a romantic history with Tony's dad."

Her mom waved a hand dismissively. "I didn't have a romantic history with him—or not much of one. We didn't go out for long.

He was flashy and fun, but his charm wore thin pretty quick."

All of which meant that her sunny, outgoing, optimistic mother had seen through Carlos a lot quicker than Dalia had seen through Tony.

She shut the lid of her laptop and stood. Well, if she had to be at La Escarpa for months on end, at least she had a tranquil personal space, even if it wasn't her Philadelphia apartment. Her childhood room could have been featured in a photojournalism piece on minimalism. The bed was neatly made with one of her grandmother's quilts. Everything was lined up, grid-like, on her desk: laptop, bullet journal, phone. A small stack of books stood beside the lamp. All else was beautifully, restfully clear.

This was the room she'd moved into after her brother vacated it on joining the Marines. Before that she'd shared for twelve years with an untidy younger sister.

Dalia had been thirteen when she'd found her first Don Aslett book in a library sale. He was the tidiness guru of an earlier generation, decades before Marie Kondo. Dalia had soaked up his wisdom like a sponge and still considered him a personal mentor. Lots of different writers had taken up the minimalist cause in the years since, but the essential message remained the same: get rid of the unnecessary items causing you stress. Keep only the things you need or enjoy.

Her apartment was streamlined and neat in the extreme. Clean, clear surfaces. Fridge contents all easy to see with space in between, leftovers stored in matching Pyrex containers. No extra lids, no overflowing Tupperware cabinet like her mom had. A coworker once saw her place and said it was like a rented condo for a vacation. It probably wasn't meant as a compliment, but Dalia had felt smug about it, anyway. She always felt smug about her clutter-free existence. Most people were drowning in excess possessions. They were not like her. No excess baggage for Dalia, physical or emotional.

Ranches were messy. There was always so much *stuff* around: muddy boots, feed buckets, tack that needed mending. Grass burrs of all varieties, from the kind that was sheer agony to step on to the small sticky ones that didn't prick but held on with some sort of plant adhesive. Spanish needle grass, sewing itself into fabric or flesh. Bits of hay that stuck to jeans, and sections of icicle cactus that broke off and attached themselves to the clothing, skin or fur of any person or animal who passed within two feet of it.

She used to sit down on the porch with Merle, her border collie, for hourlong grooming sessions, with a slicker brush, a pair of scissors and a letter opener for removing the mats in his soft undercoat. Sometimes she'd find a piece of needle grass that had screwed itself through his coat and was just starting to pierce his skin. It was so satisfying to pull it out and snap the hard sharp-pointed head with its hairy barbs and trailing spiral-shaped stem. Merle was patient, offering no resistance, only whining softly when she tugged too hard. It felt good to make his coat smooth and burr-free.

Dalia shook herself out of her reverie. She was actually smiling. What was the matter with her? Was she getting nostalgic about *needle grass*?

She roamed around the room, gloating, and opened the closet. Her luggage stood in the back, empty, because she'd already put her clothes in the closet and dresser. She could do that, because the closet and dresser weren't full of useless clutter. There was exactly one box in the closet, marked "sentimental."

The box she'd used to mail back Tony's stuff was a big box, purchased at the university post office. The weeks after that fateful spring break had been dark with misery, with Tony acting weird and her suspicion deepening with each passing day, finally culminating in one last nasty conversation, after which she'd taken everything she had of his and everything he'd ever given her, boxed it up and overnighted it to him. It helped, doing the actual packing and addressing in a public place; it made the whole thing feel like an emotionless transaction and kept her from breaking down or losing her nerve. She hadn't written an accompanying letter. What was there to say?

She'd made sure he had to sign for the package, just so she'd know beyond a doubt that he'd received it. He'd received it, all right. And he didn't call to protest or try to get her back. And although this was theoretically what she wanted—no fuss, no drama—still it stung. When it came down to it, she didn't expect him to let go so easily, even in the face of glaring truth. It hurt that he didn't fight for her. Made her wonder just how long things had been over between them in his mind, how long he'd been bored with her. She was sore about it still.

But that was just a feeling, and it didn't change anything. She hadn't sent his stuff back to get a rise out of him; she'd done it because she was through with him. His lack of reaction was evidence that she'd made the right decision.

She gave herself a little shake. That was enough thinking about Tony. Time to get back to gloating over her tidy room.

The clothes she'd brought from Philadelphia had filled only the top two dresser drawers. She opened a lower one now just to enjoy the sight of it, empty.

But it wasn't empty. There was *stuff* in there—a broken iPod, an empty leather case for a tablet, a sequined pink sweater with some of the sequins missing and a pair of ridiculous fur-trimmed knee-high socks, worn out at the heels.

Righteous indignation swelled in her. She removed the entire drawer, took it to her sister's room and dumped the contents onto the bed. Then she took a picture and sent it to Eliana, along with a message. *These things must have been misplaced. Weird, huh?*

The reply came back right away. *Oh, come on. You've got so much more space than I do.*

Dalia answered just as quickly. *False. Our rooms are exactly the same square footage. And your dresser has more drawers than mine.*

*But mine are crowded!!!*

*And whose fault is that?*

*Don't be mean!!! You won't miss one drawer, you've got 5000 empty ones.*

Dalia's fingers were flying now. *They're MY drawers, and they're empty because I have the discipline to keep them that way.*

*But what's the point of having them if they're empty?!!*

Dalia made a scoffing sound. What a question! Why did people act like empty space was some sort of anomaly, like it had no value in and of itself, like it was just waiting to be filled? Don Aslett said there was nothing wrong with wide-open spaces. Wide-open spaces were American.

But it was useless to try to explain it to

Eliana. She couldn't, *wouldn't* understand. Dalia needed to talk to someone who did understand.

She texted Lauren. Can you Skype?

The reply came seconds later. Yisss.

Dalia sat back at her desk and opened her laptop. The incoming Skype call notification was already doing its thing. She answered.

And there was Lauren, with the interior of her live-in van stretched out behind her, colorful and magical, like something out of a fairy tale.

Unlike Dalia, Lauren enjoyed an abundance of cushions and throws and artistic old architectural remnants, but there was nothing in her space that could be called clutter. They were both minimalists at heart, in their different ways; their shared college dorm room had looked like a modern still life. Lauren had made Dalia a hand-lettered rendition of the William Morris quote: *Have nothing in your houses that you do not know to be useful, or believe to be beautiful.* It hung in Dalia's apartment by her closet door.

In most other ways, the two of them were opposites. Dalia thought living in a van, even a thoughtfully fitted-up one like Lauren's, sounded awful, and Lauren thought Dalia's life in the city sounded soul-crushing. Dalia preferred to work with numbers, and Lauren, a photographer, was much more artistic. But that was fine. Each respected the other's style, space and wildly different personality.

Lauren was beautiful in a feminine, girlie way, and the rich warm colors of her van made a perfect backdrop for her chestnut hair and creamy skin, as she surely knew.

"Hey there! What's up?"

That was another nice thing about Lauren. She didn't waste time with chitchat.

Neither did Dalia.

"You'll never guess who my mom hired as the contractor for the kitchen rebuild."

"How could I possibly guess? I don't know anyone in Limestone Springs except—ohmygosh, is it Tony? Your superhot ex?"

"Wow. You guessed that a lot quicker than I thought you would."

Lauren squealed and bounced on her mattress. "Is he as hot as he used to be?"

"Honestly? More so. And I wouldn't have believed that was possible. His body is as amazing as ever, and he's got this perfect little beard now, like a Tony Stark beard, with points and swirls and things. It's like a sculpture for his face."

"Mmm, nice! Soooo, is there still a spark?"

"What does it matter? You know what happened. He cheated on me. He's nothing to me now. Less than nothing."

"Right. That's why he's the first thing out of your mouth when you Skype me without scheduling it a week beforehand."

Dalia realigned her phone with the edge of her desk. "Okay, yes. There's a spark. More than a spark. Kind of a…blaze."

"Wow. That's big. You haven't had a blaze since…"

"Since Tony. Yeah, I know. And it makes me mad at myself. It's just weakness."

Lauren looked thoughtful. "Well, it's been a long time. Maybe he's sorry. Maybe he's changed."

"He doesn't look sorry. And I was just reading this article, trying to figure out how long this rebuild is going to take, and it looks like it could take half a year easy."

"Half a year! Can you be away from work that long?"

"Oh, yeah. That's not the issue. My mom thinks I'm telecommuting. I don't telecommute. I don't have to. This is just how the job is now. With all the platforms available to financial planners—data-sharing, planning programs, videoconferencing—there is simply no reason for me or anyone else with proper licensure and credentials to go into an office unless I want to. There are still some old-school clients who prefer in-person interaction, but plenty more who'd just as soon handle it all online. The truth is, at this point I could live and work wherever I want. I just want to live in the city, in my own space. But that's not possible right now. My mom's injury is going to take a long time to heal, and there's ranch work to be done, besides looking after her and overseeing the rebuild. And it's my duty to take care of all that. So I'm stuck here until it's done."

"How are you managing without a kitchen?"

"That part's fine. We have a hot plate and toaster oven set up, and there's an extra fridge in the laundry room, and my mom's church friends have been bringing dinner. They have this whole schedule worked out. A lot of them have used Tony and his brother for home renovations themselves. I keep hearing the words *good but slow*. And I'm thinking, if he's slow, how does he make a living? Does he pad his estimate? Inflate his hours? Overcharge for materials? And this is a ground-up rebuild, not just a renovation. They're going to have to extend the foundation and frame new walls. I'm afraid he's going to milk this job for all it's worth and fleece my mom. Clearing the wreckage and preparing the site alone will take weeks. I told my mom I'd stay for the whole process, and I will, but I had no idea I was in for such a long ordeal, let alone with Tony."

"How is your mom?"

"Cheerful and sunny and upbeat as ever, and doing a lot more knitting now that she's supposed to keep off her feet. I know her ankle must hurt, but she never complains. She's just antsy because she can't get to church to help with the Wednesday-night suppers and the Fall Festival. Oh, and get this. She hosts this fundraiser for the volunteer fire department every year, this huge all-day event, and she won't give it up even though there's rubble all over the ground and she's got pins and screws sticking out of her Franken-ankle and no kitchen to cook in. It's going to be complete and utter chaos. Oh, and guess who's a volunteer firefighter?"

"Hmm, let me think. Your superhot ex?"

Dalia groaned and beat her head against her desk a few times. Then she looked up and said, "Remember that guy? You know, what's-his-name."

"Sorry, I can't quite place him."

"You know, my first boyfriend who wasn't Tony."

"Oh, yeah, that guy. What *was* his name? Wait—I know. Liam."

"That's right! Liam. He was like the anti-Tony. Nonathletic, Anglo, bookish. Even wore little hipster glasses."

"Yeah, Liam was cute."

"He was, wasn't he? But he bored me. Every man since Tony bores me. It isn't fair. He ruined me for other men, and he doesn't even want me. Not that I want *him*! I mean, not on a rational level. It's just... I don't know. Life has a shine to it when he's around that it doesn't have when he's gone."

"I know."

"What do you mean, you know? How could you possibly know that?"

"Because I know you. Your attraction to

him is something that doesn't follow logic. It's been the one consistently irregular, wild-card-type thing in your life. You like things orderly and predictable. Cause and effect. Effort and reward. Reap and sow. But then there's Tony, and he's all charm and spontaneity and improvisation. He shoots from the hip, makes stuff up on the fly. He annoys you because he upsets your notions of how the world works, and he fascinates you because he's so good at it."

"Yeah, that's about the size of it." She swallowed hard. "We had this whole life planned together, you know? Where we'd both finish college, and maybe he'd go pro and maybe not, but either way he'd have his degree and I'd have mine, and…and we'd get married. And we'd work hard and save our money, and one day we'd get a nice place in the country. And sometimes I catch myself thinking about what might have been like it *is*, like it's out there, somewhere, in some alternate version of my life. A phantom life. The life I was supposed to have, where Tony stayed faithful."

"Well, maybe it means something that you feel that way."

"Yeah, it means I'm an idiot."

"No, Dalia, it doesn't. You can't go through life shutting down your feelings all the time. Maybe you need to follow your heart for a change."

"What? No, I don't. That's a terrible idea. Follow my heart. What does that even mean?"

Before Lauren could answer, Dalia heard the unmistakable sound of a vehicle coming down the drive. The entry to La Escarpa was guarded by a coded electronic gate, so visitors were always something of an event. People didn't just drop by.

Maybe another meal delivery from the church? It was early for that, though, just past eight in the morning. Besides which, it sounded like more than one set of wheels.

"Hold on a minute," she said to Lauren.

She went to the window. A line of vehicles was coming down the winding drive. A fire truck led the way, followed by an unmistakable vintage red Chevy stepside.

Back at her computer screen, she said, "I have to go. Someone's here."

## *CHAPTER FOUR*

DOWNSTAIRS, SHE FOUND her mom on her crutches, peering out the living room window at the approaching caravan, her knitting project abandoned on the sofa.

"What's going on?" Dalia asked. "Did you call the fire department?"

"No, I have no idea what they're doing here. Look, that's Mad Dog McClain driving the fire truck. He's the chief."

They went outside. The vehicles started parking one after another. Mad Dog, a slender, bespectacled redhead in a long-sleeved button-down and a broad-brimmed straw gardening hat, got out of the fire truck and walked toward the house.

"What's going on, Mad Dog?" her mother called out. "Do I have a fire I don't know about?"

Mad Dog smiled.

"No, ma'am. We're here to work. Tony

called me and said how he and Alex are fixing to rebuild your kitchen. Said there's lots of wreckage to clear away before they can get started, so why not bring out the whole fire department to take care of it. I'm no carpenter, but I can pick up debris and haul it to the dump, and so can the rest. Then the Reyes boys can get the walls up for you that much sooner."

Tony stepped out of the Chevy. Dalia's heart gave a quick painful thump at the sight of him in his cargo shorts, cowboy work boots and T-shirt emblazoned with a Texas-shaped graphic. Tony always was wild about Texas-shaped things.

Her mom got all fluttery. "Oh, Mad Dog, that is so sweet of you all. I don't know what to say." She raised her voice. "Thank you for coming, everyone! There's bottled water and tea in the laundry room fridge. I wish I could offer you something more, but Dalia can go to town and get some drinks, and later on we'll order some pizzas."

"Oh, no, ma'am," Mad Dog said again. "You don't have to do that. We brought plenty of food and drinks with us. We know you don't have a kitchen right now, and anyhow, you're hurt. There's nothing for you to do but sit and watch."

By now other volunteer firefighters were making their way toward the house, carrying coolers and totes and covered dishes. Burly, tattooed Wallace Griggs had what looked like a seven-layer dip in a glass trifle dish.

"Thank you," Dalia's mother called out. "Thank you all! This is so very generous and thoughtful of you."

"It's only fitting," said Mad Dog. "We don't forget everything you do for us, hosting the fundraiser every year."

"I don't forget what you did for Martin," said Dalia's mom, her voice quavering.

Mad Dog's smile faded. "I only wish I'd been able to do more."

Dalia swallowed hard and looked away. She could feel Tony watching her. He'd come to her dad's funeral, along with what seemed like half the town. She'd been fresh out of college, working her first job in the city and living in her new place. All through the service, she kept remembering the last time she ever talked to her father. She'd called to tell him she wouldn't be home for Thanksgiving. She didn't say why, just that she was busy, and he didn't complain. He was busy himself, he said, putting up a third crop of hay at the end of a rainy summer that had yielded a superabundance of grass. He sounded cheerful. Two days later he was gone, struck down in the hay pasture by heat exhaustion. He'd worked himself literally to death.

At the funeral, everyone kept saying how fitting it was that Martin had died in harness, doing the work he loved. No one said how ridiculous it was for a strong, fit, healthy man to die just a few years past his fiftieth birthday. They kept coming, those people, one after another, pressing Dalia's hands, making sympathetic faces, telling her how much she looked like her father and how much he loved her, while inside her the grief rose and swelled into something close to panic. She should have come home all those Thanksgivings and Christmases instead of cowering away from memories of Tony. She might have come home without even being asked, to help with the haying.

She was balanced on a knife edge of control, wishing they would go away and leave her alone. And suddenly Tony was there, with red-rimmed eyes and a somber face. He didn't say anything, just wrapped her in his arms, and she breathed in his familiar scent and relaxed in an embrace that fit her as perfectly as if it had been made for her, and she was safe. Just for an instant, she wanted to whisper in his ear, "Get me out of here," and somehow she knew he'd do it—he'd take her away without a moment's hesitation from this suffocating mass of people, if only she asked him.

But she didn't ask, and Tony let go and moved on. And that was the last time she'd seen him, until one day ago when he'd shown up at the house.

She dared a quick glance at him now. He was watching her, all right, and his eyes looked wet. He cleared his throat.

"All right, everybody," he called. "Those who have food or drink, come through the front door and leave it wherever Mrs. Ramirez says. Those with trailers and big trucks, back them close to the demolition site. Scrap lumber goes in Andy's flatbed, drywall and insulation in Samantha's stock trailer, scrap metal in the big blue Dodge. If you come across any farmhouse-chic-type stuff, put it in Alex's stepside. We're talking old beadboard, millwork, weathered wood, any sort of good-looking scraps that someone might want to stick on a wall or make into a rustic bookcase. Alex is gonna take it to that Architectural Treasures place for salvage. Use boxes for broken glass and trash bags for the small stuff. We've got crowbars and cat's paws and sledgehammers aplenty to help with pulling stuff apart. Wear gloves, and watch out for snakes, nails, scorpions, black widows, deranged barn cats and chupacabras. If you have any questions, ask me or Alex. Oh, and be careful with Alex's pretty little truck—don't rough it up. Okay? Let's go!"

He gave a quick double clap like he used to do on the football field, and everyone hopped to it.

Dalia pulled on her old ropers and went to work alongside them. What else could she do? Sit on a deck chair beside her mom and sip bottled iced tea and watch? No way. The sooner all this mess was cleared away, the sooner the rebuild could start…and end.

THERE WAS A certain way people moved in Texas when it was really hot—spare and steady, with no wasted energy. The volunteer firefighters set a good moderate pace and stuck to it. Mad Dog made sure everyone stayed hydrated. Hats and neck cloths guarded against the brutal sun, along with long sleeves for those really inclined to burn.

Then there was Tony.

He moved fast, bouncing from place to place like a pinball—lifting, hauling, directing, joking and never seeming to tire. He shed his shirt well before noon, and Dalia stole a few quick glances at him. It was as she'd thought: he was a little heavier than in college, but not much, and his form was as beautifully sculpted as ever.

He'd always been sturdy and muscular, even as a little boy, always athletic, always in motion, always surrounded by a crowd. Dalia had kept to one or two friends at a time, and often she'd go off by herself inside one of the concrete cylinders on the school playground. They looked like culvert cylinders, and maybe they were. The insides were shaded and cool, and perfect for curling up by yourself or with a friend. Dalia was in one of these with a library book one day in seventh grade, when Tony joined her, sliding into the space across from her, in an abrupt transition from *...And Now Miguel* to *Suddenly, Tony.*

He smelled of the playground, of dust and sweat and the metallic tang of monkey bars. He grabbed the book out of her hand. "Whatcha readin'?"

"This book," she said. "It's about a ranching family in New Mexico."

It felt weird, actually talking to him. They hardly ever spoke to each other in those days, and yet she was always aware of him. No matter which direction her gaze was pointed, he was always the clearest thing she saw, and she knew somehow that he was watching her, too.

"Huh," he said. He turned it around, saw the big shiny medal on the cover and said, "Ooh, it won an award."

He laid the book facedown on his other side. Dalia would have had to reach past him to get it back, but she didn't want it back just yet.

Her braid was hanging over her shoulder. Tony looked at it, and for a moment she thought he was going to pull it, like he had done approximately once a week since kindergarten. But then he looked away. He looked at her face. And looked away again. He seemed nervous, almost jumpy, which wasn't like him.

And then he leaned over and kissed her.

It was a quick, innocent kiss, nothing salacious for a twelve-year-old boy, but it made her heart leap into her throat. The feel of his lips on hers, the sight of his face afterward, his big dark eyes startled and happy.

Then he was gone again, running back to the monkey bars with a wordless yell, twice as loud and rambunctious as before. Her heart pounded. She could still feel the pressure of his lips against hers, the brush of his damp, springy hair against her forehead.

She could feel them now, fourteen years later, watching him clear wreckage at her mother's house.

THE BUSTED PORCH swing lay on the ground amid a heap of other debris that had been cleared from the porch and kitchen and set aside for further deconstruction. Tony stood looking down at its splintered wood and broken frame. He'd been hoping to see that it wasn't quite destroyed after all, that it just needed a couple boards replaced and some gouges repaired and then it could be hung up again good as new, but there was barely a board left that wasn't smashed.

"It's a shame, isn't it?"

It was Dalia's mom, watching him from her deck chair under a live oak. She had her hands full of some sort of fluffy knitting thing.

"Yes, ma'am. If it was still in one piece, I could carry it under that tree for you, and you could sit there in it with your hurt foot up on a cushion."

"That's exactly what I keep thinking. But wishing won't make it so."

Tony was working in this area because it was where Dalia wasn't. He moved as fast as he could, trying to keep his mind occupied and his eyes off Dalia. It wasn't working.

She was wearing her hair in that long single braid like when they were kids.

"Just how old is this thing, anyway?" Tony asked. "Couple decades at least, right? I remember seeing it the first time I ever came out here, at Dalia's birthday party. The one where our entire third-grade class was invited."

Mrs. Ramirez gave him a sly, knowing look. "The one where you carved your graffiti into the siding on the house?"

Tony actually felt himself blushing. It had been ambitious of him, carving all that with the sharp tip of the weed-pulling tool he'd found next to the watering can. He could have just put *T+D* and called it good, but no, he'd gone all in. He remembered the thrill he'd felt as he spelled out their two names and that daring word *loves*. No ambiguity, no way it could mean Tamara and David, or Travis and Dancy. Still, he hadn't been quite bold enough to make his statement *completely* public. There'd been a big planter against the house. He'd shoved it forward and done his work, then pushed it back in place. The words were hidden, but they were *there*, and he knew it even if no one else did.

Only it sounded like someone else had.

"You knew about that?"

"Oh, yes."

"I thought I was being so clever, putting it behind that big planter."

She laughed. "Who do you think potted up the geraniums every year? But I kept your secret. Martin would have flipped out if he'd known Carlos Reyes's son had defaced his property."

He laughed, too. "Yeah, I guess you're right. Thank you, Mrs. Ramirez. You probably saved my life."

"Oh, you're very welcome. And to answer your question, I'm not sure how old the porch swing is. It was there long before I married Martin."

"Do you want me to put it aside somewhere? I feel kinda funny taking it to the dump. Seems disrespectful somehow."

She smiled at him. "You're a good boy."

To his surprise, tears stung his eyes and he had to look away, because no, he really wasn't.

"Put it in the burn pile," she said. "It can be fuel for the bonfire at the firefighter fundraiser. That'll be a more fitting send-off."

"Okay. If you're sure."

"Oh, yes. It was a good porch swing, and it did its job well, but it's broken now and there's no point keeping it around to look at. It'll only make me sad. That's what Dalia would say, anyway."

"Yeah. Minimalism, right? No clutter, no baggage. No living in the past."

"Mmm-hmm. I've heard her lectures so many times I know them by heart. She was always so driven and determined, even as a little girl, and she had no qualms about speaking up or reorganizing my kitchen cabinets. She was ruthless when she was sure she was right."

Tony nodded. He'd been on the receiving end of that ruthlessness more than once. But it was weirdly comforting, talking about Dalia with her mom, like they were the ones who really knew her. Mr. Ramirez had never left any doubt that Tony was not worthy for Dalia to scrape her boots on, but Tony had always suspected that Mrs. Ramirez secretly liked him a little.

He ran a hand along the porch swing's top board. He used to rest his arm there as he sat in the seat's corner with Dalia's back against his chest and her head on his shoulder.

"I hate to let it go," he said.

It was a dumb thing to say. It wasn't like it was *his* porch swing.

"So do I," said Mrs. Ramirez. "It's rocked many a baby, and many a barn cat, too. But we can't turn back the clock. Things break. Sometimes they can be fixed, and sometimes they can't."

# *CHAPTER FIVE*

DALIA STOOD BESIDE her rented SUV and stared across the street. A lot had changed in downtown Limestone Springs, and a lot had stayed the same. Tito's Bar, a fixture since the 1980s, had acquired a gentrified vibe and apparently doubled its space, but the movie theater she and Tony used to visit, together and separately, hadn't changed a bit.

They hadn't actually started dating until spring of their senior year. By then, college plans were made. Tony had his football scholarship, and Dalia had her academic scholarship to a little liberal arts school in Pennsylvania that no one had ever heard of.

In a way it was a drag they got together so late. They'd hardly had any time together before going their separate ways. The start of college in the fall had been a big, loud, ticking clock. Every time Dalia turned around there was another "last": last summer, last Fourth of July, last week at home.

But in another way the timing was perfect, because if they'd gotten together sooner, she might have done something really stupid, like go to the same in-state college as Tony and convince herself it was what she actually wanted. No, this way was better. Healthier. They would both be where they wanted to be, doing the things they cared about, not gripping each other so hard they squeezed the life out of their relationship. She trusted Tony. She wasn't jealous or possessive at all. Not the least bit worried about her gorgeous, charming star-athlete boyfriend going to school halfway across the nation from her, surrounded by adulation and temptation and girls.

Okay, so she'd had her doubts. But not Tony. He'd been dead sure of himself and her, and he'd said so.

"What's there to worry about?" he'd said. "Sure, it'll suck, being so far apart, but we've got our plan and we're sticking to it. You're gonna do amazing things at your fancy Yankee school and learn all about finance, and I'm gonna work hard and keep my nose clean and impress the coaches. And with any luck I'll stay healthy and go pro, but if I don't, at least I'll have my degree. And then we'll be together—really together, not just on holidays—and nothing will separate us ever again."

She shook her head. "You can't know all that. A thousand things could go wrong."

"Like what?"

*You could get tired of me.* "Just things. Most high school relationships don't last, Tony."

"So? We're not most people."

"We need to be realistic."

They were on that darned porch swing, Tony in the corner with one leg against the back of the seat and the other foot resting on the wood planks of the porch, lazily rocking, Dalia with her back against his chest. It was easier to say these things when she didn't have to look at him.

Tony stopped rocking. *"Realistic,"* he said. "What does that mean? We should go ahead and break up now because you think we might break up later?"

"No! That's not what I mean."

"What *do* you mean? What are you so afraid of, Dalia?"

"I'm not afraid! I just…"

She swallowed hard. "You can't know that we'll make it."

"But I do know. You would, too, if you could feel what I feel."

She wanted to believe him. But the odds were against them, and she'd never been one to indulge fantasy.

"Hey," he said in an unbelievably tender voice. "Look at me."

She didn't want to. But he shifted behind her, changing their positions so that they were side by side.

He lifted her chin. His eyes were full of love and hope and confidence. Then his face turned to a blur as her tears spilled over.

"Hey, hey, hey," he said, his voice all high and soft, like he was comforting a small child. He wiped her tears away with his thumbs.

Then he said, "Let me show you something."

He got out of the swing and knelt by the big geranium planter that stood against the house. He pulled back the planter…

And there it was, on the very bottom board of the cedar siding. A message carved roughly into the wood. *Tony loves Dalia.*

She left the swing and crouched beside him. She heard herself laughing. The letters had a childlike look to them. "When did you do this?"

"Third grade."

"Third grade! That birthday party."

"Yep. First time I ever came out here."

A flood of memories washed over her. "The kittens!"

One of the barn cats had just had a litter, and she'd shown Tony the little nest the mother had made on an old saddle blanket in the feed barn. He'd gone completely nuts over the kitties. Cuddled them gently. Baby-talked softly to them.

"Yep. That sassy calico, Calypso—she was one of them. I said you should call her that because I thought it was a cool name for a calico. And you did. I remember how pumped I was about that years later when I found out you'd actually kept the name. And your brother was running around like some kind of commando with all his machetes and things strapped on him. He was eleven years old and I thought he was the coolest. You see? I'm a part of your history, and you're a part of mine, and I've loved you since we were little kids. There was never anyone else for me, and there never will be."

He took her hand, laid it over his heart and covered it with his own.

"There. Can you feel that?"

It was a melodramatic teenage thing to do. All she could feel was the beating of his heart, which proved nothing other than that he was alive. But it thrilled her to her core.

"Yes," she said. "I can feel it." Like an idiot, like the kind of girl who fell for such things.

And then she'd kissed him. Her mind had known perfectly well that the letters carved into the siding didn't guarantee anything, but her heart had taken it as proof positive.

"Dalia! Hey, Dalia!"

The voice calling her name brought her back to the present, and her heart gave a painful lurch because it sounded like Tony. But it was only Alex, crossing the street toward her, and waving.

She put on a smile, waved back and took a deep breath. *Steady on, Dalia. You've got this.*

Alex gave her a hug. He had on a dark blue coverall with his name embroidered over the pocket.

"What's this you're wearing?" she asked.

He looked down at himself. "It's for my second job. I work for Manny at his garage. Auto and tractor repair."

"What, construction doesn't keep you busy enough?"

"I just like to earn as much as I can."

He said it cheerfully, but it made Dalia wonder. Was it possible Tony was stinting his brother's pay?

"We live in town together, me and Tony," he said, pointing. "Got a little place right over the gym. Very convenient for working out."

"Looks pretty handy to Tito's Bar, too."

"Ha ha! Yeah, we do spend a fair amount of time there, too. They have trivia on Thursday nights. Me and Tony are a team, and we do pretty well. Tony knows sports, I know history. We just need someone who knows tech."

Dalia knew tech. For a moment Alex's face lit up, as if he'd just realized that. He got as far as "Hey, you should—" before coming to his senses and finishing lamely with "—check the place out sometime."

"I don't care for bars," she said.

"Oh, it's not just a bar anymore. They

serve food now at their expansion next door. Fancy stuff. Artisanal pizzas and wraps and things. Lots of goat cheese and roasted brussels sprouts and stuff like that. The lawyer who used to have an office there retired, and Tito got the space. It's all redone inside, with the old brick walls exposed and the hardwood floors refinished. Really beautiful, if I do say so myself. Me and Tony did the work."

"How nice for Tito," Dalia said, in a voice that clearly communicated there was no way on God's green earth she was setting foot inside a bar Tony frequented, or the adjoining restaurant, no matter how artisanal the pizza.

After an awkward pause, Alex said, "So what're you doing in town?"

She held up her mom's list. "Getting stuff for the firefighter fundraiser."

It hadn't been easy persuading her mother to stay home and let Dalia do the legwork. Her mom was clearly getting cabin fever. Dalia sympathized, but she did errands a lot faster on her own. Her mom always wanted to drive by the church, and the house where she'd grown up, and the house where she and Dalia's dad had lived when they first got married.

"Oh, yeah," said Alex. "The fundraiser is coming right up, isn't it?"

"It sure is. Honestly, I'll be glad when it's all over and the rebuild is all we have to focus on."

"I'll bet. It can't be any fun living with a giant hole in the side of your house and no kitchen. But we'll get it done. Tony's at the lumberyard right now getting the order in."

*Is he, now? Well, well, well.*

So far, Dalia's plans to monitor the rebuild hadn't borne much fruit, though not for lack of trying on her part.

"I want to see the bid," she'd told her mom. "The minute he sends it, forward a copy to me. Okay?" And her mom had said, "Sure!"

It came later that same day, while Dalia was in the living room answering some work emails. She experienced a jolt at seeing the ReyesBoysConstruction email address, but she forced herself to finish what she was doing, and not rush through it, before opening the forwarded email from Tony.

Satisfied that she'd shown adequate unconcern, she clicked the message. It was formatted nicely, with the same house graphic from the truck decal as a letterhead image.

She opened the attachments. Floor plan, elevation drawings. They looked…good. *Very* good. Not ostentatious but tasteful, comfortable. Now that she actually saw the reconfiguration of master bath, master closet and laundry room, she had to admit it made a lot of sense. The old layout was awkward, with the washer and dryer accessible only from the side porch. The new floor plan had an enclosed laundry room adjoining the kitchen. And the proposed bath and closet shared a single entry from the master bedroom, which would look a lot better than the two weirdly spaced doors in there now.

She went back to the body of the email and realized for the first time that rather than simply forwarding the message, her mother had added her as a recipient to her reply of *Looks great! Can't wait to get started!* The reply was time-stamped two minutes after the arrival of the original message. Her mom would have barely had time to open the attachments, much less study them.

"Mom! You already accepted the bid?"

"You bet I did! Don't those plans look amazing?"

"But—but we didn't go over it together yet."

"Oh, I didn't want to bother you."

"I'm right here in the same room with you! And I have an MBA in finance!"

Her mom waved a hand dismissively. "I don't want to get all bogged down in the details. I want to get a move on."

"But you love details! I thought we'd be deliberating over this for days!"

"I'm bold and decisive now. It's my new thing."

"Well, don't you want to make sure you aren't getting ripped off?"

"Ripped off? The Reyes boys would never rip me off! And people wouldn't recommend them if they were dishonest. City life has made you cynical, honey."

Dalia silently opened the next two attachments, for scope of work and payment schedule. The materials list looked reasonably detailed; she saw no obvious red flags. But she knew fraud was rampant in the construction business. With so many moving parts, so many project participants at different levels, overcharges were easy to hide.

And who would suspect someone as charming as Tony? Someone who brought out the entire volunteer fire department to clear away debris for free? A magnanimous gesture like that was a classic misdirect.

If he could put one over on hard-nosed, suspicious Dalia when he was just a callow teenager, how much more capable was he now, as a mature man, of bamboozling her sunny, optimistic, people-loving mother?

All right, then. She'd just have to keep close watch on the process. Demand copies of receipts, compare them with the bill of materials actually used, and make sure Tony wasn't billing her mom for expensive materials while using substandard ones and pocketing the difference.

She forced a smile now. "It was great seeing you, Alex, but I'd better be on my way."

"Okay. I'll see you later."

The lumberyard was at the end of the block. Dalia wouldn't get a better opportunity to check on Tony.

*Fool me once, shame on you. Fool my mother? Not on my watch.*

# *CHAPTER SIX*

TONY BREATHED DEEP of the sweet, bright scent of lumber. He felt all right, in spite of a late night at Tito's and slightly more beer than was good for him. He'd spent a second day at La Escarpa, with memories flooding his brain and Dalia looking at him like he was a hornworm on a tomato plant, and another day drawing up the plans for the rebuild. Then yesterday, Mrs. Ramirez had accepted the bid and sealed his fate. After all that, he'd needed consolation.

At least, that's what he kept telling himself.

He hadn't gone over his limit by much, and what he now considered his limit would have been just warming up back in the day. His tolerances had changed for sure. That first year back home was a haze in his memory now. But even then, no matter how sloshed he'd gotten the night before, he'd get up in the morning, down his hangover remedy and head to Bart's Gym. Alex used to say it was a good thing Tony was so vain, because it kept him from completely letting himself go. It wasn't only vanity, though. He cared how he looked, sure, but he also just plain liked physical exertion and performance. He partied hard and worked out hard. The trade-off worked well enough, for a while.

But then it started to wear on him. He didn't bounce back as fast as he used to. And one morning at the gym, Bart himself shook his head at Tony and said, "Son, you have got to start taking better care of yourself. You won't be able to cruise along on youth and a good genetic package forever."

And he realized Bart was right.

So that was the end of that. Overnight, he'd put hard drinking behind him and hadn't looked back. He'd quit altogether for several months, gone cold turkey, and then cautiously started having an occasional beer or two. He'd been relieved to discover that drinking in moderation was something he could do, and he'd never drunk to excess again, not once.

He didn't want to go down that road again. He wouldn't.

He'd walked to the lumberyard straight from Bart's after his morning workout. It was handy living within easy walking distance of the grocery store, the gym and Tito's, and within sprinting distance of the firehouse. He was almost always the first to reach the firehouse after a call, with a personal best of thirty-four seconds.

He had a hard copy of Alex's meticulous materials list in his back pocket. He could've made the order online, but he liked doing it in person. That way he could make sure it was perfectly clear exactly what was being ordered, and where it was to be delivered, and when. Plus, it was nicer this way. He got to shoot the breeze with Arturo and Wanda at the pro desk, and have a cup of the San Antonio Blend coffee that always seemed to be brewing there.

That was how they divided the labor on the business side of things. Alex had always had a better head for figures, so he handled that part. Tony was the visionary and front man. They made a good team.

A porch swing hung on display near the

front of the store. Five hundred bucks, and plastic, no less. *Sheesh. Outrageous.* It looked so cheap and flimsy compared with the one from La Escarpa. And that free-standing A-frame supporting it? Please. A porch swing belonged on a porch, hanging from the rafters.

"Running up a tab?"

The voice sounded really close, like barely a foot away. Tony jumped and let out a yell.

He'd always startled easily and showily, to the delight of everyone who knew him. It was a running joke with his college teammates to prank him by sneaking up on him, or jumping out at him, or even just making sudden loud noises. Eventually someone had started filming the results. There was a YouTube compilation video made of scene after scene of Tony being startled. Last he'd checked, it had over three hundred thousand views.

He didn't mind—at least, he hadn't back then. It was hilarious; he could see that as well as anyone. He'd laughed at that compilation video every time he'd watched it, laughed *hard*. But these days it didn't take as much to startle him, and it really wasn't funny anymore.

Especially when the other person was standing there staring at you without a hint of a smile.

"Dalia!" He held a hand to his chest and tried to laugh. It was hard to look cool when you'd just shot straight into the air like a scalded cat. "You scared me."

"Mmm-hmm, I see that. What are you doing?"

"Oh, just tryna get my heart rate back to normal. How 'bout you?"

"I came to town to run some errands for my mom. I saw Alex a few minutes ago, and he said you were about to place the order for the construction at La Escarpa. So I came over to have a look."

"You don't have to do that. I handle materials purchase at my end, with my contractor discount. Then the stuff gets delivered in stages. I'll notify your mom when the first delivery is scheduled."

It was a pretty standard, and intuitive, way of doing things. Was it possible that she'd *actually* come here because she wanted an excuse to spend time with him? Her facial expression made that seem unlikely, but with Dalia you never could tell.

"If you have nothing to hide, you won't mind if I double-check."

"Nothing to hide? Why would I… What are you saying?"

"You know what I'm saying."

And suddenly he did know, and it made him sick.

"I'm just here to make sure things get done right and my mom gets what she's paying for," she went on. "It's nothing personal."

"You're accusing me of trying to rip off a customer," Tony said. "It's personal."

"Don't be such a baby, Tony. Let's get this over with."

"You don't trust me."

"No. I don't."

"What about Alex? You don't trust him, either? You think he'd be part of some underhanded deal?"

"I don't know what Alex might or might not do, or be tricked into doing. It doesn't matter. La Escarpa is my home, my responsibility. Not his."

Tony made a scoffing sound and shook his head. "You always were a control freak,

Dalia, but this is taking it to a whole 'nother level."

"Calling me names? Wow. Very mature."

"Yeah, well, you started it."

The words sounded stupid and childish, even though it was true. She *had* started it. She'd called him a baby and accused him with no cause. And yet somehow she made it seem like she was in the right. She *radiated* righteousness, standing there looking at him just like her father used to when Tony would pick her up for a date.

He couldn't win with her. He never could.

"I can't believe this," he said. "I can't believe you actually think I would try to cheat your mother."

"It wouldn't be the first time you cheated."

"What? How can you say that? I never threw a game, and I never juiced."

"I'm not talking about *football*." She spat the word out like something foul. "I'm talking about spring break."

He should have taken a deep breath, counted to ten, whatever it was people did to keep their tempers in check and not do things they'd regret. But he was mad at being made out to be some sort of miscreant, mad at having his nice morning ruined, and he said the first thing that came into his head.

"I never cheated on you. *Never.* And it's not like I didn't have lots of chances."

The words hung there in the air, big and plain and with no way to take them back. Time seemed to stop. Dalia stood there staring at him with this wide-eyed blank look on her face and her mouth fallen open a little like she had no idea what to say. And then Tony knew he had to get out of there before that changed.

He turned and walked off...and collided with some sort of display. He heard it crashing down behind him, but he didn't look back. He kept walking, fast, out of the lumberyard and into the harsh Texas sunlight.

What was *wrong* with him? For once in his life, why couldn't he think before he spoke? He should have kept his mouth shut and left well enough alone, even if well enough was still pretty bad. But he didn't, because he was mad. And he didn't have any right to be mad or hurt here. He was the one who'd burned the bridge. He'd pushed her into breaking up with him, and he'd meant to do it, meant to make her think he was a selfish screwup and she shouldn't waste any more time on him. He was okay with that, sort of. But for her to think he cheated on her—well, apparently he wasn't okay with *that*.

His anger was gone. All he could think now was how he would have felt if he'd thought *she* cheated on *him*. That was the feeling he'd given her, for over six years.

*Tell her the truth*, Alex had said, over and over, right from the start. But Tony hadn't, because he thought things would get better and she'd never need to know. And by the time he realized that was never going to happen, it was too late, he'd gone too far and was in too deep, and it didn't matter anyway because at that point, truth or not, the two of them were through.

And now—now it was too big a tangle to sort out.

He wasn't walking anywhere in particular. He just wanted to get somewhere safe and private where no one could look at him or talk to him. He turned into the alley behind Navarro Street where he and Alex had a rented garage, more or less downstairs from their apartment.

He unlocked the door and slid it up. Their two trucks were parked there, his Dodge and Alex's Chevy, both with their Reyes Boys Construction decals. The stepside's bed was still piled high with stuff from the firefighters' cleanup day at La Escarpa—old weathered siding and beadboard and such. The remains of the porch swing were in there, too. Mrs. Ramirez had told him to burn it, but painted wood wasn't really safe to burn because it gave off toxic fumes, so he'd put it in here instead. It was all jumbled together with siding and painted porch boards.

He started pulling it out. He didn't want the porch swing going to strangers.

*Things break. Sometimes they can be fixed, and sometimes they can't.*

## *CHAPTER SEVEN*

"HE LIED," DALIA SAID. "Just straight up lied to my face. Can you believe the *nerve* of him? After all these years, after everything he put me through, he has the gall to look me in the eye and act like the whole thing never happened."

"Hmm," said Lauren.

She was gazing off camera and frowning thoughtfully. A quiver of irritation ran down Dalia's spine. Lauren wasn't supposed to be thoughtful right now. She was supposed to be outraged on Dalia's behalf. Furious. Livid.

"What do you mean, 'hmm'? You remember. You were there."

"I remember your side of things, what you said at the time."

"My *side* of things? Are you saying I made it all up?"

"No, no, of course not. It's just...well,

Dalia, in fairness, neither one of us was *there*. You don't have any actual proof. Forensic evidence. Photos. Witness testimony."

"Forensic evidence? Witness testimony? What are you, CSI? Where is all this even coming from?"

"Well, I read this article recently about memory and how unreliable it is. I don't remember exactly what it said—ha ha, that's funny, isn't it?—but it was something about how there are all these gaps in what we truly know about a situation, and how we fill in those gaps with whatever fits our preconceived notions. And over time those made-up bits become part of our memory of the event, and we think they really happened, but they didn't."

"That may be how most people operate, but not me. I look at facts. I'm not led by emotion."

"Most of the time you're not. But when it comes to Tony, you kind of are. Anyway, I don't think this has anything to do with a person's temperament. It's something everyone does. Confirmation bias, that's what it's called. We see things through these lenses of prejudice, and we make the narrative fit what we already believe."

The words felt like a slap in the face—all the more so in light of Lauren's own history of wildly distorted perceptions regarding matters of the heart. Lauren had all the relationship savvy and decision-making acumen of a strawberry daiquiri. Every time she latched onto a new guy, she came up with a fantastic web of garbled logic to explain why this one was destined for her on some cosmic level—and there'd been hordes of guys, all more or less losers. But Dalia had never mocked. Her policy was to say what she thought one time, and then zip it. Over and over, she'd listened with the patience of a saint and waited for Lauren to realize the truth for herself—and she'd always helped pick up the pieces after the inevitable heartbreak.

And *this* was what Lauren served up now, in Dalia's hour of need?

"Okay, so I don't have *forensic evidence*. What about a confession? Is that good enough?"

"Did he really confess, though? What exactly did he say? Did he say, 'Yes, I cheated on you'?"

"He didn't deny it."

"But that's not the same thing, is it?"

Dalia opened her mouth and shut it again. What *had* he said, exactly? Was it possible Lauren was right? Had she somehow misjudged the situation all those years ago?

"I've got to go," Dalia said.

"You're mad, aren't you?"

"No."

"Please don't be mad, Dalia. You're my best friend."

"I'm not mad!"

Dalia heard the sharpness in her own voice, stopped and said more calmly, "I just have to go. I've got things to do. I'll talk to you later. Have fun rock climbing."

She signed off before Lauren could say anything more and sat at her desk for a while, staring out the window. Outside, the flatbed from the lumberyard was depositing a load of strapped-together two-by-fours and two-by-sixes and such. It was a long, noisy process, with lots of beeps and clanks and hydraulic hisses, lots of ooching forward and pausing and ooching forward again, as the bright lumber came rolling backward along some metal pipes, then gradually tilting off the end of the trailer. Tony and Alex ran around putting four-by-four boards underneath where the lumber was going, to keep it from resting directly on the ground. Then Tony shouted something at the driver, the truck went forward and the edge of the load dropped off the back of the trailer.

And suddenly Tony turned around and was looking straight at her.

And smiling.

The smile wasn't intended for her. He was probably just glad to have the lumber successfully unloaded, or maybe he was laughing at something Alex said. But it sent a shot of pure sweetness through her. Her anger fell away, and all at once it was like the past didn't matter at all. Nothing mattered but that smile. Those eyes. How it would feel to be in those arms, right now.

It lasted less than a second. Then his eyes clouded, the smile faltered and he looked away. If that wasn't guilt, then what was it?

All the sweetness she'd felt turned into a hard lump of lead in her chest. She turned her back to him. She had to get out of here.

She pulled on her riding boots and took her .357 Magnum down from the top shelf, along with her thigh holster. A few minutes later she was heading out the back door, away from the lumber and Tony.

The grass was unusually lush and green for September, with patches of abnormally tall sunflowers. A cool front had come in overnight, taking the edge off the late-summer heat.

A horse was grazing in the paddock north of the house—a golden-brown horse with black points and a black dorsal stripe running from mane to tail.

Dalia put her fingers in her mouth and whistled.

The horse's head shot up and his ears perked. He let out a whinny and ran to her.

Dalia's dad had trained all the livestock to come when called. For cattle, he used a long, piercing yell that rose in pitch at the end. She used to love to hear that high whooping cry ring out across the pasture and see the cows come running.

Buck reached the fence and put his head close to Dalia's, whuffling softly, as if it had been only a few days since she'd last called him to her, instead of more years than she cared to count. Nothing wrong with *his* memory. Her throat got tight as she scratched his chest and felt his whiskers tickling her face. He smelled of grass and sunshine.

She led him through the gate to the feed barn, where the tack was stored in a lean-to. His feet looked all right, but it was about time to get the farrier out, and he clearly hadn't been groomed in a while. She added a reminder to her phone to ask her mom when his teeth had last been floated. Maybe she'd arrange for the equine dentist to come out while she was here. Dealing with horse health care would be a lot more relaxing than dealing with Tony, and it needed to be done.

By the time Dalia had Buck saddled and was riding him along the fence line, the last lingering tension over her conversation with Lauren had dissolved.

La Escarpa was divided into two distinct elevations and topographies. Northwest was all rolling hills and rocky soil, typical Hill Country. Southeast was flatter, with a mixture of red-and-black clay and sandy loam.

In between, following a rough diagonal, was a slope, abrupt in parts and gentler in others. This was the "scarp" of La Escarpa, basically the Balcones Fault in miniature.

The house and barns stood on the hilly side, safe from floods. There was good pasture in the lowland, what her mother always referred to as "the Houston-y part." Fewer cedars, more oaks and elms.

They followed the horse trail east, to a fence that separated the home pasture from the lower elevation. Dalia opened the gate, rode through and closed it again without dismounting, keeping her eyes open for danger—rattlesnakes, wild hogs, rabid skunks.

They headed down the switchback that made the slope manageable, and south to the first fork in the trail, where Buck flicked his ear back, ready to be told what to do. They went left, crossed the creek and went left again to loop around the low acreage.

It was so restful, being around animals. You didn't need many words with them. You communicated with them mostly through body language and energy, the same way they communicated with each other. They didn't expect you to make small talk, or tell you how you ought to smile more. They didn't push you to share your feelings. They didn't lie or cheat or make ridiculous speeches about the unreliability of memory. They were the best company. Some of the most peaceful hours of her life had been spent riding this trail, with Merle loping behind in his tireless border collie gait.

"A merle-coated dog called Merle, and a buckskin horse called Buck. Seriously?"

Tony's voice twined its way through her thoughts, gently playful. He'd been appalled by the lack of imagination in her animal names. He'd teased her about it a lot, but never in a mean way. That was one thing about Tony: he was never mean. He kept up an unending stream of bizarre alternative names—Merle Haggard, Merlin the Magician, Merlin Brando. Bucky, Buckster, Buckleberry Finn, even Sergeant Barnes, as in Bucky Barnes. They always made her smile.

She was smiling now.

She gave her head a shake, trying to knock Tony out of her mind.

The trail curved more or less northward, around a big stock pond with a pair of ducks out for a swim. She and Tony had their first kiss here, if you didn't count that one in seventh grade. She'd brought him here during Marcos's last-ever pasture party, that sweet-scented spring evening before Marcos left for Marine boot camp. They'd sat together on the grassy bank and watched as a family of raccoons came to wash their food at the edge of the moonlit water.

And then she kissed him—or he kissed her. Afterward, she wasn't sure who had made the first move, and anyway, it didn't matter. All that mattered was they'd both wanted to do this for a long, long time, and it was finally happening. And then his arms went around her and her hands were in his hair, and just as he started slowly lowering them both to the ground, a rutting axis buck showed up, crashing through the brush, stamping his hooves and bellowing—and Tony shot straight into the air and let out a scream unlike anything Dalia had ever heard before. She had never laughed so long or so hard in her life. He'd looked so funny, with the whites of his eyes showing all the way around the irises, and his hair standing on end like a cartoon character.

"Stop it!"

She said the words out loud, startling Buck, who shied a bit and glanced back.

She took a deep breath, forcing herself to calm down, and laid a reassuring hand against Buck's neck. She had to get a grip. This was *her* childhood home. Tony had no business hijacking her memories.

At the top of the curve, the trail was joined by a second switchback coming down from the scarp. Then it turned southward, following the east fence that ran along Ybarra Road.

Once the trail rounded the bend, she forgot about Tony for a while. Something was off. And the farther south she rode, the worse it got. It was like she'd strayed onto someone else's property, or into some *Twilight Zone* version of La Escarpa. She actually looked around to make sure she was in the right place, but no, the fences were all where they were supposed to be, and the general topography was right.

But everything else was wrong.

The low acreage had its own road access, was off the highway and couldn't be seen from the house—all of which made it an ideal partying spot for rural teenagers. Marcos's friends used to drive on in, turn their music up, let their tailgates down and bring out kegs and coolers of cheap beer.

But anyone who tried that today would just get his tires punctured and his paint scratched from all the encroaching mesquite brush.

You had to be vigilant with mesquite. It was incredibly hardy, drought-resistant and quick to resprout. Without proper management, it could dominate a pasture, drastically reducing forage and generally getting in the way and making a nuisance of itself.

This pasture hadn't quite been taken over yet, but it was well on its way. Already it looked like the sort of pasture that used to make her dad shudder when he drove past.

When did this *happen*? How had things gotten this bad? She felt a surge of anger at Marcos and Eliana for not telling her, for not doing more to help out. But that wasn't fair. Why should everything be their responsibility? La Escarpa was her home, too, and she'd stayed away longer than either of them.

Okay, then. She was here now, wasn't she? She'd get things sorted.

For starters, this whole southeast pasture needed to be root-plowed. That would mean less grass for the cattle in the short term, and holding on to the hay from the south parcel instead of selling it, but in the long run it meant better grazing. The cattle guard was more than half-filled with gravel—runoff from those low spots in the roadbed, no doubt. It should be dug out and relaid, and the roadbed regraded, with a yard or so of fresh gravel. The fencing was a mess, overgrown with hackberries and icicle cactus. It ought to be cleared and restrung. Wasn't there some new alternative to barbed wire, some sort of superstrong smooth wire that was stretched incredibly tight? She ought to look into that. Run cost comparisons. Weigh pros and cons.

If she and Tony had gotten married, maybe they'd be casually shopping for acreage of their own by now.

If they'd had the same week off for spring break, sophomore year, maybe they'd have spent it together in boring old Limestone Springs, instead of her going home with Lauren to Pennsylvania one week and Tony heading to South Padre on a football team debauch fest the next. A guy with his looks and personality, on a beach filled with partying college students—he'd have had to fight tooth and nail *not* to cheat.

He'd called her one night from the island. She was back in school again, studying hard, forcing herself not to call or text too much, because she was not a weak, silly, clingy, insecure girlfriend.

Right away she knew something was wrong. It was nothing obvious like wild party sounds in the background or blatant inebriation. But there was something off in his tone, something almost excessively sweet and affectionate. Exactly how Tony would sound if he *did* cheat, as she later realized. He'd be sorry after, of course he would, but he couldn't take it back.

Then things got weirder still. Tony's end of the conversation got disjointed, with random questions, and answers that didn't fit what Dalia was saying, finally ending with, "Ha ha, yeah, that sounds great. Look, I gotta go, okay? I'll talk to you later. Love you."

The *love you* sounded strange, kind of forced and tacked on, and he hung up before she could say *I love you, too.*

The weirdness didn't end there. Tony kept acting off in their conversations, with a strained quality to his affection that had never been there before. Tony, the most spontaneous and transparent person she knew, actually sounded *fake*.

Finally, things came to a head in that fight over the phone, and the next day she boxed up his stuff and put it in the mail.

*I should be grateful*, she'd told herself. *I'm lucky it happened now and not later, after I'd actually married him.*

It wasn't much consolation. She wouldn't have believed it was possible to hurt like that and still function. Lauren was a godsend, unfailing in sympathy and comfort. Now Lauren had betrayed her, as well, casting doubt on whether Tony had cheated at all. It was ridiculous, but...what if she was right?

That flare of temper Tony had shown at the lumberyard had looked so *real*. Tony was a lot of things, but a hardened pathological liar wasn't one of them. If he'd done it, he'd be embarrassed, defensive, deflective. Not angry.

And what if he hadn't cheated? What if

the phone call and the behavior afterward meant something else entirely?

They were heading westward now. They closed the loop, crossed back over the creek where they'd crossed it before, and reached the fork again. Buck flicked his ear back, waiting for the go-ahead. They could go home the way they'd come, or make another left and loop around the low acreage to the southwest.

Dalia turned him toward home. She'd ridden long enough for her first time back in the saddle.

They climbed the switchback and reached the scarp gate. The truck from the lumberyard was gone, and there was no sign of Tony or Alex. As Dalia closed the gate behind her, she saw something moving around in the orchard that looked suspiciously like her mother. She rode on over and halted Buck at the orchard fence. Yep, there was her mom, scurrying around on her crutches, with chickens fluttering along behind her like she was the Pied Piper.

"Mom, what are you doing out here? You should be inside resting your foot."

She'd said the same thing so many times that it was starting to lose its meaning.

"One of my Brahmas is acting funny," Mom said. "I think she's hiding a nest somewhere. I've got to find it and make her stop."

"I could have done that for you."

"I couldn't wait for you to get back. I've been trying for days to catch her in the act. Just now I was taking the trash out when I heard her give a loud celebratory squawk, and I just *knew* she'd laid an egg. I had to hurry out before I could forget exactly where she was when she did it."

Dalia suppressed the urge to remind her mother that she could have taken the trash out for her, too.

"Did you find the nest?" she asked instead.

Mom sighed. "No. I guess she was just having me on."

Buck chose that exact moment to blow loudly through his nose, as if to say, *Chickens. Honestly.*

"So," Dalia said, "I just rode down to the low acreage and—"

Mom cringed. "I know, I know. The mesquites are taking over. Travis was supposed to take care of that, but clearly he had better things to do."

"Who's Travis?"

"My latest former hired man. He lit out for Texarkana back in June."

"June? That's three months ago! Why haven't you gotten anyone else?"

"Well, I don't exactly have applicants beating my door down! Hired men are hard to find and harder to keep. The ones who're any good always want a place of their own, and sooner or later they get it. And the ones who aren't any good, aren't any good! I've had thirteen hired men in the past four years, and half that time I haven't had any hired man at all."

"Well, hired man or no hired man, something's got to be done about that pasture."

"I know. I'll get the Mendoza boys to come out. They do land clearing."

"You ought to get them to clear the fence line and redo the cattle guard while they're at it."

Her mom shook her head. "No. I can't afford all that."

*You can't afford for the cattle to get out, either*, Dalia thought, but she held her tongue.

If the money wasn't there, then it just wasn't there. It didn't seem right that the kitchen rebuild could go forward while the ranch work stalled out for lack of funds. But the rebuild was coming out of insurance money.

"Go back inside and put your foot up," Dalia said. "I'll get Buck taken care of and then heat up some dinner. And tomorrow I'll make it my mission to outsmart your egg-hiding Brahma."

She dismounted outside the feed barn, led Buck to the door—

And there was Tony.

"What are you—" Dalia began, then stopped because it was obvious what he was doing. He was arranging bales of coastal Bermuda hay onto the trailer, no doubt in preparation for the hayride at the firefighter fundraiser.

"Oh, sorry," Tony said at almost the same moment.

He had on yet another Texas T-shirt, one where the shape of the state was formed by the various city names all written where they belonged.

"No, that's okay," said Dalia. "I just need the tack room."

"I know it's a little early to get the trailer

ready," said Tony. "But, well, we were already out here, and your mom asked us to go get the small bales from the feed store, and Alex said why not go ahead and load 'em up and put 'em on the trailer while they're still nice and bright. But I don't have to do this now. I'll just—I'll get out of your way."

That flash of anger he'd shown at the lumberyard encounter was gone without a trace. Now he just looked unhappy. Because he felt guilty?

"I said it's fine," said Dalia.

It wasn't fine. It was painfully awkward. But it was also a perfect opportunity, probably the best she'd ever get.

Maybe memory *was* unreliable. But the truth was real. And the truth mattered.

She steeled herself, opened her mouth—

"Don't," Tony said.

"Don't what?"

"You're getting ready to talk about—about what happened. And I…I just can't do that, Dalia. I've got to keep my head on straight. When we—when things ended between us—that was the worst time of my life, and it was no picnic for Alex and my mom and grandparents, either. I can't get sucked back into the way things were then. I've got too many people depending on me. I know you have good reasons for thinking I'm unreliable. But I'm good at what I do. And I don't rip people off. You can go over my bookkeeping if you want, check receipts against delivered materials, talk to Alex, whatever. Just let me do my job."

She swallowed hard. "Okay. I, uh, I'm sorry I was so…hostile before, in the lumberyard. That was uncalled for."

"Thank you for saying that."

A long uncomfortable moment passed, and then Dalia turned back to her horse.

She took off Buck's bridle, clipped his halter to a rope and tied the rope to the hitching post near the tack room door. Buck kept his head turned, eyeballing the hay with mild interest.

"Never mind that," Dalia told him. "You've got plenty of green stuff in your pasture."

Working from the left, she undid the back cinch, then the breast collar, reaching around Buck's neck to drape it across his back, and then the front cinch. As she was tying up the latigo, Tony came up to the horse's other side and hooked the cinch straps over the saddle horn.

"Is this Buckleberry Finn?" he asked.

She felt a smile coming on but managed to hold it back. "Sure is."

"Whoa! What is he now, twenty? He looks amazing! What's your secret, huh, buddy?"

His voice sounded all high and sweet, like it had that day in the barn with the kittens. He'd always been goofily affectionate with animals.

"Remember when I rode him?" Tony asked.

Their eyes locked across Buck's back. In an instant, the years fell away and they were eighteen again, Tony in still another graphic T-shirt with the state of Texas on it, Dalia pulling him to his feet and brushing the dust off him, both of them stumbling and laughing and falling into each other's arms.

She couldn't hold back the smile anymore, but she turned her head to hide it. "I don't know that I'd call it *riding*."

For about two seconds after Tony had gotten into the saddle, Buck had stood there with a comically shocked look on his face. Then he'd lowered himself to the ground and begun to roll.

Tony dragged off the saddle and pad and put them away on their racks. “Half a ton of angry horseflesh tryna crush me into the ground,” he said. “I thought I was dead for sure.”

“It was your own fault,” said Dalia. “You weren’t confident enough, and he could sense that.”

“Well, of course I wasn’t confident. I was nervous.”

“Nervous? What do you mean? You’d been riding since before you could walk. You rode a *bull*.”

His eyes lost focus, and he chuckled. “Yeah, I did, didn’t I? And I won, too.”

“I know you did. I was there.”

She remembered how it felt, watching him from the stands that night—that hot choking mixture of excitement, fear and pride. His first time out, eighteen years old, barely old enough to qualify, and he’d taken home a prize.

“I was lucky,” he said. “It was a small rodeo, and other guys, guys who were really better than me, were having an off night.”

“You still made it to eight seconds. Luck was part of it, sure, but you were good.”

He smiled at her. "Thanks. Anyway, yeah, I could ride. But with the Buckster, here—that was different. He was *your* horse. It was a big deal, meeting him. Almost as bad as meeting your dad. Maybe worse, since your dad didn't actually try to kill me. So yeah. I'm sure I was giving off some sort of vibe. And Buck Rogers here was like, 'Whaaat? Get this riffraff outta here. You can do better than this loser, girl.'"

His tone was light, but there was something sad in it. Dalia didn't know what to say. For some reason it had never occurred to her that Tony could have been nervous about meeting her horse. He'd seemed so big and strong and unbeatable to her back then, but he'd only been a boy.

Tony went back to the hay trailer, and Dalia took a towel from a shelf and started wiping the sweat off Buck's coat, trying not to think of the smooth fit of Tony's jeans or the contoured fade pattern of the denim over his thighs.

By the time she finished with the currycomb, Tony had gone.

She felt relieved and disappointed at the same time. Being around Tony was…

unnerving. He made her lose her head. It was good that they were on better terms now, probably the best terms she could hope for, but all things considered, she ought to stay away from him as much as possible. And she was about to have a full day of him at the FFF, starting with an early-morning football game between Limestone Springs and another department.

But Tony wasn't the only firefighter in Limestone Springs, and plenty of people besides firefighters would be at the fund-raiser, spread out over several acres. How hard could it be to avoid one man at a huge community-wide event?

She'd manage. She had to.

## *CHAPTER EIGHT*

A WHOLE LOT of compressed action took place in the three seconds between the snap and the throw. It was like time slowed down, or Tony suddenly acquired superspeed. Every detail stood out sharp and clear—the end-to-end lengths of fire hose outlining the playing field in the smooth stretch of mown pasture, the pale blue of the early-morning sky, the relative positions of the players on both teams, the weight and texture of the football in his hand.

Directly before him, a mass of blockers in red and blue jostled and grunted. Downfield, potential receivers struggled to get free.

His attention narrowed to a single receiver in a red Limestone Springs VFD T-shirt, arms wildly waving, eyes wide with hope.

Tony raised the ball to ear level and threw.

The ball spiraled cleanly through the air.

Clint sprang, arms stretched way above his head, rising higher and higher.

His fingertips just grazed the ball before it sailed past.

A collective groan rose from the crowd.

Tony clenched his teeth, biting down on his anger. At himself, mostly, and maybe a little at Clint for not being a few inches taller. But there was no point in showing it. The purpose of the annual exhibition football game between the volunteer fire departments of Limestone Springs and Schraeder Lake, as Mad Dog insisted on reminding Tony year after year for some reason, was really three purposes. First, to foster team spirit within each department. Second, to get to know the guys on the other side. The two departments often cooperated on big fires and floods, so it helped to interact regularly in a different context. Third, as a draw to the community. The residents of Limestone Springs turned out in droves to watch this game, and that meant more money in the coffers, which meant better equipment and potentially more lives saved.

All pretty worthwhile goals, the kind that didn't leave room for personal ego. So prior to the start of the game, on Mad Dog's orders, he always gave the guys the whole all-in-good-fun, teamwork-is-what-counts, just-give-it-your-best-shot speech. And it *was* fun. It felt good to play again, even at this level. Losing football had been like losing part of himself. Of course, he'd lost other things at the same time, not least of which was his girl, so for a while it'd been an all-around depression fest. Just being out of that dark fog was reason enough for gratitude. Playing football with his guys was icing on the cake.

Still, winning would be a lot more fun than losing—especially with Dalia over there by Mad Dog, watching. And they weren't going to win if Tony couldn't place the ball where it needed to go.

"Looks like Reyes is hearing footsteps," said one of the Schraeder Lake players, loud enough for Tony to hear.

The common taunt meant the quarterback was so scared of getting tackled that he kept fumbling the ball. Tony ignored it. He'd never been afraid of being hit, but there wasn't much he could say in the way of a comeback. *I didn't fumble, I just overthrew*—that wasn't much of a defense.

Then another Schraeder Lake guy, a Mitch Somebody, said, "Or maybe his old man bet against him and got him to throw the game."

Tony threw back his head in a long, hard, exaggerated laugh. He even added an actual knee slap. "Oh, man, that is so *funny*! You're cracking me up here. How do you come up with this stuff? Have you been waiting all year to use that?"

Mitch didn't laugh, just smiled a smarmy sort of smile. "Come on, man. Don't get mad. You know I don't mean it."

"Sure, I know. You're just kidding, right? It's all in good fun. We're all here to encourage a spirit of cooperation between departments for the good of the community, so we can do a better job at stuff like, you know, *saving lives*. Nobody would want to ruin that by being an egotistical jackass. Right?"

As he spoke, Tony stepped up to him, closer and closer, until their faces were only a few inches apart. Mitch took a step back. Other guys started to gather around, Limestone Springs on one side, Schraeder Lake on the other.

"Come on, Tony," Wallace Griggs said. "Let's just play."

"Yeah," said Tony, with one last look at Mitch. "Let's just play."

Mitch gave Tony another smarmy smile before oozing off. He was in Tony's head now, and he knew it.

Because the thing was, there really had been a scandal with betting on high school football during Tony's day, and to no one's surprise, Tony's dad had turned out to be right in the middle of it. It wasn't the worst thing his dad ever did, not by a long shot, but it did not look good. The best thing that could be said about the nasty episode was that contrary to what Mitch said, there was never so much as a hint that Tony had thrown a game. Limestone Springs had been undefeated that year. And Tony knew without asking that his father had never, would never, bet against him.

Still, it stung. Tony was just glad Alex wasn't around to hear what Mitch said, because no way would his brother have kept his cool.

It was rough on both of them, growing up with a smooth-talking, conniving, unreliable compulsive gambler for a father, but in different ways. Alex was such a completely different kind of guy. He'd been at odds with their dad for pretty much his whole life, and as soon as he was old enough, he'd all but severed ties with him. For Tony, it wasn't that simple.

*Just like your father.* How many times had Tony heard that growing up? It'd taken him a while to realize it wasn't always a compliment.

The funny thing was, his football obsession actually did start with his father. Long before Tony understood the game, he'd enjoyed the sense of closeness he'd felt watching games on TV with his dad. Alex didn't care for it, so it was just Tony and his dad's special thing. Carlos was the kind of guy whose emotions were contagious. If he got excited about something, the people around him got excited, too. He'd been a good player himself in high school, and when it became clear that Tony was going to be *very* good, he was ecstatic.

On the next play, Mitch hit Tony just after

the throw, driving him into the ground. It was a cheap shot, but that couldn't be blamed for Tony's bad pass, which was even wider of the mark than the one before. Tony spat out some dirt and got back on his feet. He would have rolled his shoulder some to work out the soreness, but he didn't want to give Mitch the satisfaction. It was a minor ding, along with some bruised ribs and a scrape down the side of one leg—nothing that couldn't be fixed by a hot bath, some New-Skin and a couple ibuprofens.

He darted a quick glance at Dalia and caught her looking. She used to watch him play when they were little, but even back then it was hard to catch her in the act. Used to drive him crazy. He'd wanted her to look at him for real, the way other girls did, in more than quick cool glances. He'd wanted to matter to her.

He still wanted that.

Well, he'd just have to give her something worth watching.

Some of the guys were dawdling on the field, wiping the sweat off their faces, complaining about the heat. Tony clapped his hands together twice, quickly, and said, "Line up!"

This time, when Mitch came after him, Tony deftly spun away, leaving Mitch to dive into empty ground. Tony threw, and as the ball made its arc he thought *please, please, please*, and Clint caught it.

The Limestone Springs fans erupted in cheers. Tony looked over toward Dalia again, but she was gone.

What wouldn't he give to be eleven years old again, throwing the ball around on the playground? All those possibilities, all those things he hadn't messed up yet. Dalia doing her best to ignore him, same as now, but for different reasons.

"All in good fun," Tony said softly.

Right.

LA ESCARPA LOOKED all wrong, like a surreal version of itself in a fever dream. Everywhere Dalia looked she saw wooden signs, hand-lettered in that fancy, loopy, uneven cursive that was so popular nowadays, grandly proclaiming the way to the pumpkin patch, the corn maze, the hayride, the mechanical bull. The feed barn had raffle prizes and items for sale laid out on tables and booths, while the machine shed, unnaturally clean and festive, had been converted to an eating area. A wooden platform stage stood ready for the band, the Chicharrones, next to an outdoor portable dance floor, which Dalia hadn't even known was a thing before today. Even the house itself looked wrong, with the two-by-sixes of the newly framed kitchen standing up against the sky, as bright and clean as fresh hay.

Weirdest of all was the actual football field marked out on a one-acre stretch in the low pasture.

How many times had she watched Tony play? She started to calculate—eight games in a high school regular season, times four years, plus playoffs, plus middle school, plus playground ball in elementary school… On second thought, she didn't want to know.

Had he always done that head-swiveling thing before he threw the ball? He looked like a cat getting ready to pounce. It was outrageously adorable.

But it could not be denied that his game

had seen better days. He still had plenty of power, but his accuracy had suffered. It hurt, seeing him misthrow the ball and then try to act like it didn't bother him.

Someone called her name. Mad Dog was sitting in a camp chair, waving to her. He had on his big straw hat and a long-sleeved shirt, and there were white streaks of sunscreen on his face.

"Come on over and set a spell," he said.

It was kind of hilarious how Mad Dog affected all these Southern idioms, when everyone knew he was a latecomer to Texas. Moved there as an adult from Iowa.

Dalia took the camp chair next to him.

"Looks like a good turnout," she said.

"Oh, yeah. All the admission tickets sold out weeks ago, and we've still got folks showing up at the gate. Raffle items are bringing in a good bit, too."

"Great! You'll be able to buy yourself a nice new fire hose."

He chuckled. "Yeah, and maybe knock a few other items off our equipment wish list. I got my eye on a fancy defibrillator machine."

"Good for you. My dad was always very particular about using the right tool for the job and investing in high-quality equipment."

"I know he was, and he was right. Trouble is, you can't always afford what you really need. It's a juggling act for the department, keeping our existing equipment in good trim and adding new stuff. Some years it's all we can do to keep our heads above water, financially speaking, but once in a while we get to buy us some new toys that'll help us do our job better. But some things don't change. Our response time is about as low as it's gonna..."

He trailed off. Something was happening on the field. A Schraeder Lake player, a big ox-like guy, said something to Tony, and Dalia could tell it was something nasty. First Tony was laughing in an exaggerated way, then he was bowing up and getting in the guy's face, and players on both sides started gathering around like something was about to go down.

But suddenly it was over and the teams were lining up again.

Dalia let her breath out slowly. She'd forgotten what a rush it was, seeing Tony's warrior side. He was usually so friendly and funny and good-natured, but that all fell away in an instant on the field, or whenever someone got out of line.

Mad Dog let his breath out, too, and took a draw from his craft beer.

Then Dalia said, "This is long overdue, Mad Dog, but I want to thank you for what you did for my dad."

"Well, thank you for saying so, Dalia. I only wish it'd been enough." He paused, swallowed and said, "He was my friend."

"Yeah." She cleared her throat. "You did everything you could."

"Still."

Another silence passed.

"What was the name of that border collie y'all used to have?" Mad Dog asked.

"Merle."

"Yeah, that's it. When I came out here to work on your dad, that dog met me at the gate and gave me an escort down the driveway. Then while I was trying to, you know…"

"Revive him?" Dalia said steadily.

"Yeah. Well, that dog did laps around the two of us the whole time. 'Round and 'round and 'round."

"Herding behavior," Dalia said. "Border collie instinct."

"Exactly. Only in this case, completely useless. Sometimes in this job, I feel like a border collie doing laps. Busy, but not accomplishing anything."

"But you accomplish a lot, Mad Dog. You have to know that. All the people you helped during the storm. My mom."

"You're right, I know. Some you win, and some you lose, and some wake you up in a cold sweat in the middle of the night. You have to make your peace with that in order to stick it out and be of any use to the community. Not everyone can. Some guys join up for the wrong reasons. It's playtime to them—it's fun. Messing around with fire, operating fancy equipment, driving trucks real fast. That aspect draws in a lot of reckless, physical, showy guys. But when the fire's out, the real work starts, with checklists and cleanup and inventory and equipment repair, not to mention training. The flashy ones get bored and drop out. You know the type, all hat and no cattle."

"I do," said Dalia. "That must be frustrating."

"Used to be. Nowadays I just sit back and wait for the chips to fall. You can't predict who's gonna hang in there and who's not. I've been surprised lots of times. Now, you take that guy right there."

He pointed at Tony. "I thought for sure he'd be a one-hit wonder. But he turned out to have a whole lot of staying power. He doesn't just *endure* the hosing down and long tedious after-fire work and other boring nonglamorous parts of the job. He makes a game out of it, keeps everyone's spirits up. I never saw anything like it. He's real good with trauma victims, too, and with kids. I've started sending him to do the yearly presentation at the elementary school, and they love him there. And he's the best I've ever seen at getting surly people to cooperate. I thought at first they were just intimidated by his size, and maybe that's part of it, but it's not all. There was this one time, we had a drunk and disorderly mixed up in this incident involving a beer keg, a crossbow and a Kubota tractor—long story. The guy needed to go to the hospital, but he didn't want to, and it wasn't like we could take him against his will. He got more and more agitated, and he finally punched Tony in the jaw. Tony didn't retaliate or even seem to get mad. He just kept on, all friendly and persuasive and nonthreatening. Ten minutes later, the guy was spilling his life's story to him, bawling his eyes out, like Tony was his last friend in the world."

Dalia looked at Tony on the field. "He always was a charmer."

"Yeah, I guess I don't have to tell you, do I? You two are about the same age. You probably went to school together."

"Yeah. Yeah, I've known Tony all my life."

She really needed to change the subject.

"This is a good game," she said. "No wonder everyone comes to see it year after year. It's impressive that you have so many decent players."

Each team had ten men on the field. That allowed for blockers, making the game a lot more interesting to watch than if there'd been just a quarterback plus a handful of potential receivers running around hoping to catch the ball.

"Well, it's Texas," said Mad Dog. "Football is king here. Plus, there's a whole lot of a certain personality that joins a volunteer fire department."

"Why don't you play?"

He laughed and shook his head. "Oh, no. I was never a jock. I was a band kid in school. I played the saxophone, you know what I mean? I used to sort of scoff at sports, but looking back, I realize a lot of that was sour grapes. I see the value in it now, or in the sort of person who's good at sports. Like Tony, there. All the qualities that make him good at football carry over to firefighting and rescue work. Physical strength, always a plus. Leadership. Infectious enthusiasm. And that ability to take in a complex situation at a glance and make a quick decision and act on it."

She got up. It was really too much, listening to Mad Dog sing Tony's praises while having to sit here watching him in all his glory.

"I'm going to go get a drink," Dalia said.

"Alrighty, then. See you later."

She walked away. A burst of cheering sounded behind her, but she didn't look back.

## *CHAPTER NINE*

"GOOD MORNING, ALL you beautiful people! Thank you for coming out today for the fifth annual fall fundraiser for the Limestone Springs Volunteer Fire Department!"

The crowd clapped and cheered, and Tony gave a nice loud whistle to keep things lively. Claudia Cisneros smiled down on them all from the portable stage, looking like a queen. She had a legal practice in town—property law, mostly—and she was like an honorary aunt to Alex and Tony, and a lot of other people, too.

"The department has many, many fundraisers throughout the year—the fajita cook-off, the chili cook-off, the bake sale," she went on. "But this event right here is by far their biggest revenue generator. It's the brainchild of our hostess, Renée Ramirez, and her work and tireless dedication make it possible. This was her idea, y'all. She *volunteered* to open up La Escarpa to the community, and even now, less than three weeks after her house was nearly demolished by softball-sized hail and hurricane-force straight winds, she hasn't begged off. That's the spirit that made Texas, folks. Let's give it up for Renée!"

Wild applause. Claudia raised her own hands above her head to clap. Mrs. Ramirez, in her chair with her injured foot resting on a camp stool, held up her insulated cup and waved.

"The day's festivities started early this morning with an exhibition football game between the volunteer fire departments of Limestone Springs and Schraeder Lake, and I'm proud to say that we mopped the floor with them for the fifth year in a row!"

Claudia's voice rose near the end to be heard above a fresh swell of cheering. People chanted Tony's name. He glanced over at Dalia. She was clapping, but in a polite sort of a way, and she wasn't chanting.

Man, she looked good in that deep red tank top, those dark jeans and riding boots, with that long, thick braid of hair hanging down her back. He remembered the rush of pride he used to feel whenever they were seen in public together. Looking around at other people, strangers in a restaurant, like, *Can you believe it? A girl like this, in love with me?* Heck, just being near her was a high.

Claudia waited, giving the crowd time to show their excitement and settle down on their own.

"Now for some history and statistics about our fine department. Pay attention, because there *will* be a test later."

The crowd laughed, and then Claudia started in with a vengeance—all about how the Limestone Springs Volunteer Fire Department was one of the oldest in the state, and how many residents it served over how many square miles and how many miles of state highway. "That's a lot of territory for twenty men and women," she said. Then she told how many medical calls the department had done last year, how many engine company runs, how many for brush trucks, water supply and technical rescue.

"I can already tell you this year's stats are going to be higher because of this month's hailstorm. All that for a department that's manned by citizen volunteers—and that really is the spirit of Texas, isn't it? Texans have always been quick to step up and do what needed to be done to protect their community—whether that meant guarding the cannon at Gonzalez, joining up with Travis at the Alamo, enlisting in General Houston's army to keep this great land of ours out of the hands of tyrants, or rescuing neighbors from fire or flood."

More applause.

"Our firefighters are all volunteers. You know them. They are your friends and neighbors and family. I wish, folks, I *wish* they could be compensated fairly for their time and effort. But the coffers are strained to the limit trying to keep up with equipment and training. That money doesn't come from taxes. So this department needs our support. Now, given everything they do for us, it would not be at all unreasonable for them to ask you to open up your wallets right now and give. But that's not what they're asking you to do. You get to support them by having a fantastic time! Go on a hayride. Ride the mechanical bull. Buy a pumpkin from the pumpkin patch. Match your wits with the corn maze. Have your picture taken with Scarecrow Bill. Cool off and chill out with a delicious craft beer from one of our local breweries. Enjoy live music by the Chicharrones. Take a look at our raffle items and buy a ticket for a chance to win. We have many, many other items for sale under the tent—books, crafts and, of course, the much-anticipated photo calendar, featuring actual members of the Limestone Springs Volunteer Fire Department."

More applause, louder and wilder than ever. Eardrum-piercing wolf whistles and woo-hoo noises.

Claudia's voice rose over it all. "Enjoy your day, and remember, every dollar you spend goes to support this department and the men and women who run it."

The crowd broke apart. Claudia stepped down from the stage, and the Chicharrones started to play. Couples gathered on the dance floor.

Tony took a quick look at Dalia. How would it be if he asked her to dance? Would it be weird? Would she slap him or throw a drink in his face or something? Probably not, since they'd made their sort-of truce.

Probably she'd just look at him like she felt sorry for him.

But what if she said yes?

There was no point even thinking about that, though. If they danced, they'd most likely talk. And if they talked, she might start asking questions that he'd have a hard time answering.

No. Things were better off the way they were.

A movement close to his right side made him startle, and when he saw what it was, he startled even more and let out a shout. It was a man-size creature with a burlap face, wearing patchwork clothing with straw sticking out at the wrists, neck and ankles. The hands were gloved, with no human skin showing. Even though the mouth on the burlap face was painted in a smile, the overall effect was creepy as heck.

People nearby laughed at Tony's reaction, and the creature itself jumped backward in an exaggerated motion.

Tony held a hand to his racing heart and caught his breath. Everyone was watching him now, so he said, "Good job, Scarecrow Bill. Carry on."

Scarecrow Bill cut a caper, something like a soft-shoe dance move, if soft-shoe dance was performed by a straw-stuffed bundle of clothing in human form. Then he slunk off, to Tony's relief.

"Freaky, huh?"

The words came from right behind Tony's shoulder, making him startle all over again. He spun around and saw big blue eyes with eyelashes so long they didn't seem real, and a bright, red-lipped smile.

She held up her hands in an I-come-in-peace gesture. "Sorry! Didn't mean to scare you."

"That's okay. You're a much pleasanter surprise than Scarecrow Bill."

She laughed. "I'd say I was flattered, but a lot of things are a pleasanter surprise than Scarecrow Bill. He's kind of terrifying."

"I know, right? I mean, I realize that's Bill Darcy from Darcy's Hardware, but *man*, does he freak me out in that getup."

"I feel the same way. That blank burlap face, those button eyes. And he never talks."

"Nope. Just shuffles around like some soulless entity."

"Pretty sure you and I are the only ones who feel that way. The town loves him."

"Probably 'cause he's doing some mind-control thing on all of them. We're the only ones who're free from his spell."

"Then we'll have to stick together." She smiled and tossed a long curl over her shoulder. "Hey, I know you, don't I?"

"Maybe. Where do you think you think you know me from?"

He hoped she wouldn't say she recognized him from old football pictures in the trophy case at the high school. She didn't look young enough to still *be* in high school, but she was definitely younger than he was. And he was getting tired of recent graduates asking, "Hey, didn't you used to be that football star?"

She looked him over, taking her time about it, then nodded. "I have it now. I know exactly who you are. You're Mr. July."

Tony smiled. "I am indeed. But I'm much better-looking in person."

"You know, I wouldn't have thought that was possible. But you are."

"Well, thank you very much. And you are...?"

"Clarissa."

"Clarissa Thompson? I remember you. I went to school with your sister Miranda. You were a few years behind us."

"That's me. So are you going to ask me to dance?"

"Why, yes. Yes, I am."

He held out his hand, and she took it. "About time," she said.

As he led her to the floor, he looked around again for Dalia, but he didn't see her.

He'd have to settle for different highs now.

## *CHAPTER TEN*

SLOWLY, CASUALLY, DALIA moseyed over to a table under the tent, picked up a calendar and started leafing through the pages.

There they were, the volunteer firefighters of Limestone Springs—and a remarkably fine-looking group they made, too. Being friends with Lauren had made Dalia something of a photography critic. The pictures in the calendar were good, if a bit on the nose with the whole strong-but-sensitive-rural-rescue-man theme. She saw arrangements of firefighters in old downtown buildings, on local ranches, in the fire truck, on tractors, on old trucks, in barns, with fire hats, with puppies, kittens, guitars, horses, longhorn cattle, baby goats and chickens.

She was careful to spend the same number of seconds on each page. Anyone watching would think she was showing polite civic interest, nothing more.

Then she reached July.

*Whoa.*

Tony's image was in a class by itself. The other guys had looked campy or embarrassed in their over-the-top settings and poses, but not Tony. He looked happy and confident, as if it was the most natural thing in the world for him to be standing in front of a prickly pear cactus, wearing his fire pants with dangling suspenders and no shirt, holding a fire ax over his shoulder. She was amazed by the sheer power of him. All that muscle, and yet so graceful and relaxed. His hair was a perfectly shaped sculpture, shining with gel. Tony always did like plenty of product in his hair.

She tossed the calendar back onto the table and walked away fast.

And there, on the folded-out dance floor, was the original, looking even more spectacular in the flesh, and dancing with a long-legged girl in a short skirt and rhinestone-studded cowboy boots. Dalia's face flushed hot, and her hands curled into fists. She wanted to march over to that girl, grab a fistful of her fake curls, yank her head back and throw her to the ground.

This was exactly how it used to feel back in high school, even before they started dating, whenever she saw Tony talking to another girl, or another girl talking to him, or even looking at him, or heard other girls talking about him the way they did, gushing over his body like he was some *thing*.

She'd told herself it was a matter of principle, that she just didn't like for him or any man to be objectified, any more than she liked for women to be objectified. But maybe those flares of temper were about more than principle. Maybe she was just plain jealous.

It was an unnerving thought. She'd always considered herself a calm, levelheaded, even-tempered person. And she was…mostly. Just not when it came to Tony.

Come to think of it, that was pretty much what Lauren had said.

She went back to the tent, passing up the calendars this time, not stopping until she reached a display of books. She picked one up without really seeing it, or the couple manning the table.

"Dalia Ramirez. What a pleasant surprise."

The voice made it clear that the surprise

wasn't a pleasant one at all. Dalia knew that voice. It was the voice that had lectured her about Goliad, and the Alamo, and Father Hidalgo, and the six flags over Texas, way back in seventh grade.

And it belonged to Tony's grandmother.

"Mrs. Reyes," Dalia said. "And Mr. Reyes. How are you?"

Mr. Reyes smiled. He had a stern face but a nice smile. "Hello, Dalia. It's been a long time."

"You're looking well," said Mrs. Reyes, with a look that added, *you coldhearted witch.*

It stung a little. Mrs. Reyes had never been one to play favorites, but she'd liked Dalia. She was the strictest, most exacting teacher Dalia ever had, undergraduate and graduate years included. Her Texas history class was legendary, with its endless demands for definitions, biographical sketches, descriptions of battles, and maps to color and label, with points taken off for streakiness. This had not made her a popular teacher, though most seventh-graders of Dalia's year were too smart to complain in front of Tony. Dalia didn't complain. She did the work, kept the required notebook in meticulous shape and got one of two As Mrs. Reyes handed out that year. The other had gone to Tony. It hadn't been nepotism, either. Tony wasn't the most diligent student in general, but he sure toed the line in his *abuela's* class.

For the first time, Dalia actually looked at the book in her hand. *Ghost Stories of the Texas Hill Country*, by Annalisa Reyes.

"Our grandniece wrote that," Mr. Reyes said. "She's about your age."

"She was two years ahead of you in school," said his wife. She knew the graduation year and academic record of every student who'd gone through the Limestone Springs school system in the past forty-five years.

"Oh, yes, I remember Annalisa." Dalia wasn't interested in ghost stories, but she opened the book and scanned the table of contents.

"You'll see our common ancestor gets a chapter to himself," said Mr. Reyes.

Ah, yes. There he was, in chapter eight. Alejandro Ramirez, Texas Revolutionary veteran, firefighting ghost—and great-great-great-great-grandfather to Tony and Dalia both.

Before dying at the Battle of Béxar, this

Alejandro had fathered a son, Gabriel. Gabriel in turn had two surviving sons by two different wives. Juan, the firstborn, was Dalia's ancestor. Antonio, the younger, was Tony's. That made Tony and Dalia fourth half cousins.

Dalia's line went on to become prosperous ranchers, influential in local politics, while Tony's side of the family struggled and dwindled.

Anyway, Alejandro's career had supposedly not ended with his death. He'd reportedly shown up in spirit form some years later, when a fire broke out at La Escarpa, and helped save people, property and livestock.

"Oh, right," said Dalia. "I remember that story."

Something must have been off in her tone, because Mrs. Ramirez bristled. "You don't believe it?"

Caught between the truth and a deeply ingrained habit of respect for elders, Dalia hedged. "Well, it's a little hard to verify, is all. It's just oral tradition."

"*Just* oral tradition? So were the Homeric poems."

*Yeah, well, the* Iliad *has some stuff in it that's probably not strictly factual, either.*

Dalia hedged some more. "A story that old, though, passed down through so many people, is bound to get embellished over the generations."

"It's not *that* many generations." Mrs. Reyes jerked a thumb at her husband. "Miguel here had the story from his grandfather Antonio. Antonio had it from his grandmother—Romelia, Alejandro's widow. An eyewitness. Antonio's father, Gabriel, was there, too. He was just a little boy, but he knows what he saw."

*Sure, you bet. Little children always make superreliable witnesses.*

Gabriel had been born after his father's death. Supposedly Alejandro had vowed, before setting off for the siege of Béxar, to come back in time to lay a sprig of esperanza in the cradle of his child.

Why had Annalisa chosen to write about ghost stories, anyway? Why not research Romelia's life and write about that instead? A single woman running a ranch in the mid-nineteenth century? Now, *that* would be a story worth reading.

"Well," Dalia said, "I guess it's fitting that you have firefighters in the family now."

Mr. Reyes smiled. "Yes. Alex is a good boy."

His wife gave him a look. "Tony is a good boy, too."

"He's all right," said Mr. Reyes. "Might not have turned out half-bad if he'd never picked up a football. I hardly ever got a proper day's work out of him after that. All that muscle and bone, wasted. You were too good for him, Dalia. I always knew it wouldn't last. I'm sorry he let you get away, though."

Mrs. Reyes made an exasperated sound. "You underestimate him. Everyone does. No one understands what a warm heart he has, or what he'd be capable of if he just had a motive."

She glared at Dalia.

*Sure, blame me. It's all my fault he flunked out of college, because I didn't believe in him hard enough. You probably made excuses like that for your son, too, and look how well he turned out.*

"How are things on your ranch, Mr. Reyes?" Dalia asked.

The Reyes place was a good piece of property, but a bit small to make a good living off of. It had been whittled down over the years, and even in its heyday it had never been as profitable as La Escarpa.

"Oh, can't complain. Got a long list of the usual chores to be done—fence to mend, brush to clear. Should keep me busy 'til Christmastime."

"Don't forget, you promised to paint the house this year for sure," Mrs. Reyes said.

He replied in Spanish, and then she replied to him, also in Spanish, a little sharply. Soon a rapid-fire exchange was going on, which Dalia could not understand. Unlike Tony and Alex, she had not been brought up bilingual, and she'd taken German in high school.

"Dalia! Come over here and give me a hand with this, please."

It was Claudia, calling from the display of raffle prizes.

"Excuse me, Mr. Reyes, Mrs. Reyes," Dalia said. "It was lovely to see you both."

"Are you going to pay for that book?" asked Mrs. Reyes.

Dalia pulled out a twenty and handed it over. "Keep the change."

She made her escape and hurried over to Claudia.

"What can I help you with?" she asked.

Claudia chuckled. "Nothing. You just looked like you could use an extraction."

"You got that right. Tony's grandmother sure can hold a grudge."

"Ah, yes. Family loyalty. It does keep life interesting around here."

"Yep. One of many reasons I like living in the city."

Dalia had already seen Claudia once since arriving back in town, when she'd brought over some *mole poblano* for dinner. Unlike most of her mother's friends who'd brought food, Claudia hadn't asked about Dalia's love life. She'd asked about her job. She'd seemed truly interested in Dalia's work in finance, and she asked intelligent questions.

"I can understand that," Claudia said. "It might be nice to live someplace where people don't know your family history for the past five generations."

"Exactly."

"Any idea how much longer you'll be in town?"

"None whatsoever. Tony has been pretty vague about the rebuild timetable, but it's clearly not going to be a quick job."

Claudia looked at her with those piercing black-browed eyes. "It must be hard."

Dalia knew Claudia didn't mean just the rebuild.

"I don't know how I'm going to get through it, Claudia," Dalia said. It was no use trying to pretend with Claudia, and Dalia didn't even want to. It was kind of restful, being seen through so completely.

"I look at him now, and it's been so many years and so much has happened, we're light-years apart. But then at other times it feels like it was all yesterday. When I came down here to help my mom, I was *not* expecting to have to deal with him. Honestly, I don't know if I would have come at all if I'd known. I was just blindsided by the whole thing. I didn't even know Tony was a general contractor."

"Yes, he's really gotten his life in order these past few years, and I'm so glad. I was worried about him for a while, when he first moved back and was living with Carlos."

"I didn't know he moved in with Carlos. That must have been a train wreck."

"Oh, it was. But at some point he seemed to wake up and come to his senses and stop circling the drain. I think it was a rock-bottom kind of thing. He worked hard, kept his nose clean and slowly climbed out of the hole. Started working construction and turned out to be good at it."

"I'm glad," Dalia said, and she was. It hurt her to think of Tony falling to pieces. "I just hope he keeps it together long enough to finish my mom's house."

"He will. Not as quickly as you'd like, but he will finish, and he'll do beautiful work."

"If he's so good, you'd think he could set a schedule and keep to it."

"Oh, *mija*, builders always go over schedule, at least in my experience. If they don't, they're probably cutting corners."

She trailed off as her eyes strayed past Dalia's shoulder, then gave a bright smile. "Hello, *mijo*."

Dalia's heart gave a painful throb. She steeled herself for a Tony encounter, but it was Alex's voice that said, "Hello, ladies. Enjoying the day?"

"Oh, yes," said Claudia. "Raffle ticket sales are going strong."

"Glad to hear it. Hey, Dalia, would you like to dance?"

"Um..."

Dalia scanned the dance floor. Tony was twirling the ringleted girl and smiling down at her.

"Sure," she said.

She took Alex's hand, walked him briskly to the dance floor and got right down to business.

"Hey, who's leading here, anyway?" Alex asked.

"Sorry."

It took a lot of effort, letting Alex lead and keeping her eyes off Tony, but somehow she managed it.

After a few minutes, she said, "So?"

"So what?" said Alex.

"What do you want to say to me?"

"Nothing. I just wanted to dance, and you're a good dancer. So I asked you. Why?"

"It just seems like everyone is on a talk-Tony-up-to-Dalia kick today."

"Oh, yeah? Like who?"

"Mad Dog, Claudia. Your grandmother."

"My *abuela* talked to you about Tony? Bet that was fun."

"Yeah, it was a blast."

"Well, I can talk Tony up if you want. It's not hard. He's a good guy. Maybe not the steadiest guy you'll ever meet, but..."

"Brilliant when he shows up," Dalia finished. "Yeah."

Alex frowned. "It's not like that. It's not that he's unreliable. He just likes excitement. He's had some rough patches for sure, especially after...you know. But he's evened out. When I remember how things used to be, when he first came back home and was living with my dad, I know I have a lot to be thankful for."

"I can't even imagine what it must have been like, the two of them living together, as alike as they are."

"They're not that much alike."

She gave him a look.

"No, I mean it. Yeah, they're both charming and fun-loving and all that, but in one way at least, they couldn't be more different."

"What's that?"

"Tony's not all smooth and slick like my dad is. Talking to my dad is like trying to rope an eel. He's slithery and slippery enough to get out of anything. You know who he is and what he's done, but somehow he manages to make it sound like he's the victim and everyone else is to blame. But not Tony. When he messes up, he says so, and he's sorry. And he's a terrible liar. He can keep a secret, sort of, but if you ask him point-blank, he blurts out the truth."

Dalia thought of Tony in the lumberyard, looking her straight in the eye and saying he'd never cheated on her. He'd looked and sounded like he meant it. But if he was telling the truth, why didn't he follow up? Why had he been in such a hurry to get away?

And why had he ever let Dalia go to begin with?

Then something in Alex's expression changed. Dalia followed his gaze.

Tony was dancing with *two* girls now—Short Skirt and Too Much Eyeliner.

Short Skirt's curls were the artificial kind, sleek and crisp and perfect—not much like Dalia's natural soft waves. Tony used to be wild about her hair, though. He would run his hands through it and wind his fingers through the waves and beg her to never cut it short. She had no intention of cutting it short, but it was nice to be begged.

Maybe his tastes had changed. Or maybe he'd never meant it at all.

She didn't say another word for the rest of the song, and neither did Alex.

"Thanks for the dance," she said when it was over. "I'd better go. Almost time for the first hayride."

The hayrides weren't scheduled to start for another hour, but it was as good an excuse as any to get away.

## *CHAPTER ELEVEN*

TONY WASN'T SURE how he came to be dancing with two women at the same time. One minute he was watching Dalia steer Alex to the dance floor, and the next thing he knew someone had taken hold of his free hand, and suddenly he was twirling her, too.

They were both very pretty in their way. But something about Dalia made other women seem overdone.

Why was he thinking about Dalia now, anyway? What was wrong with him? Here he had not one but two very attractive women working hard for attention. Why couldn't he just go with that, instead of stealing glances at his ex-girlfriend?

What were she and Alex talking about? Whatever it was, she sure looked serious about it. Course, with Dalia, that could mean anything, because she almost always looked serious. But maybe this really was. Maybe she was thinking what a good, solid guy Alex was. Smart, hardworking and handsome.

It made sense, the two of them together, Alex and Dalia. A lot more sense than Tony and Dalia ever did.

No. No! Alex would never do that to him. It was a time-honored rule that you never, *ever* dated your bro's ex—and that went double when the bro was your actual brother.

Didn't it?

But all's fair in love and war. And any guy with eyes and a brain would have to be crazy not to get with Dalia if he had the chance.

The sick feeling in the pit of Tony's stomach made it hard to smile, but he did it, anyway.

Then one of his dance partners, the newer one, stumbled and fell against him. He tried to steady her, but she kept wobbling and clutching him and laughing in a breathless way.

"Oh, I'm so dizzy! All that spinning around made my head go funny!"

Clarissa fake-laughed and rolled her eyes at Tony. "Sure, that's the reason," she said.

"I think we better get you to a seat," Tony said. "Wouldn't want you to take a spill."

Clarissa fake-laughed again. "He's right, Kenzie. You'd better sit down before you turn an ankle in those flimsy shoes."

Kenzie put up a protest, but she still let Tony take her to a seat. Clarissa went along, keeping up a stream of talk to Kenzie that sounded sweet and mean at the same time. How did girls *do* that? Guys didn't act that way. To be fair, though, not all girls did, either. Dalia didn't. She was never catty to other girls, and never fake nice, either.

Kenzie kicked off her shoes. "There! Now my ankles are safe. I can dance fine now."

"Your toes aren't safe, though," said Clarissa. "They'll get stepped on."

"Oh, Tony won't step on my toes. He's too good a dancer for that."

"How'd you even know my name?" Tony asked. "Have we met?"

"You're in the calendar! And I already knew you anyway from the trophy case at the high school. So you're practically an old friend. Come on, let's dance."

"I don't think that's a good idea," Tony

said. "I think you're done dancing for the day."

"Well, then I'll let you buy me a drink."

"I think you're done drinking, too."

Clarissa laughed like this was the funniest thing anyone ever said. "He's right, Kenzie. You can't help it. It's not your fault you're a clumsy drunk. That's just how you are."

"Well, you're an amorous drunk," said Kenzie.

"Mmm-hmm, I am, I really am." Clarissa cocked her head at Tony. "What sort of drunk are you? No, wait, don't tell me. I can see it in your face. You're a happy drunk."

"Wrong. I'm a reckless drunk."

"Ooh, that sounds intriguing," said Clarissa. "What does reckless look like to you?"

"If I told you, it might make you cry."

"Awww! Now I really want to know."

"Well, you're not gonna find out."

"Why not?"

"Because when you're a reckless drunk, the best thing you can do is not get drunk anymore."

Alex wasn't any kind of drunk. Alex always kept himself under control. Alex was perfect. Everyone loved Alex.

"I gotta go," Tony said. "There's a thing I gotta do."

"All right," said Kenzie. "We'll catch you later."

*I hope not.*

He left fast, not caring where he went as long as it was away. He heard another female voice calling, "Hey there, Mr. July!" But he just kept walking.

He could still hear the Chicharrones playing way behind him by the dance floor. They finished one song and started another. Was Dalia still dancing with Alex?

"Tony. Hey, Tony!"

A thickset bull of a man, with a shaved head and a handlebar mustache, waved at him from over by the mechanical bull. He held up a big can with a slit cut in the lid and a label on the side that said Bull Rides $10. He shook the can at Tony.

"Get over here and support your community! We're raising money for firefighters here!"

"Mr. Mendoza!" Tony went over and gave him a good strong handshake. "It's been a while. You weren't at Trivia Thursday last week."

"I had a job that went late, making a pad site for a guy's barn in Schraeder Lake. Looks like I'll be working out here pretty soon, though. Land clearing."

"Yeah, I noticed the low acreage was getting pretty brushy. So you're the one manning the mechanical bull, huh?"

"Not just manning it. I'm the owner-operator. Been renting it out for parties and such. But for the FFF, I waived my fee."

"Business venture, huh? Dirt work and land clearing not keeping you busy enough?"

"More than that. I'm actually hoping my grandsons might show some talent. None of my boys ever did, but maybe it skips a generation."

"What? You used to ride? I didn't know that."

"Oh, yeah. Wasn't half-bad, either. Cleared ten grand my best year."

"No kidding? When was that?"

"Same year Rigoberto was born." Rigoberto was what Mr. Mendoza called Tito, his youngest son, owner of Tito's bar. "Then I tore up my shoulder and broke my cheekbone, and Rose said just what did I think I was doing, and was I trying to get myself killed and leave her to raise five boys on her own, 'cause that wasn't *her* idea of a good time. So that was the end of that."

"That's too bad. I rode myself once, my senior year of high school. Didn't get hurt, but Coach Willis lit into me good when he found out."

"Yeah? Well, I don't see no coach stopping you now." Mr. Mendoza shook the can again. "C'mon, do your civic duty."

Tony checked out the setup—a bull head and body mounted on a thick pole and surrounded by inflatable pads for a soft landing, a big tarp overhead for shade and a control console for Mr. Mendoza.

"Well," Tony said, "I might have a little cash on me."

He dropped a ten in the coffee can, stepped up, grabbed the strap and swung on.

The bull was covered with brown-and-white cowhide and had a nice leathery scent. Tony got himself situated, raised his left hand and nodded.

It started with a jerk. The bull pitched forward, and Tony leaned back, acting on instinct more than anything else. Then it reversed, fast enough to make his head snap.

He had to lean forward and grip hard with his thighs to keep from sliding off the end.

Then he found his rhythm, and everything fell into place.

There was nothing quite like that bucking bull motion. A back-and-forth, seesawing kind of thing, with some spinning action thrown in. He watched the back of the bull's head for directional cues, drilling his gaze right between those sawed-off horns, but he didn't think too hard about it. This was one of those things where, by the time you thought what to do, it was too late. You had to feel what to do, and do it, all in the same instant.

And it was a lot to do, in a very short time. One second he was leaning way back, with his spine in line with his thighs and almost touching the bull's back, and the next, the bull's head loomed up right in his face, and all the while his arm was swinging as a counterbalance.

The bull changed directions.

Everything that wasn't Tony or the bull was a blur. All that mattered was right here, right now, this pitching, spinning six feet or so of space, with him at the center of it.

And suddenly he was flat on his back, with the striped tarp whirling overhead and a sound of cheering, though he couldn't remember there being a crowd when he started.

Mr. Mendoza's face appeared above him. "Hey. How you feel?"

Tony was laughing. "I feel fantastic," he said.

"Good. 'Cause you held on for nine-point-two seconds."

"Really? It felt like longer."

"Yeah, it always does for me, too. But you did good. And I may have turned up the difficulty level a notch or two for you, bud."

"You did? Thanks, Mr. Mendoza."

Tony got up and back onto solid ground. All the dings he'd gotten in the football game this morning were making themselves heard again loud and clear, plus a few new ones, but it was a good feeling, because he'd done the thing. He hadn't been beaten.

Someone else was already taking his place on the bull, and a line was forming.

"Looks like you drummed up some business for me," Mr. Mendoza said.

"Ha ha! Happy to help. I'll be back later

if things slack off again. Got to fill that cash can."

"Yeah, and get some training in while you still can." Mr. Mendoza smiled. "County fair's just a week away."

"Yeah, it is, isn't it?"

He thought of all the equipment he'd bought for his one rodeo ride. After that night, he'd stuffed it all back in his brand-new riggin bag and taken it to his grandparents' place. Was it still there?

So JUST HOW hard *could* it be to avoid one man at a big community-wide event?

When the man was Tony, next to impossible.

He was *everywhere*. Playing football. Calling out names of winners in the raffles, making everyone laugh with his hilarious improvised one-liners. Grilling fajitas in that Texas flag apron of his. Riding the mechanical bull.

*Dancing.*

She thought she'd get a break when she drove the tractor for the hayride, but there was a ridiculously smitten high school couple snuggled down among the hay bales on the trailer, and *that* reminded her of the hayride out at the Mastersons' place back in tenth grade, when she and Tony sat next to each other, her hip and thigh close against his, each of them acutely aware but ignoring each other with all their might. They managed to go the entire ride without making eye contact or exchanging a single word.

She couldn't get away. Even when he wasn't there, she couldn't stop thinking about him. She longed to feel Tony's arms around her, and for him to kiss the top of her head like the stupid adorable high school boy with his stupid adorable girlfriend.

And the worst part of it? This was how it was *all the time*. This was her *life*. Even in Philadelphia, he was always popping up in her imagination, making random snarky remarks about whatever was happening at the moment. Every time she leafed through a *Texas Monthly*, she thought about the place in the country the two of them might've settled down in one day in their phantom future.

She didn't like daydreams. She liked real things. And in spite of all that had happened, in spite of knowing better, she wanted Tony for real—and she couldn't have him.

BY THE TIME Dalia sat down at a table in the eating area with her mother, she was exhausted. She deserved a break. She'd been working nonstop, she'd been helpful and courteous, and she hadn't clawed the eyes out of any of Tony's dance partners.

The sun was on its way down, but there were hours yet to go. Another hayride. The bonfire.

People around her were chowing down on grilled brats and fajitas, drinking craft beer from kegs kept cold in trash cans filled with ice. The food looked good, but she was too stressed to eat. All she wanted now was to rest her feet for a while.

"Oh, sweetie, would you get me some of that green salsa? It's in those ketchup-type bottles with the nozzles cut down. They're behind the bar."

Dalia stifled a groan. "Sure," she said as cheerfully as she could.

The guy behind the bar was around seventy, with a thin cotton snap shirt and a cowboyish swagger.

"I'd like one of those green salsa bottles, please," Dalia told him.

He grinned. "Well, darlin', I'll give it to you on one condition, if you'll give me a smile first."

Dalia took a step back. Bad enough to be called "darlin'" by a man older than her father—but this? How many times in her life had she been ordered, directly or indirectly, to smile? The variations were endless. "It takes fewer muscles to smile than to frown." Or "Smiling makes you more attractive." Or "Can I get a smile?" Or "You forgot your smile!" Or just "Smile!" It always came as a rude shock, with Dalia not bothering anyone, just sitting there minding her own business with a neutral expression on her face, maybe thinking about some task she needed to do later, or trying to remember the name of a song, or noticing a potted plant, or just zoning out. And then someone jerked her out of her own head with a command to smile—like telling her to smile would make her *want* to smile. It was like being dowsed with ice water.

Did sober-faced men get told by complete strangers to smile, or was it just women? She really wondered about this. Someone ought to do a study.

When she was a kid, whenever pictures were being taken, her mom used to tell her, "Smile naturally!" The illogic of the command always bugged her. If the smile really was natural, she'd be doing it without being told. Otherwise it was just a convincing fake smile. But Dalia couldn't do a convincing fake smile. She tried, but she couldn't. She cringed at the sight of those pictures now, of her stiffly curving, fractionally parted lips. Now she was grown up, and she would not smile unless she wanted to. Certainly not on the command of some stranger. Much less when there was so little to smile about.

"Thanks, anyway," she said to the guy. "I'll find it somewhere else."

And she turned and walked away.

It felt pretty satisfying, except now she had no salsa, and what was she going to tell her mom? That she refused to get it on principle because some moron told her to smile? A man of her grandfather's generation, who ought to have allowances made for the sexist assumptions of an earlier time?

She scanned the area. Surely there was a surplus salsa bottle somewhere in this place.

And there was…at Tony's table.

This time she did groan out loud. Really? *Really?*

He wasn't alone. He was sitting there with *three* girls—Short Skirt, Too Much Eyeliner and Halter Top. Short Skirt had her hand on Tony's arm and was leaning way forward, smiling into his face.

*Okay, no reason this should be a big deal. Just go on over quietly to Tony's table and get the salsa. I don't even have to speak to him. It's not* his *salsa. He's not using it—he's just drinking a beer. I'll just reach past him—*

Tony whirled around with a quick shout, colliding with Dalia, sloshing beer down her jeans.

"Sorry," Dalia said. "Didn't mean to startle you. Just wanted the salsa."

Tony held a hand to his heart, breathing hard. "I'm sorry. Did I spill on you?"

"No," she lied.

"Why are you so jumpy, Tony?" Halter Top asked. "You need another drink."

Dalia took the salsa back to the table. A

woman had joined her mother, one of her church friends who'd brought food, but Dalia didn't hear what they were talking about. She was thinking.

Years ago she'd seen a horse at the equine veterinarian's. Another horse approached it from the side, not menacing or all of a sudden or anything, just there. But the first horse reacted all out of proportion. It snorted, shied and drew itself up, tall and daunting. Then it whipped its head around really far toward the other horse.

It calmed down right away after that. By the time Dalia saw the cloudy film covering the horse's eye on the near side, she didn't need the veterinarian's explanation. And she didn't need an explanation now for Tony's performance, which had echoed the horse's so eerily.

Of course, Tony had always been ridiculously easy to startle. That had been a running joke throughout their school years. But this was something more.

There was no cloudy film over Tony's right eye. But there was a sort of flat, unfocused look to it. And the way he'd startled, whipping his head around far enough to see her with his other eye, was exactly the same.

She didn't know to what degree, or how it had happened, or when. But there was one thing she knew for sure.

Tony was blind in one eye.

## *CHAPTER TWELVE*

THINGS THAT HADN'T seemed significant before suddenly clicked into a much bigger picture. The way Tony trailed his right hand along the wall while walking through the house at La Escarpa. The catlike swiveling of his head before he threw the football. The way he'd startled when she'd approached him in the lumberyard—much like the way he'd startled just now. How he'd collided with the display in the lumberyard when he'd walked off after she accused him of cheating on her.

She'd thought he was just being childish and dramatic.

In fact, he couldn't *see* the display.

It was his right eye, his dominant eye. That must be a hassle, though clearly not too incapacitating. His peripheral vision and depth perception were obviously lacking, but apparently he could see well enough to do construction work. And while he couldn't throw a football with the same precision as in his heyday, he was still an above-average player.

What could cause loss of sight in so young a man? Diabetes? Glaucoma?

And why hadn't anyone ever said anything about it to her? She'd certainly heard enough details from her mom and her mom's friends about the medical conditions of other people in town—Mike Jeffries's irritable bowel syndrome, Hannah Jacobs's kid's peanut sensitivity. No physical ailment was off-limits for discussion. Why hadn't they told her about this one? Maybe they were being considerate, not talking about Dalia's ex in front of her?

Or maybe they didn't know. Maybe it was a new thing.

Was Tony sick? He certainly looked healthy enough, but who knew? He could be in the early stages of...something.

There was nothing obviously wrong with the eye. It tracked right along with the other eye, and it didn't look filmy. Was there anything off about the pupil, like it was too dilated or not dilated enough? She didn't know.

Tony's eyes were dark brown, almost black. Any problem with the pupil would be hard to spot unless she was really looking for it, and really close.

She was itching to take out her phone and do some Google research. But that was dumb. There was an easier way to find out.

*Just ask him.*

She looked at Tony. He was in high spirits, talking and laughing, and Short Skirt was pawing at him.

Correction: just ask Alex.

"I JUST LOVE BONFIRES," said Clarissa. "Don't you?"

"Sure!" said Tony. "All firefighters love bonfires."

The kindling crackled away beneath the carefully constructed teepee, with the flames licking the bigger logs. A loose crowd hung around, some in camp chairs, some with roasting sticks. People were handing around bags of marshmallows.

"It's always a toss-up, the triple-F bonfire," he said. "Some years there's a burn ban on and we don't get to do it, which is sad. But this has been a wet summer, so we're good to go."

Clarissa nodded like this was really profound.

The wreckage from the Ramirez kitchen hadn't bulked up the burn pile all that much after all. Most building waste wasn't safe or practical to burn. Painted wood and pressure-treated lumber were full of toxic chemicals, and wallboard was mostly gypsum, which was a mineral and pretty much fireproof except for the paper coating. So the old two-by-fours went to the dump, along with most of the porch deck boards and siding from the house.

A lot of the more stylishly weathered wood got held back for resale at Architectural Treasures, a new place in town that sold salvage from old houses. It was a great idea, Tony had to admit. That stuff was hot right now. People ate it up, and with good reason. You couldn't beat old craftsmanship, for one, and a lot of old flooring and siding came from better wood than what was available today. Modern trees just weren't as old or dense. The old stuff might be worn and weathered, but it was solid. Plus people liked the idea that there was a story there, a history—especially with all the throwaway culture around them. Modern stuff tended to be slick and cheap and crude—here today, gone tomorrow. But if something was old enough to be scarred by honest wear, it was probably worth keeping.

"We use the same area for the fire every year. See that ring of stones? And that whole cleared space outside of it? That keeps the fire contained. And those fire hoses are all hooked up and ready to go so things don't get out of hand. That'd be real cute, if the volunteer fire department started a Class G wildfire at our fundraiser and ended up burning half the county."

Clarissa giggled. "*You* were real cute this morning, lugging those fire hoses over here after the football game. You made, like, a little dance out of it."

He remembered that, but it felt like a long time ago. A fire hose was heavy, and moving all those lengths of it was a hot, boring job, so he'd decided to liven things up for himself and the other firefighters by turning the whole thing into a hose drill.

"You were watching me, huh?" he asked.

"Oh, I've had my eye on you all day."

That should have made him feel good, but the truth was, he was getting bored. Flirting with Clarissa was too easy. She flattered him too much. He liked it better when there was a layer of insult involved and he had to unpack the words and twist them around.

As it was, all he could think of to say back was "Glad to hear it." Which sounded lame, but Clarissa giggled again—giggled hard, like he'd said something really clever. Honestly, he was embarrassed for her.

The truth was, he wasn't drunk enough for this to feel like a good time, and he didn't want to be.

"ALEX, CAN I talk to you?" Dalia asked.

It had taken her the better part of an hour to track him down. She'd finally found him working on the bonfire.

"Sure!" he said. "What's up?"

"Alone, I mean."

"Oh. Okay."

She led him away from the crowd, to a spot behind some brush. She was probably being silly. Just because nobody'd told her about Tony being partially blind didn't mean it was some big secret. Alex would probably say something like, *Oh, that. I thought everyone knew about that.*

Probably. But somehow she didn't think so.

"This all seems very mysterious and hush-hush," he said. "What's on your mind?"

"Actually, I'm...a little concerned about Tony."

"Why? Has he had too much? He seemed all right when I saw him last. But don't worry. I'll keep an eye on him and get him home safe. We came in my truck, anyway."

"That's not what I mean. I want to know what's wrong with him."

"What do you mean, what's wrong with him?"

"I mean he's blind in one eye."

Alex was visibly shaken. "How did you know about that?"

Her heart sank. So much for it not being a big deal.

"I just figured it out. What's wrong with him? Tell me."

Alex raised his hands, palms out. "Hey, that's between you and him. You want to know, you ask him yourself. And remember, I told you nothing. *Nothing.*"

"What do you mean? Why is it a secret?"

He shook his head hard. "Uh-uh. Not telling."

"Is he sick? Is it progressive? Is it... serious?"

Alex opened his mouth, then shut it.

Dalia grabbed his arm. "Alex! Come on. You're scaring me."

He almost looked ready to tell her then. But instead he said again, "Ask him yourself," and then hurried away.

She stared after him. She felt sick to her stomach. Why wouldn't he tell her? Just how bad was it?

Was Tony sick? Dying?

She walked slowly back to the bonfire. Tony was in the same place as before, laughing with Short Skirt, but suddenly she could hear how forced the laughter sounded. The whole thing was an act.

Then he looked at her, and there was something in his face that looked like fear.

What was going on? What was Tony hiding?

# *CHAPTER THIRTEEN*

CLARISSA HELD UP her beer to the sky.

"This is the best night of my life!"

"Oh, yeah?"

Tony tried to sound interested, but it was uphill work. As far as he was concerned, the night wasn't all that great. Maybe not the *worst* of his life, but then it did have a lot of competition for that spot.

"Of course it is!" said Clarissa. "You know why?"

"Uh-huh," Tony said, not really listening, because Dalia was talking to Alex *again*, and whatever she was saying, she sure looked intent about it.

Clarissa moved into his sightline. "Well, then? Tell me."

"Tell you what?"

"Why it's the best night!"

"Oh. Um… I don't know."

"Because it's when I met you, silly!"

"Thanks," he said.

Now Dalia was leading Alex away from the bonfire and behind a stand of huisache trees.

"Where's your truck?" Clarissa asked. She was standing way too close to him and starting to get on his nerves.

"How do you know I drive a truck?"

"I know it *instinctively*." She mangled that last word, but he figured it out. "And I'll bet it's big and strong and…and shiny, just like you."

"It's pretty nice, yeah. But it's not here. I came with my brother."

His brother, who at this very moment was off somewhere behind the huisache with the girl Tony had loved all his life.

"Do you live in town?" Clarissa asked.

"What? Yeah, me and my brother have a place together."

"Well, I live alone."

Then Alex came back around the huisache, walking fast and looking grim, and Dalia came back, too. She looked at Tony, and there was something in her face that he didn't know how to read, but it might be the way she'd look if she'd just tried to come on to his brother.

Clarissa moved into his field of vision and gave him a look like she was waiting for something.

"Sorry," he said. "Did you ask me a question?"

"Has anyone ever told you you have a gorgeous smile?"

"Yes."

He didn't mean it to be funny, but she laughed, all high and fake and way too loud. Then she hooked her fingers into his belt loops and said, "Well, I want to be the reason you're smiling tomorrow. Let's get out of here."

His attention shifted, and he saw her, really saw her, for the first time—a very attractive young woman who was very into him and also very drunk. He thought a minute, then said, "You wanna go home, huh?"

"I do. I do want to."

"All right, then," he said. "Let's go."

He walked her to the makeshift parking lot.

"Here, gimme your keys," he said, and she handed them over, just like that.

He scanned the parking lot and saw…

Aha! Perfect.

“Hello, Claudia,” he said.

He walked Clarissa over to Claudia and introduced them.

Claudia looked at Clarissa and smiled. “Oh, yes, I’ve known Clarissa since she was a little girl.”

Clarissa stood up a little straighter. “Hello, Ms. Cisneros.”

Tony handed Clarissa’s keys to Claudia. “Clarissa is ready to go home now. Will you make sure she gets there safely?”

“Absolutely. Come on, *mija*.”

“Good night,” Tony called as they walked away.

“Good night,” they both replied. Clarissa didn’t sound all that happy with him, but oh well.

TONY LAY ON his back with his eyes shut, listening to the wind rustling in the elm branches overhead. The sounds of celebration were dim out here, on the bank of the stock pond where Dalia had led Tony eight years ago at her brother’s party, where they’d seen the raccoon family and heard the rutting axis deer, where they'd had their first kiss. Or *was* it their first kiss? Did the one back in seventh grade count? What was he supposed to call it? Their first official, legit, grown-up kiss? They'd never really settled the issue, and he guessed they never would.

"Tony?"

Tony sat up. "Alex. What're you doing here?"

"Looking for you. The bonfire's out and it's time to go home."

"How'd you find me? This place isn't exactly on the beaten path."

Alex shuffled his feet and looked down. "I, uh, I put a tracking app on your phone."

"Are you serious? Why'd you do that?"

"In case you ever got lost."

"You mean in case I ever got wasted and you had to find me and get me home."

"Well, you gotta admit it'd save time."

Tony stood up. "Listen. I'm grateful to you for all the times you looked out for me, and I'm sorry for everything I put you through in the past. But you can stop worrying. All that stuff is behind me now, and that's where it's gonna stay."

Alex sighed. "Good, 'cause you're way too big to haul."

"Oh, I don't know. I bet you could still put me in a fireman's carry."

They walked in silence for a while. Then Tony said, "Anyway, you did carry me, lots of times. You took care of me after…you know. You were the only one I could trust. You're my best friend."

Alex smiled. "You're mine, too. Always were. We got each other's back, right?"

"Right. And I…" He took a deep breath and steeled himself. "I release you."

"You what, now?"

"I release you. From the bro code. I won't make any trouble or stand in your way. You're better for her anyhow. You deserve each other."

"Wait, hold on. Are you talking about *Dalia*? You think I…?" He made a face. "Ew, no! Tony, I would *never* do that."

"But it's okay. That's what I'm saying. You can. I won't stop you. I just want you to be happy. Both of you."

"No, no, listen to me. It's not just the bro code, okay? I don't feel that way about

Dalia, and I never could. She's great and all, but she's not my type."

"Why not? What's your type?"

"I…don't know exactly. But she's not it. And I'm not hers."

"Are you sure about that? I saw you together. Dancing. Talking. Sneaking off behind the huisache. She sure looked determined."

Alex laughed. "What, that? Yeah, she was determined, all right. Determined to talk about you. The same thing we've talked about every other time I've seen her since she's been back in town, and probably every single time we ever spoke to each other in our lives. You, you and only you."

"Really?"

"Yes, really. She still cares about you."

The cold, sick feeling that had been in Tony's stomach since the dance floor suddenly went away.

"She doesn't care about me," he said. "All she cares about is making sure I don't mess up the rebuild on her mother's house."

"I don't think that's true," Alex said.

"Yeah, well, I do. Hey, did you ride Mr. Mendoza's mechanical bull?"

"I gave it a go."

"And?"

"Don't worry, I didn't beat you. Your record still stands. You got the high score of the day."

"Yesss!" Tony pumped his fist.

He'd gone back for three more rides after that first one, and improved his score each time. He was good. Not world-champion good, but still good. He knew perfectly well that he'd never be great. For one thing, he was too big. Bull riding was one sport where his size was no help to him; in fact, it was a drawback. Nimbleness, speed and compact strength were the necessary qualities. Almost all the champions topped out at five-ten at the most.

But that only made it all the better when he did perform well. It was something he wasn't even the right physical type for, something he hadn't even worked that hard at, and still he managed to be pretty good.

"Remember Suerte and Bizcocho?" he asked.

Alex gave him a sidewise look. "You kidding? I think about them every day."

When they were kids, Tony and Alex used to spend long summer twilights in the paddock at their grandparents' place, riding Bizcocho, their grandfather's seal-brown gelding, and Suerte, their father's flashy chestnut mare. They used to talk about doing team roping one day. But it never happened. Football started taking more and more of Tony's time, and Suerte got sold to pay gambling debts, and Bizcocho got sick and had to be put down. Alex talked about saving his money and buying a horse of his own, but that never happened, either.

What if football and other things hadn't gotten in the way? What if they'd done rodeo, and Tony had gone on spending long stretches of time at their grandparents' ranch like Alex did? It might have made all the difference.

Well, there was no use wondering what if. But maybe it wasn't too late, for some things at least. Maybe his best years weren't behind him after all.

## *CHAPTER FOURTEEN*

Tony was standing on the Ramirez front porch, in the corner just off the kitchen, thinking what a perfect place it would be for a mechanical bull. Then suddenly Dalia was there, saying, "No, that's where the porch swing goes."

And Tony said, "But it got all busted up, remember?" And he pointed at the heap of splintered wood on the porch decking.

And Dalia said, "Nothing a little elbow grease can't fix. Look, I'll show you." And she took the nail gun out of his hand and started nailing random boards together.

*Bam. Bam. Bam.*

He opened his eyes.

*Bam. Bam. Bam.*

He groaned and rolled over, burying his face in his pillow.

"Alex, get the door," he called.

*Bam. Bam. Bam.*

He covered his head with the pillow to smother the noise. "Alex!"

No answer. Where was Alex? And who was out there pounding on his door at this time of the morning? He didn't know what time it was exactly, but it was too early for visitors, especially the morning after the FFF.

*Bam. Bam. Bam.*

"I know you're in there, Tony. Come on, open up."

He sat straight up. *Dalia?* What was she doing here? How did she even know where he lived?

"Just a minute," he answered.

Yesterday's jeans were lying across the foot of the bed. He picked them up, pulled them on and stumbled to the bathroom, where he did a quick emergency hygiene-and-grooming session, knocking things over in his clumsy hurry.

Dalia kept knocking. "Is that running water? Are you brushing your teeth? Come on, Tony, let me in."

He ran his hands through his hair one last time and opened the door.

She stood there, looking calm and cool

and perfectly put together, with her boot-cut jeans and tank top and lightweight jacket. She held her tote on one shoulder with her hand gripping the base of the handle. Her sleek braid of hair fell over the other shoulder.

"Can I come in?" she asked.

He stepped back and waved her inside.

She'd gone only a few steps when she stopped short and looked around at the living room in obvious surprise.

"What?" he said.

"Nothing. It's just…nicer than I expected."

It did look pretty good. Throw pillows, a little wall art, a pewter pocket watch clock. Tidy, too.

He shrugged. "I like nice things. And I clean up after myself. Alex is the messy one."

She took a seat in the exact middle of the sofa, and he sat on the club chair, facing her.

She looked so serious. It wasn't just her regular serious face, either. There was nothing strange about her giving him that look. But coming to his apartment to do it? That took effort.

Then she said, "How did you lose the sight in your right eye?"

It was like she'd hit him upside the head with a sledgehammer.

"What did Alex tell you?" he heard himself ask.

"Nothing. I figured it out for myself. I asked him about it, but he wouldn't say anything. He said if I wanted to know I should ask you."

"Uh…"

He ran a hand through his hair and looked around the room. Seconds ticked by on the pewter clock. He saw his arms moving in a nervous way that didn't make sense. He was *squirming*, like an insect pinned down by one wing.

"Tony, what is it? Please tell me. Are you sick?"

"Sick? No. Why would I be sick? It was an accident."

"When?"

"Six and a half years ago."

Silence. Then, sharply, "Spring break?"

He nodded. He had his head bowed now; he couldn't look at her.

When she next spoke, her voice was calm again, or almost. "How did it happen?"

He swallowed hard. "Um, I was at the hotel with the guys." His voice was shaking; he stopped, swallowed again. "We were, uh, drinking and goofing off. Filming each other with our phones. You know, stupid human tricks. Phone video was kind of a new thing back then and we were excited. And somehow I decided that it would be a great idea not to just jump off the hotel balcony into the pool…but to *dive* in."

He heard her suck in her breath.

"I know, it was a bad idea. But I did it. And I would've been okay, except something startled me at the last second, and so I was a little off my rhythm. I didn't miss the pool or anything, but I guess my eyes were open when my face hit the water, or maybe it was the angle or something, I don't know."

"It's a detached retina, isn't it?"

He laughed a little. "Why am I not surprised? Of course you would know that. But I didn't. I didn't know anything was wrong. I mean, my eye didn't feel great after it hit the water, but I didn't think I'd actually injured it. There was no blood, the eyeball was still in place, so how bad could it be? I didn't know retinas got detached. I just thought I was a little shook up, is all. I didn't have any really scary symptoms until it was too late."

"That phone call," Dalia said.

He didn't have to ask which one. "Yeah. That was three days after it happened."

"You were being so weird," she said. He could hear the accusation in her voice. "So vague about what you'd been up to. You sounded guilty."

"I felt guilty. I *was* guilty. I knew it was stupid, getting wasted and acting crazy. I knew you wouldn't like it. But I didn't know then how bad it was. I was grateful I didn't get hurt, like blow out my knee or break my back or something. I'd learned my lesson, and I was never going to mess up that way again."

"But it was already too late," she said softly.

"Yeah. My vision had been a little wonky since the accident. You know those floaters people get in their eyes? I had more of those than usual, and things looked kinda dim. But I didn't know anything was up. I thought I was just hungover. But then that day, while we were talking on the phone, things started getting *really* messed up, with lots of big floaters, blobs and rods. And the lines in the wallpaper turned all wavy. It was like I was tripping balls. Then everything turned red. I found out later it was blood flooding my eye from the tear in the retina."

Dalia put her head in her hands.

"That's when you ended the call," she said.

"Yeah." *I gotta go. Talk to you later. Love you.*

"I've never forgotten the doctor who did the surgery. He was so *mad* at me. He said if I'd come in right away, it would've been no problem. But with things as far along as they were, the prognosis wasn't good. He said I wouldn't know how much vision I had left in the eye until after recovery. As it turned out, I lost it all." He cleared his throat. "And that was the end of football, and the end of college."

*And the end of us.*

"Why didn't you tell me?"

"How could I? What would you have said if you knew what an idiot I'd been? That I'd gotten drunk and jeopardized my future—*our* future—just to show off?"

"It would have been better than thinking you were with another girl!"

"Would it?"

She stared at him with her mouth hanging open.

"Look," he said. "You don't have to worry, okay? I've been living with this a long time now and I know what I'm doing. I'm not going to mess up. There are a lot of things that a lack of depth perception will prevent a person from doing, but carpentry isn't one of them."

"You're talking about the rebuild on the house? That's what you think I'm worried about right now?"

She got up. "I'm sorry. I can't. I have to go."

And she did, just like that. Got up and walked out without another word, before Tony could do more than instinctively get to his feet.

The door slammed. Rapid footsteps clomped down the stairway and faded away.

He dropped back to the chair with a sigh.

The clock ticked, and ticked, and ticked.

## *CHAPTER FIFTEEN*

TONY HEFTED THE window into the opening, rested its bottom edge on the sill blocks and pushed it gently into place. He checked for level and plumb and measured both diagonals, adding shims as needed to square things up. It felt good to be back at work. The FFF was usually one of the high points of his year, but this time around it'd been emotionally exhausting, and the aftermath was even worse. He was happy to be back here with his tools and materials, putting things to rights, and not getting ambushed by women.

"Good morning, Tony."

The tape measure flew out of his hand.

He spun around and saw Dalia standing behind him on one of the plywood panels that had been laid across the porch joists.

"Sorry," she said. "My mistake."

"That's all right," he said. "I'm just glad the tape measure didn't hit you."

*Good morning, Tony?* What was that supposed to mean? Why did she sound so businesslike and polite? How long had she been standing there watching him, with her hands folded in that weirdly formal way?

"Um… Would you care for some coffee?" she asked. "A bagel?"

A *bagel*? What was this, New York City? He almost made a crack about how she'd lived in the big city too long. But no. He couldn't joke with her like that. Their last meeting had been, well…

"No, thanks, I'm good. We went to that taco-kolache-espresso place in town, you know, the one with the big metal rooster next door? They've got a boudin kolache that's really good. I mean, I haven't actually tried it, but…I hear it's good."

Why was he rambling? He wasn't even sure what boudin was.

"Could I speak with you alone, please?"

"Sure."

She took a quick look around at Alex and the other workers. "Alone."

Okay, she was starting to seriously freak

him out, with her bagels and coffee and *Could I speak with you alone, please?*

"All right," he said. "Alex, would you take over for me here?"

"Sure thing," Alex said.

Dalia walked through the empty door opening into the house. He followed her across the living room, into the short hallway…

Tony gulped. She was holding open the door to her old bedroom.

He'd never actually been inside this room before, never caught more than a glimpse of it through the open doorway. Mr. Ramirez had laid out some vivid and painful consequences that would befall Tony if he ever set so much as a toe across the threshold.

He squared his shoulders and walked on through.

The room was severely neat, with what looked like the same furniture she'd had in high school, and the same quilt on the bed. Dalia turned the desk chair around to face the bed and sat there, while gesturing for Tony to sit on the bed itself. He did, gingerly, on the very edge.

This whole thing was surreal. It felt a lot

like that time he'd been called into his elementary school's principal's office—with his mom, no less—after he'd climbed onto the roof of the cafeteria. That man sure could put some menace into bland words. *Antonio needs to find a more constructive outlet for his energy and develop better impulse control.*

Dalia took a deep breath.

"I want to apologize for whatever I did—and I don't doubt that I did it—that made you think you couldn't tell me the truth about what happened on spring break. What you said about being scared of how I'd react—I wish you hadn't felt that way, but I understand why you did. I know I can be a rigid and uncompromising person. I made you afraid of me, and I'm sorry. Not that what you did wasn't really stupid! It was. But being stupid isn't the same as being unfaithful. I know this doesn't change anything that's happened, but I want you to know how sorry I am."

Tony's eyes stung. For her to be humble and sorry was something he'd never looked for, never imagined. Dalia had never apologized to him before, for anything, ever.

Nothing strange about that; he was the one who was always messing up. But now that he heard her say the words, he suddenly felt like a weight had been lifted off him.

Then she said, *"However."*

She packed a lot into that *however.* After she said it, she took a long pause. Tony just kept quiet and waited. He was pretty sure he knew what was coming.

She spoke slowly, like she was choosing her words carefully.

"I want to know how we got from you being afraid to tell me the truth, to me thinking you cheated on me. That day in the lumberyard, you said you never did. Is that true?"

"It's true."

For a second there was a break in her self-control. She took a quick breath, let it out and lowered her head.

Then she looked him straight in the eye again.

"Okay. I believe you. So why did I think for six years that you did? I might have jumped to conclusions, but that can't be the whole story."

"Yeah, it's not. I, uh— You have to understand, I didn't know right from the start that I was going to lose the vision in the eye completely. I held out hope for a long time. Weeks. I thought I'd heal up good as new and you'd never need to know. But then—Wow, I don't even know where to begin."

"Why don't you pick up with that one phone call, when your vision started to go? What happened after that?"

"Okay, yeah. Well, so I went to the ER in Corpus Christi, and then they admitted me to the hospital, and an ophthalmologist came in to do the surgery."

"What was it like?"

"Oh, man, it was the worst. Did you know they don't put you under for eye surgery? They give you a local, and a sedative, but that's it. They're operating on your *eye-ball* and you're awake for the whole thing! I talked the entire time, just a string of nonsense. I don't think the surgeon liked it much. He didn't like *me* much, period. He was pretty grim—he had, like, the worst bedside manner ever—but he said there was really no way to give a prognosis until the post-recovery vision test. I just had to wait and see."

"How long?"

"Two to four weeks. The recovery period was rough. My eyes were all red and swollen—both of them, because the good eye did this sympathetic thing where it swelled up, too. There was all this stuff to do with ice packs and weird sleeping positions. The one bright spot was I got Percocet. Ha ha!"

It had seemed funny enough before he said it, but once the words were out, they just sounded sad, and Dalia did not look amused.

"Did you go through all that alone?"

"Oh, no. Alex was with me. I called him from the ER, and five hours later he was there. He's the only one who knows, actually. Well—other than you now."

"Seriously? You never told anyone? Your grandparents? Your mom and dad?"

"Mom had just gotten remarried. I didn't want to bother her. Dad would've been worse than useless. And my grandparents had enough to worry about on the ranch. Honestly, I just didn't want to talk about it. Plus, at that point I was still hopeful. Like I said, I…I thought I'd get my vision back and everything would be okay."

"But what about the guys who went to North Padre with you? What'd you do about them?"

"Told 'em I was sick. That wasn't hard to believe, the way I'd been drinking. They were too busy partying to pay much attention. And as soon as it was okay for me to travel, Alex got me back to the dorm. My roommate had dropped out of school by then, so Alex stayed in my room. Made sure I took my meds and did everything the doctor said."

"But didn't you miss class?"

"Well, sure. But for a college athlete to miss a lot of class and then show up with bloodshot eyes is not that unusual. I could've made it up later. The coaching staff could've arranged something, assuming I'd be able to play again. At that point I wasn't able to do much of anything, other than sit around and think, and talk to you on the phone once in a while."

"I remember. No wonder you sounded so weird."

"Yeah. Well, so the recovery period ended, and I had zero vision in my right eye. And I kept right on grasping at straws. I still had time before summer training camp, and we wouldn't have our physicals until after that. I thought maybe I could memorize the eye chart, I thought I could adapt, I thought my eye could still heal. But I couldn't keep fooling myself forever. It didn't matter how great of shape the rest of me was in. With no depth perception, I couldn't land the ball anymore. And with no peripheral vision on my right side, I was a sitting duck for getting sacked. I was finished. So I tried to feel you out about the whole thing. We were talking, and I said, what if I didn't go pro? What if I didn't even play college ball anymore? What if I didn't finish school? And you asked if I was flunking out. And I said no, I was just thinking out loud. And you said, 'Well, don't. You're not good at it.'"

He could hear the bitterness in his own voice. He'd never forgotten those words. They'd felt like a slap in the face.

Dalia picked up where he left off. "And then *you* said, 'You know what? Never mind. I don't know why I even try to talk to you.'"

Apparently he wasn't the only one who could still recall the exact words of the conversation.

"I thought you were just picking a fight," she said. "And so I said, 'This is about spring break, isn't it?' And you...you didn't say anything. There was just this long silence that made me feel sick to my stomach. And then you hung up. You hung up on me, Tony."

"I wasn't picking a fight, not at first. It was a last-ditch effort. I was asking because I really wanted to know if the two of us still had a shot. You could have said that it didn't matter, that you loved me no matter what I did for a living. And then I could have told you, and maybe, just maybe, you would've forgiven me and things would have been okay. But that isn't what you said. And I knew then that we were finished. So yeah, I pushed you away. There was no point in telling you the truth about what happened. I'd just have to hear a lecture about how stupid I was, and then you'd break up with me anyway, so why not skip to the credits? It was better for you not to be dragged down by me."

"Better? How can you think that? I thought... Tony, I thought you cheated on me. I mean, come on. It sure sounded like an admission to me."

"Yeah, but you know what? I think you were ready to believe it because you expected it all along. And that's what I don't get. Out of all the things I could have done, all the reasons I might have been acting weird, the one thing you zeroed in on was that I'd been with another girl."

"Well, yes. Naturally that was the first thing I thought of."

"Why *naturally*? Do I have *Cheater* printed on my forehead?"

"Well, no, of course not. It's just..."

She looked at him like it should be obvious. He waited. She held out a hand toward him, gesturing, like he was Exhibit A. He held both of his hands out, palms up, like, *What?*

She stood, looked up at the ceiling and sighed in that impatient way that meant Tony was being obtuse.

"Well, look at you, with your outrageous good looks and your ridiculous charm. I don't think you even *mean* to flirt half the time—it's just your way. You can talk to anyone and make them like you without even trying. You've got this…this body, and this face, and this charm, and I…I'm not all that. I'm just me. I'm not…pretty enough for you. I never was."

He felt his jaw fall open. "Not pretty enough? Are you kidding me? Why would you think that? Didn't I tell you how beautiful you are, like, a million times when we were together?"

"Of course. But you *would* say that, and make it sound sincere. That's just how you are."

He rose to his feet. "It's just the truth, is what it is! Dalia, you are the most amazing woman I have ever known. You're beautiful and smart and hardworking and disciplined. You're the whole package. I'm the one who's not enough. I'm not smart enough for you and your successful family. But I never cheated on you, and I never wanted to. There was never anyone for me but you. Never. Not then and not now."

Those last few sentences came out before he knew he was going to say them. The air seemed to shudder with the shock of it. Dalia stood there, all stiff and taut like she'd fall to pieces if she relaxed even a tiny bit.

Then her eyes filled with tears.

Tony could count on one hand the times he'd seen Dalia cry. On the playground in fourth grade when she broke her arm. On the front porch that time when he'd shown her the board where he'd written *Tony loves Dalia*. At her dad's funeral. And now.

He put his arms around her and felt hers go around him and hold on tight. It felt *good*—like getting into a hot shower the morning after the first cold front of the year. It was the most amazing feeling of comfort and release. He laid his cheek against the top of her head and breathed deep of that juniper berry scent. He could have stayed that way forever.

But then she took a deep shuddery breath and pulled away, and it was like the hot water ran out after two minutes, leaving him shivering. He ached with wanting to hold her again, but he let her go and stood there quietly while she got her face back under control.

An awkward, excruciating silence passed. Tony wasn't good at awkward silences. He always wanted to fill them, but he couldn't think of anything to say to fill this one.

Dalia sniffed and drew herself up straight. "But I heard you got cut from the team because you were skipping workouts and stuff."

"Yeah, that's not wrong. I did. The coaching staff never knew what the real problem was."

"What? Why on earth not? Why didn't you tell them about your eye?"

"Because I'd rather have them think of me as a brilliant but undisciplined player than know the truth—that I just couldn't do it anymore. It's one thing to be the guy who refuses to get his act together. It's another thing to be the guy who can't perform no matter how hard he tries."

"And you think the first one is *better*?"

"Well, yeah! I mean if you're just a goof-off, then there's still hope for you. Everyone believes that if you'd just buckle down and apply yourself, you'd be great. But if you go all in, if you do your best and your best isn't good enough, then what else is there? You're just some guy, nothing special. And everyone knows it."

She shook her head, clearly not convinced

but willing to let it go for now and get on with the story.

"So you got cut from the team. And without your scholarship, you were finished in school also."

"Well…it was a combination of things. Alex thought there might still be a way to work out some sort of arrangement, financially. He was researching grants and stuff, and making me study for finals. But then that plan tanked."

"Why? What tanked it?"

"Your package. It showed up Monday morning, just before my first exam."

She dropped her face in her hands.

"Nothing else felt important after that," he said softly. "I was just…done. So I flunked out, came back home and moved in with my dad. I know, terrible idea—but I didn't have a lot of options. My mom and her new husband were living in Longview. Rick's a pretty good guy, but I don't think he would've been thrilled at taking in his wife's washed-out twenty-year-old son at that point in their marriage. Alex was living with my grandparents, and he tried to get me to move in with them, too, but that would've meant getting up at the crack of dawn, working cattle, mending fence, and I just wasn't up to it. Not the work itself so much as my grandfather. He's a good man, but he's not the easiest person in the world to get along with, especially when he thinks you're a slacker. Dad was basically the only one who was excited to have me around. At that point I didn't have much left to lose, and the idea of a nonstop party seemed pretty good. There was nothing to rein me in, no reason whatsoever to stay in shape or keep my nose clean. Just good times."

"That sounds awful."

"Yeah, it was. It didn't take me long to find out that I could sink lower, that I did have something left to lose. Finally I realized I had to do *something* productive with my life, and the first step was getting away from my dad. That was hard. Not just, like, the emotional side of it, but the logistical side, too. I didn't have enough money for a place of my own, so I actually lived out of my truck for a couple months. I hired on with a roofing crew. Man, was that rough. I have never worked that hard in my entire life. It was mind-numbingly hard. But somewhere along the way, I started to like it and get good at it. I learned to frame and trim. Then I started taking on small jobs on my own, and one thing led to another. By then Alex was going to automotive technology school and wanted to live in town, so we moved in together. And it got to where I was bidding bigger and bigger jobs, and before I knew it, I was a general contractor."

"Hold on a minute. You started out as a roofer? Wasn't that dangerous, walking around on roofs when you didn't have any depth perception?"

He shrugged. "Not any more dangerous than firefighting."

She stared at him. "I forgot about that. You're a *firefighter*, and you're blind in one eye. How is that even allowed?"

"Allowed? You realize we're volunteers, right?"

"Well, yeah, but it's not safe. Surely you have to make some sort of disclosure of any preexisting physical conditions before they accept you."

"Nope. Anyway, it's not that big a deal. Once you put that helmet and SCA mask on, your peripheral vision's pretty much shot, anyway. You have to keep your head on a swivel to watch for flames sneaking over your shoulder."

"You are *not* making me feel better."

He smiled. "You worried about me?"

It came out sounding flirtier than he'd intended. *Careful*, he told himself. *Don't be dumb. Don't ruin it.*

Dalia scowled. "I'd prefer that you not die a fiery death, yes."

"Ah, well. Thanks for that."

What was he doing? The way he said it, the way he was smiling at her—this was what she'd meant. He flirted when he didn't even mean to, when he was trying *not* to.

Well, he wasn't going to mess up now. He'd just won back some respect from her—at least that was how he was reading the situation—and he wasn't about to throw that away. He'd show her he could be mature about this.

"I'd better get back to work," he said.

His hand was on the door latch when she said, "So what's it like, being blind in one eye?"

He turned back around.

"It's not that bad. You adjust. You know that cars aren't the size of playing cards, so if they look real small, they must be far away. You guess, and experiment, and figure it out. I'm mostly used to it now, but there are still times when the world just looks… wrong. Everything's sort of dim and flat, and the colors aren't right. Oh, and then there's this weird thing where you feel like the center of your body has shifted, like your good eye is in the middle of your face. For a long time I used to lean a little to my left without knowing it, but I don't do that anymore, I don't think. I do still tend to run into things on my right. I'm clumsier than I used to be. And pouring drinks is a challenge, because you can't tell how far back the glass is. I have to hold the glass I'm pouring into with my other hand, or rest the bottle on the edge of the glass, or stand up and look straight down to make sure everything's lined up. Otherwise I miss the glass and pour onto the table. It's hard to look cool after that, so I was motivated to figure it out pretty quick. And sometimes it takes me a little longer to recognize people. I don't know why, but it does."

"How well can you see me right now?"

Something in her voice made his heart leap into his throat. "Well, um, not real well.

You're kinda backlit by the window. I can see, like, your outline. I can see that there are, uh, contours there."

She took a step toward him. "How about now?"

"Yeah, well, uh, better. I can see your face. I can tell it's you."

That was a stupid thing to say. Of course he could tell it was her. Her voice, her face, her shape, her scent, everything about her had his senses filled to overflowing.

"How far away am I?"

"I don't know. I'd have to touch you to be sure."

He started to reach for her but pulled his hand back. *Don't be dumb. Don't mess this up.*

Then Dalia took his hand, pulled it to her and settled it in the lean curve of her waist, and ran her own hand slowly up his arm—her whole hand, fingers spread, feeling him. When she reached his triceps, he flexed like he used to whenever she'd touch his arms, and she smiled like she remembered.

He had just enough time to think, *What is happening?*

And then Dalia was kissing him and he wasn't thinking at all anymore.

SHE HADN'T MEANT to kiss him.

Had she?

No, definitely not. Okay, maybe the whole thing did seem a little planned, getting him alone behind her closed bedroom door. But all she'd really wanted was to clear the air. Only a day earlier, she'd learned some things that radically altered her view of the past six years, exonerating Tony of serious fault, and casting her own behavior in a new and unflattering light. Whatever mistakes he'd made, he hadn't been unfaithful to her. But she'd made assumptions, and pushed him into a corner, and added to his suffering, which had been bad enough already.

She'd wronged him, and she had to say so. That was only justice.

But once she had him there, the way he looked, the things he said and the memories that had a different meaning than what she'd thought came together in a powerful way.

And underneath all that was something more powerful still.

What it came down to was that she loved

Tony, and she wanted him now as much as she ever had. She'd never stopped, really. And there was no reason to fight it anymore. All the things keeping them apart had vanished like August dew in a Texas sunrise.

Just for a second or two, a voice inside her head said, *It's been too long. Too much has happened. We're too different.*

And then she was kissing him, and the voice didn't have anything more to say.

She heard a soft thump from the closed door as Tony's back pushed it against the jamb. He smelled of sawdust and silicone caulk. His faded T-shirt was soft under her hands, and the artistic sculpted beard that had drawn her attention so often over the past several weeks rubbed against her chin.

A knock at the door made them both jump. "Dalia? Are you in there?"

It was her mom.

"Uh, no. I mean yes. I'll be out in a minute."

Tony was trying not very successfully to muffle a laugh. His eyes were bright, his face shining with joy and mischief, and for a second he looked a lot like the Tony of fifteen years ago.

"Shh!" Dalia whispered. "We've got to get you out of here. You can climb out the window."

"And have my guys see me sneaking out like some punk? That's way worse than just walking out the door."

"Yeah. Yeah, you're right. We're not teenagers anymore."

"No, we're not. We're two responsible adults with nothing to hide. We'll just saunter out all cool like there's nothing to see here."

"Okay," she said. "But don't open the door yet. I need a second."

It would take more than a second to restore her calm. Her heart pounded, and she was shaking.

She didn't want to go. It felt so abrupt, ending the encounter this way. Nothing was resolved or talked through properly—it *had* been, but then the kiss had raised a whole fresh set of issues. And she didn't want to address any of them yet. She just wanted to kiss Tony again and again.

But there wasn't time for that. She was in her childhood bedroom with her high school sweetheart, with whom she seemed to have just gotten back together, with an entire construction crew and her mother waiting outside the door.

And the longer they waited, the weirder it was going to be.

"I guess I'll go out first," she said. "Then you follow in a few minutes. I'll try to distract everyone."

"Okay."

She reached for the door latch, but Tony put a hand on hers and said, "Wait a minute."

He turned her around to face him. "Dalia, will you go with me to the county fair?"

It melted her heart, how eager and earnest and formal he looked, how he was rushing the words out like he had to hurry before he lost his nerve. So much for not being teenagers anymore.

She laughed, then kissed him again.

"Is that a yes?"

"Yes. Now go. I mean stay. I'm going first. No, wait! I have a better idea." She picked up a file folder from her desk and handed it to him. "Take this, and we'll go out together. That way it'll look like we were discussing some sort of legitimate business in here."

"Yeah. Yeah, that's good."

He reached for the door latch—there'd been a lot of reaching for the door latch in the last few minutes—then turned and kissed her one more time.

Then he squared his shoulders, opened the door and walked out, looking just the same as when they'd gone back to her brother's pasture party after kissing at the stock pond.

She'd missed him so much.

# *CHAPTER SIXTEEN*

DALIA WATCHED FOR Tony's truck from her front-facing bedroom window like some infatuated sap, the same way she used to watch for the Dodge Charger he drove back in high school, before it got repossessed in the fallout from one of his dad's losing streaks. And just like back then, she felt a thrill of pure sweetness when she saw the dust cloud on the driveway that meant he was almost there.

She took a last look in the mirror. She'd spent more time on hair and makeup than usual, and she knew she was looking good. Her eyeliner was especially on point.

With so much advance warning, she could have gone out to meet him, but it was a pleasure to watch him drive up, park and get out with that spring in his step. Besides, she couldn't deprive her mom of the opportunity to revel in delight. Her mom had been giddy since finding out Tony and Dalia had an actual date.

Then she heard the front door open and her mom calling out a greeting, which meant she was hobbling around on her crutches.

Dalia grabbed her purse and hurried out to the living room.

"Sit back down, Mom. You didn't need to let Tony in. After all these weeks and years of coming here, I'm sure he knows his way around."

"Oh, I'm tired of resting. And it's only two weeks until I'll be walking in my walking boot. Dalia made a spreadsheet to keep track of my recovery process," she told Tony as he crossed the threshold. "She makes the most beautiful spreadsheets."

"I know," Tony said. "I've seen them."

He smiled at Dalia, put a hand to his chest and looked her over. "I, uh—mmm. Wow."

"Thanks," she said, with an appraising glance of her own. "You, too."

"You both look lovely!" her mom said. "You won't mind if I take some pictures, will you?"

"Okay," Dalia said. She made it sound like she was giving in, granting her mom a favor, but she was glad. She *wanted* a picture of them on this day, wanted a tangible reminder to help her lock down every detail to keep in her memory forever.

The pictures were taken, then they said their goodbyes and headed outside. Tony opened the passenger-side door for Dalia, then ran around to the driver's-side door like there was no time to waste. He always did it that way.

Once they were past the cattle guard and heading down the highway, he reached over, took her hand and brought it to his lips, all in one swift motion.

"What are you smiling about?" he asked.

She hadn't even realized she was smiling. "I was thinking about our first date."

"Ah, but *which* first date?"

He was still holding her hand. The feel of his fingers laced between hers was so perfect and right.

She chuckled. "This again?"

"Of course. We never really figured it out."

They'd spent a lot of time talking it over. Dalia always said Marcos's pasture party didn't count as a date because they didn't go to it together or plan to meet there. Tony said if it ended with the two of them making out, it counted as a date. She said no, it didn't, because that wasn't what "date" meant. A date was something you arranged beforehand. That was the *definition*. Then he pointed out that once they were both *at* the party, she'd invited him out to the stock pond and he'd accepted, so that part right there was a date, even if the party as a whole wasn't. She said this was splitting hairs.

"You were always so adamant about it," she said. "I never understood why it mattered to you so much."

"You want to know a secret?" he asked. "I didn't really care. I just liked talking about it—partly because it was fun to wind you up, and partly because the idea of a first date meant there would be a second and a third. A history. And the fact that you argued so hard for your own way meant you thought so, too."

"Wow, that's…really sweet, actually."

"Yeah, I'm a sweet guy. That's also why I pushed so hard to drive you to school, that first Monday after we got together. Remember? You didn't see the point. You said it was a waste of gas, with me living so close to the high school and you living out in the sticks. And I said—"

"You said we had to make a grand statement. You didn't want there to be any doubt in anyone's mind that I was your girl. Oh, yeah. I remember."

She picked up his hand and kissed it. "You want to know another secret? That was just token resistance. I was actually thrilled. I'd been half-afraid that once the weekend was over you'd blow me off and pretend like nothing ever happened between us. But you *wanted* people to know. You wanted it *official*!"

"Well, sure. I was proud of you."

"You were! You really were! And that was the most incredible thing. Because I was proud of you, too. Fiercely proud."

"Fiercely? Wow. Well, how 'bout now?"

"Even more now."

He pulled over onto the shoulder, put on his hazard lights and kissed her.

It was so good to be holding him again. His lips on hers, his hair in her hands—it was all so familiar, but so *now*.

Later, when they were driving again, he

said, "You want to know another secret? I've been wanting to take you to the county fair since seventh grade."

She looked at his amazing profile, dark and sharp against the afternoon sky. "You're kidding me."

"I'm not! Every fall, from seventh grade to senior year, I thought it would be the year it happened. And every year I was wrong. And when we finally got together it was spring, which was too late, and then after that we were away at school. And then…we broke up. But I never forgot. I've thought about it every fall since, but, you know, in a sad way. And now here we are, actually going. So this is the fulfillment of a fourteen-year wish for me."

"Seriously? You really wanted to go with me? You sure didn't act like it, with all those beauty queens and barrel racers hanging on your arm year after year."

"Heh, heh. You noticed that?"

"Of course I noticed. I noticed everything you did."

"Well, I had to amuse myself somehow, and show you what you were missing."

"Show me what I was missing? You never asked me to go with you, genius."

"Because I knew you wouldn't say yes."

She leaned closer to him, slipped her arm through his and gave him a quick sidewise glance and a smile. "Says you."

THEY STROLLED AIMLESSLY around the fairgrounds, just taking in the sights and sounds. Tony couldn't stop smiling—not that he tried very hard. He liked seeing all the wildly different-looking people, the jumble of full-sleeve tattoos, snakeskin-print leggings and hair dyed in nonnatural colors, plus all the traditional country-looking people. Western shirts with pearl snap buttons, Wranglers and plaid, cowboy hats and big belt buckles. Lots of glorious mustaches and beards, as well as big hair on women and men. Sometimes, entire groups walked by all wearing maroon A&M shirts.

Lots of younger men wore the traditional jeans, boots, hat and belt, but with T-shirts instead of button-downs. That was the route Tony had gone. He had on his favorite Texas graphic T, the one with an outline of a United States map with an oversize

Texas, so big that the panhandle reached all the way to where North Dakota ought to be.

Tony liked all the noise and action. More than that, he liked walking around with Dalia on his arm. Sometimes they ran into people they knew, and it was always fun to see their faces register surprise at the sight of the two of them together. *That's right*, Tony wanted to say. *We're a couple now. This is my girl.*

He stopped in front of a mechanical bull. "Mr. Mendoza got himself one of these," he said. "I rode it at the FFF."

"I saw."

"You did?"

"Of course. I couldn't take my eyes off you—and I was really trying, too."

"I actually rode it more than once."

"I know. Four times. I saw. Looked real good doing it, too."

He tried to look modest but gave up. "You wanna see me do it again?"

"That line is pretty long. Besides, I've already seen you ride a real one. That was even better."

"Oh, yeah? You liked seeing that?"

"It was amazing. I didn't even know you

were going to ride, and suddenly there you were. You were always such a natural athlete. Everything physical that you ever tried, you succeeded at. You just had an instinct for it."

"You're kind of a natural yourself. I bet you'd have been terrific at barrel racing."

"I thought about trying, but I was too busy with sheepdog trials. I didn't want to be dealing with a horse *and* a border collie."

"Remember that one time when your dog busted loose, barged into the arena while another dog was doing the course and tried to take over?"

She laughed. "Yes! I haven't thought of that in years. That was the craziest thing."

"I know! Those dogs were so *into* it, so dead serious about their work. There was poor Merlin Brando, just straining to get loose, crying out with those anguished yelps 'cause there were sheep to be herded and he wasn't there to do it. And then he slipped his hold and burst in and told that other dog, *Outta the way, fool! Watch and learn.*"

"I was horrified. I thought Merle and I would be banned for life. But everyone thought it was hilarious. Just a border collie being a border collie. Passionate about work."

He pulled her to him and kissed the top of her head. "You're kind of a border collie yourself at heart."

She smiled. "You silver-tongued devil, you."

They browsed vendor booths. So many things for sale—hummingbird feeders, earthenware mugs, wooden steins, etched-glass pint and pilsner glasses. Throw pillows covered with leather or hair-on animal skins, trimmed with studs and concha shells. Purses, spangly and fringed, studded, embossed, bejeweled, be-crossed. Lots of crosses in general. Boots, hats. Clothing for humans and dogs. Decorative rocks with designs or words carved or etched into them.

And, oh, the Texas-shaped things. Tony kept saying, "We need that. We need that." Like there was a *we* to consider, like the two of them were going to have a household together.

And Dalia kept saying, "No, we don't."

He never got tired of that *we*.

As their Ferris wheel cart rose into the

sky, Dalia said, “So I’ve been reading up on monocular vision.”

Tony let out a shout of laughter. “Monocular vision?”

“That means when you only have vision in one eye.”

“I know what it means. I just never call it that.”

“What do you call it?”

“Being a cyclops.”

She smiled, cupping his cheek with her hand. “A cyclops has one eye in the middle of his head. Whereas you have two beautiful dark brown eyes placed exactly where they’re supposed to be.”

He smiled back and gave her a quick kiss. “I’m glad you like ’em. But only one of ’em works.”

“Right. Which means you have twenty percent less peripheral vision, and no depth perception at all. None. Zero.”

“Yep. Which stinks for quarterbacks and fighter pilots, but for most other folks it’s fine. There are a few challenges, especially at first, but you get over it. You adapt.”

“I’m sure you do, to a degree. But there’s a limit to how much you can adapt when the raw sensory input just isn't there. Your brain can make new neural pathways, but it can't make you a new eye."

"I know all that. Let's not talk about it now, okay? Look."

He swept an arm over the busy fairgrounds, the rooftops and water towers, the tree-covered ridges and rolls fading into a blue haze at the horizon.

"We've got all this beautiful country spread out around us, and it's a beautiful day, and we're together. I just want to enjoy that."

"Okay."

She settled against him the way she used to, with her head against his chest at just the right height for him to rest his chin on it.

He knew she hadn't really let go of the subject. She was just giving it a rest for now. But that was okay. Before she had a chance to pick it up again, he'd show her what he could do. She'd see.

## *CHAPTER SEVENTEEN*

"THIS WHOLE OBSESSION of yours with the state of Texas shape is getting out of hand," said Dalia. "It's almost pathological."

Tony gave the Texas-shaped cutting board a cheerful pat. "Thanks!"

He'd actually bought it, though Dalia thought it was wildly overpriced and said so. Now he held it out at arm's length to admire all over again.

"Solid mesquite, with a little knothole right where Limestone Springs should be. Isn't that great?"

And she had to admit it was. In spite of how hard a time she was giving him, she was secretly delighted. Cutting boards were so *domestic*. She'd thought at first he was interested in it as a gift, maybe to butter up her mom, but no, he wanted it for himself.

"What's so surprising about that?" he said. "I cook."

*He cooks. My boyfriend cooks.*

"You grill, sure, but that's just playing with fire."

"That's not all grilling is. But I don't just grill. I do regular kitchen-type cooking, too."

He tucked the cutting board under one arm and took her hand. "One night soon, I'll make some chimichurri sauce and marinate us some steaks and cook 'em out at your mom's. My chimichurri sauce is fantastic."

*My boyfriend makes a fantastic chimichurri sauce.*

She could picture him, chopping and dicing and sautéing, singing along with whatever music he had going, half dancing as he moved around the kitchen. She could picture the Texas-shaped cutting board, rinsed clean and standing up to dry behind the sink, in a kitchen that looked a lot like the one he was building at La Escarpa.

She loved listening to him talk. It was so restful. He kept up a running stream-of-consciousness monologue about all the things they saw. Once in a while she interjected a dry pithy remark, which set him off in a new and freshly hilarious direction, but there was no pressing need to keep up her end of the conversation like with most guys.

About a year ago she'd gone out with a web developer she'd met on a dating site. He'd peppered her the whole evening with icebreaker-type questions that sounded like he'd gotten them off an online listicle with a title like "Fifty Million Great Conversation Starters for a First Date." *What's something I wouldn't guess about you? What are you most passionate about? What has been the most significant event of your life so far? What five places would you visit if money and time were no object? What's the most spontaneous thing you've ever done?* It was exhausting, like a job interview or police interrogation. It made her brain freeze up. Her answers made her sound stodgy and unimaginative, which was exactly how she'd felt. The guy didn't call again and she didn't care. She didn't even remember his name.

She felt more at home now, and more fully herself, than she had in years. She never had as much fun with anyone as she did with Tony.

They went into a big metal barn that held all the best-in-show entries—quilts, hand-made clothing, knitting, crocheting, photography. The winners already had ribbons on them.

"Your mom should enter this," Tony said. "She's always knitting."

"That's just because she hurt her foot," Dalia said. "She loves knitting, but usually the ranch takes too much of her time for her to finish many projects."

The subject was a pretty good lead-in for something she wanted to talk to him about, but should she do it? Or was it too soon? She didn't want to assume too much, come on too strong, make Tony think she was angling for a commitment on their first back-together date.

Anyway, it was too late now. The moment was gone.

The food entries came next. Plates of eggs, pies with one slice missing and various home-canned goods.

"So many pickles!" said Tony. "Pickled okra, pickled garlic, pickled carrots, pickled grape olives."

All the food items were protected behind sheets of chicken wire, but Tony stuck his fingers through to touch the jars.

"Why are you doing that?" Dalia asked, chuckling.

"I just want to."

"Well, you're not supposed to."

"How do you know? I don't see any rules posted."

"They have that chicken wire there for a reason."

"Yeah, so you don't smash the jars or try to shoplift 'em outta here. They don't mind if you touch 'em a little."

They came out of the best-of-show barn into a galley-style food court area with stalls lining the sides. Tony stopped dead, clapped a hand to his stomach and took a deep breath.

"Mmm, smell that good fried-food smell. Are you hungry? I'm starving."

They ate at a picnic table with a plastic tablecloth clamped on—pork chop on a stick for Tony, a gyro for Dalia and a funnel cake to share.

"Eating outdoors is the best," Tony said.

"You should see the Italian Market in Philadelphia," Dalia said. "It's this big outdoor market spread out over twenty city blocks. My favorite taqueria is there."

"A taqueria, in an Italian market, in Philadelphia? That doesn't sound right."

"It's really good, though! Anyway, the market isn't just Italian anymore. There's all kinds of food. Vietnamese. Seafood. And cheesesteaks, of course."

"So there's more to Philly than concrete and Eagles fans, huh?"

"Oh, yeah, lots more. We've also got a higher murder rate than New York."

"Ha ha! I bet they put that on all the brochures."

"There are actual attractions, too. Lots of American history stuff, too, of course. Alex would love it."

"Oh, *Alex* would love it? Well, then. I should book a trip right away, for me and Alex. I wouldn't want him to miss out on an opportunity to see some American history stuff. I mean, if it's there to be seen, then he ought to see it."

She gave him a sly smile. "Yeah, you should. It would be educational. And culturally enriching. And while you're there, you could, you know, come see me, too."

"Yeah? Well, forget Alex, then. You're the only attraction I need."

They finished their food and headed to the stock barn, a big metal building with stalls formed by gate panels lashed together, and plenty of fresh wood shavings on the floor, all very clean and spacious. Just inside the doorway, Tony stopped and took a deep breath, just like he'd done in the food court.

"Don't you love the smell of livestock?"

"I do love it," Dalia said. "Livestock, and farms in general."

"Yeah, farms smell nice. Like hay and sunshine and feed and healthy animals. Old leather, a little machine oil. Ripe compost when you spread it over the garden."

"Exactly! A healthy farm smells wonderful. It's only when animals are sick or overcrowded that there's a stink. I went out with this guy once, and when he found out I'd grown up on a ranch, he acted like it was some low-class thing, like I'd spent my childhood wallowing around in stinky muck and mire."

"He sounds like a real jerk. You should avoid people like him. In the future you should never go out with anyone who isn't me."

For a second she almost said, *You're right,*

*I shouldn't.* But maybe that would be too much too soon, and reading too much into what might have been a flippant, impulsive remark on his part.

Before the silence could get awkward, Tony said, "I've been thinking a lot about when I was little, how me and Alex would go to our grandparents' place, and it was so…so *safe* there, you know? At home there was always tension over money, and you never knew what Dad was gonna do next. Mom tried hard to hold things together, but she was always so stressed, and sometimes the best she could do was take us to the ranch and leave us there for the weekend. Everything was so different there. Harmonious. My grandparents could be pretty cantankerous, but they were on the same side, working for the same goal. Partners. They respected each other. Plus there's this freedom to life on a ranch. You get up in the morning, and nobody tells you what to do. You figure it out for yourself, whether you're gonna mend fence, or cut hay, or burn brush, or worm cattle, or shore up the wall of the feed barn where it's getting a little rickety. 'Course, a lot of the time you're responding to emergencies or the demands of the season or what kind of weather you're having that day. But you get to make the call. And you can change things up if you want. Reconfigure the pastures. Try a new breed of cattle. Put in a field of lavender for a cash crop like that one guy over on Darst Field Road. You're your own boss, and what you decide matters, so you better make good choices and work hard. You know what I mean?"

"I do," she said. "I know exactly what you mean."

"I didn't appreciate it at the time the way I should have, the way Alex did. But looking back, I'm grateful I had that experience. I wish I'd had more of it. I think I'd be a better man."

Well, she'd never get a better lead-in than that. *Quit being such a coward and tell him.*

"I've been thinking a lot, too," she said. "La Escarpa is getting to be too much for my mom to run on her own. Really, I think it's been too much for a while now. I just didn't see it because I was away. But I'm at a point with my work where I can live wherever I want, and—"

"You're moving back home? That's fantastic!"

"Hold on! I haven't decided yet. I'm still thinking about it. But at the very least, I'm going to be spending more time here, you know, helping out. A lot more time."

"What'd your mom say to that?"

"I haven't told her yet. I didn't want to bring it up until I had things settled in my mind."

"Well, I don't know if this counts for anything, but I vote that you move back full-time, and soon."

She smiled at him. "It does. It counts for a lot."

They worked their way through the petting zoo, where they petted some rabbits and baby goats, and two palomino horses standing just close enough to the panel for an adult or older child to reach but out of grabbing range for little kids. They petted black pigs and spotted pigs and one white pig with a pink snout and pink skin showing through its bristles, like a pig in a storybook.

Most of the goats were Boers, with long floppy ears and short coats of white and reddish brown.

"Aren't Boer goats funny-looking?" said Tony. "They always look like beagles to me. A whole pack of beagles out in a pasture, grazing."

"Browsing," Dalia said. "Cattle graze. Goats browse."

"Hey, look at those animals with the long spiral curls. Are they some sort of sheep? They kinda look like English sheepdogs."

"There's a sign on the gate where that couple is sitting. *Cedar Ridge Angora Goats.* Huh. You know, I think La Escarpa used to have Angoras, way before my time. My dad told me about it."

"Oh, yeah? Cool. Well, then we should go talk to these people."

Dalia would have been content to slowly walk past the pen, with maybe a smile and a nod to the attractive older couple, or even a remark like *Good-looking animals*. Talking to strangers was a risk. You never knew what you might be letting yourself in for.

But before she could stop him, Tony had gone right up to them and said, "Hey there! These sure are some fine animals you've got here. Look like they ought to be starring in a hair-product commercial. I'd use whatever they're using."

The man stood. He was a big, solid guy with bright blue eyes and a kind face. "Well, thank you! They've got good genetics, but it does take some doing, keeping their fleeces in good condition."

"I'll bet. You can't have 'em rolling around in grass burrs or brushing against icicle cactus, can you?"

"No, you cannot."

Tony put out his hand. "I'm Tony, and this is Dalia."

"Ray Schmidt." He had a good firm handshake. "And my wife, Syndra."

Syndra had her hands full of knitting, so she just waved her needles and said, "Hi!"

"What are you making?" Dalia asked.

Syndra raised her arms to unfold a yard or so of light, frothy fluff with a sort of floral shape radiating from the center. "A bridal shawl."

"It's beautiful. Is the fiber from your goats?"

"It is. This is first-clip kid, which means it's from the first clipping of a six-month-old kid. It's finer and softer than the adult fibers.

Mohair fiber—that's what it's called—has a lovely drape to it, and it knits up beautifully, but it doesn't have a lot of elasticity, so the yarn is typically blended with silk or wool. This one has a silk core."

"It's very lustrous, too."

"Yes, that's because the scales are so tight. That means it holds dye well, too. Do you knit?"

"No, but my mom does. She did it a little when my brother and sister and I were small, but never as much as she would have liked. Too much work on the ranch, plus riding herd on us kids. But about a month ago she hurt her foot, and ever since she's been laid up, she's been knocking out projects left and right."

"I first started knitting when I broke my ankle coming off a horse. I could never stand not to be active, so I had to find something to do."

"Syndra's a born-and-bred country girl," Ray said. "I came to rural life a little later, but I love it. Do you folks have a place?"

"Not right now," said Tony. "I live in town, and Dalia lives in Philadelphia, of all places. She's home helping her mom. But she grew up on a ranch that's been in the family since before the Texas Revolution. She and her brother and sister are the seventh generation to live there."

"Your family's place wouldn't be called La Escarpa, would it?" Ray asked.

"Yes," said Dalia. "Do you know it?"

"I worked there, the summer before I started medical school. Never forgot it. Beautiful place. It was my first experience with Angoras, and the Hill Country, and rural life in general. I worked for a man called Marcos Ramirez."

"That was my grandfather!"

"Then Martin must be your dad."

"You knew my dad?"

"I did indeed. Of course, he was just a little bitty boy back then, strutting around in his Lucchese boots. He was the most meticulous kid I ever saw. Always as neat and pressed as if he'd just stepped out of a bandbox. Always had his shirt tucked in and his hat on straight and his boots clean. Good worker, too. Is he still a rancher? Is he here today?"

Tony saved her from having to answer.

"Unfortunately, Martin passed away a few years back."

Ray frowned. "Oh, it doesn't seem right I should live to hear that. I'm so sorry. He was such a self-contained little guy, quiet and polite, with this intensity about him. He always seemed to know exactly who he was and where he belonged."

"Very true," said Tony. "He wasn't the most fun person in the world to deal with for anyone who wanted to date his daughter, but he was tough and hardworking and fair. He had integrity."

Ray told some stories about Dalia's dad as a boy, and they talked about the care of Angora goats and the market for mohair.

Finally Tony said, "We'd better get going if we want to get good seats at the rodeo."

Syndra gave Dalia a business card, and Dalia gave Syndra her email address. Ray thought he might have some pictures from his summer at La Escarpa. Syndra also gave Dalia bags of yarn and roving to take home to her mother.

As they walked away, Dalia took Tony's hand in hers. "Thank you."

"For what?"

"For talking to those people. I never would have done it on my own, and I'd have missed out on all that."

"Ah, it's no problem. I liked doing it."

"I know. That's the best thing about it. You were just being yourself. So thanks for that."

"Well, you're very welcome. And there's plenty more where that came from. I can be myself all day long."

"Good. Because I…I like who you are."

It wasn't quite what she'd wanted to say, but it was close enough for now. She wanted to say she needed him, but it was a little early in the day for that sort of talk.

But was it? They'd known each other all their lives. Hadn't they waited long enough? They had enough missed opportunities behind them—at least, she thought so. Did he think it, too? She wanted to know, but she wasn't about to ask.

He smiled. "Thanks. I like who you are, too."

He brought her hand up to his face and kissed the back of it.

"Don't you just love talking to people like Ray and Syndra?" he said. "They're old enough to have lots of knowledge and experience, but they have so much energy and drive still, and they're so in love and not afraid to try new things. That's how I see us down the line."

The last sentence took her off guard. Did he really say it? Did he mean it the way it sounded? Or was it just a half-baked remark that he'd tossed out before thinking it through?

Then he gave her a quick sidelong look.

"Yeah," she said. "So do I."

Maybe they didn't have to wait until they were old enough to retire. They were young and strong and debt-free—at least, Dalia was debt-free. She wasn't sure how solvent Tony was, and this probably wasn't the best time to ask. But he'd spent the past several years running a successful small business, and he was respected and well liked in the community.

Just as important, they already had land access.

Was her mom up for a new agricultural venture? Dalia knew she would love the fluffy, sweet-faced Angora goats. Starting a mohair operation would be a lot of work—

building new pens, acquiring a herd, learning about a whole new species, dealing with shearers and mills.

But she wouldn't have to do it alone.

What if Dalia actually did it, moved back to Limestone Springs, maybe back to La Escarpa itself?

What if she and Tony got married after all? It could happen. Stranger things had happened. So what if they'd been interrupted, if things weren't quite like they'd planned? Things were better now. *They* were better now, grown up. Tony wasn't a professional football player, but he was a responsible community member, a business owner. He'd messed up, suffered for it and come out stronger, and so had she.

She kept the thought inside her, warm and glowing.

## *CHAPTER EIGHTEEN*

THEY SHOWED UP in what they thought was plenty of time for the rodeo, but the general-admission area was already packed. Dalia would have been all right with it, but Tony grandly swept her back through the gate and upgraded them to the fancy seating in front, which still had plenty of room. They each got a different, bigger stamp on the back of their hands from the richly mustachioed man who stood guard at the gate, ready to pounce on anyone who might try to sit in the fancy seats without paying for them.

"Oh, yeah," Tony said as they took their new seats. "This is much better. Only problem is, there's no back to the seat for me to rest my arm along as an excuse to put it around my girl."

He mimed the action, stretching both arms over his head with an exaggerated yawn and then bringing one slowly down behind Dalia with a comical expression of round-eyed innocence on his face as he looked pointedly away from her.

She took his hand as it landed on her shoulder and pressed it there.

"Do you need an excuse?" she asked.

He kissed her. "Well, no. I guess I don't."

It had been years since Dalia had been to a rodeo. It was hard to pay attention now, hard to look at anything besides Tony, all that lean strength of him, sitting there in his perfectly faded jeans. He kept in near-constant motion. Sometimes he picked up her hand, brought it to his lips and kissed the back of it in that swift, natural motion of his. Sometimes, when the rodeo clown was especially witty, he put his arm around her and squeezed her close to him, and she felt his big laugh booming through his chest. The clown's routine wasn't *that* funny, but Tony's laugh was so irresistible that she laughed, too. She'd forgotten how much he liked slapstick. It was oddly endearing. She'd glance over at his eager, attentive, grinning profile as he waited for the next comedic gem, and she loved him so much her throat ached.

There was lots to talk about, like where

the competitors came from—Buda, San Antonio, Wyoming, New Mexico, Australia—or how well they performed, or how they were going to have to visit the chiropractor the next day. Every so often, one of the calves had figured things out, and stopped just outside its chute instead of running, so the competitor rode right past it in a burst of momentum. Then the calf trotted smugly off to the pen.

Just after team roping, Tony suddenly said, “All right, listen. I gotta go do something. You wait here.”

“Where are you going?”

“I can’t tell you. It’s a surprise. But I’ll be back. You just sit tight, okay?”

He said it all in a rush, like he had to get away fast before she dragged the truth out of him, which probably wouldn’t have been all that difficult if she’d tried.

“Okay,” she said. She’d let him have his surprise, whatever it was.

He kissed her and was gone.

She chuckled. Alex was right: in the ways that really mattered, Tony wasn’t like their dad after all. He could never be a gambler; he was too transparent.

What was his surprise? She couldn't remember seeing anything she'd particularly wanted at any of the booths. Maybe it was something nice to eat. She *was* getting hungry again.

She made herself stop thinking about it. Whatever it was, she didn't want to figure it out and spoil it for him.

It was a clear night with a deep blue sky. When they'd first taken their seats, the golden crescent moon had just started rising above the bleachers opposite them. Now it was sailing high, and the stars were coming out.

Tony hadn't made it back by the end of saddle bronc. He'd be sorry he missed that; he loved all the rough stock events. He must be stuck in a line somewhere.

Tie-down roping began, and ended, and still Tony didn't come. By the time barrel racing started, Dalia was getting annoyed. Where was he? Did he get caught up in a conversation somewhere and lose track of time? It was no fun sitting here by herself. She wanted him here beside her, wanted to hear his comments and see him laugh at the clown.

Barrel racing ended. It was time for bull

riding now. Surely he'd be back for this; it was his favorite event. Dalia found the whole thing pretty terrifying. Exciting, sure, but so much could go so wrong, so fast. Vests offered some protection to internal organs, and some competitors wore head protection, but most didn't.

Seeing Tony compete during their senior year had been eight seconds' worth of mingled excitement and terror, with a big dose of pride. He'd looked so *good.* But she'd been relieved when Coach Willis had found out about it and put a quick end to Tony's bull-riding career.

The pickup riders and even the clowns seemed to have a more watchful, serious air now, as they waited soberly to do their part. Rodeo was fun, but there was always the risk that a rider—or a worker, for that matter—would get injured, maimed or killed.

A screen showed a close-up of each competitor in his chute before he rode, poised just above his bull, waiting. A couple of them wore helmets, but most just had their hats. Typical cowboy vanity.

It must be a tense time for them, that wait in the chute. All that preparation and training, years' worth in some cases, and in a matter of seconds the whole thing would be over, one way or the other.

Dang it, where was Tony? She wanted him here, with her, commenting on the over-the-top names of the bulls. Bruiser, Demon, Cochise, Frequent Flier. Now the announcer was introducing one called Dust Devil.

Then he said the competitor's name.

*Antonio Reyes.*

TONY HELD TIGHT to the top rail of the chute, keeping his weight off the bull and his toes tucked in so he wouldn't poke him with his spurs. Dust Devil was a red, tiger-striped brindle, a Brahma-Hereford cross, nineteen-hundred pounds. Tony had checked him out earlier, just after bronc riding was done, when the rodeo workers first started rolling the bulls up the alleyways and into the chutes.

Dust Devil was a massive, meaty animal. He'd even made eye contact with Tony as he passed him. His eyes were small and angry, set deep in the sides of his head with fleshy rolls and wrinkles above them—like he was raising his eyebrows at Tony, like he was sizing him up and didn't think much of him.

Now the bull was puffing and snorting, unable to look at Tony but communicating just fine with him all the same. *I know you're there, bud, and you're goin' down.*

All the metal pipes that formed the chute had advertising on them, bumper stickers for the various rodeo sponsors. Tony had his left hand over an ad for Justin Boots, and his right hand gripped the rope that circled the bull's girth—his own rope, which he'd retrieved from his grandparents' place yesterday, along with his chaps, spurs, vest and gloves. The equipment had been stored indoors in his riggin bag and was still in good shape. His gloves felt just right, grippy and flexible at the same time.

He had a weird, gone sort of feeling in his stomach. Things were about to get pretty wild. Anything could happen. Every bull had its tendencies; some were north-to-south buckers, some were spinners, and there were other, individual quirks besides. It was up to the rider to do his research and prepare himself.

But preparation could do only so much.

Once the chute opened, it was anyone's guess. You couldn't make a strategy, really, because you couldn't dominate the situation. The bull was going to do whatever he was going to do, and everything you did would be some sort of response to that. Like when the other team changed up its alignment in the last moments before a play, and you had to adjust. Only, this was not a defensive line but an animal, an angry animal that weighed not much less than a 1979 Volkswagen Beetle. And instead of seconds, you had *fractions* of a second to react, and there were more serious consequences if you failed.

There was no time to think. Your body had to act on instinct.

And underneath that feeling in his stomach, Tony felt something else, a cold calm certainty that said, *I got this.*

He nodded to the worker. The chute opened.

Almost the same instant, he was pitching forward, the name of a motor oil manufacturer suddenly huge before his eyes. Not even out of the chute yet, and the bull was trying to brain him against an iron pipe.

Then the bull left the chute, and Tony was

jerked backward and spinning hard to the right. A slamming jolt shuddered through him, from the soles of his feet to the top of his head, and then he whipped around fast to the left, feeling the twist in his spine.

He was laughing. No fear now, just a savage joy.

Another jolt, another twisting jerk. He held tight to the rope, but it was slipping out of his grip. He saw his left leg passing over the bull's back to the right. It spun around like the spoke of a wheel, like something not connected to him.

Something hit him hard on his left hip. The sky rolled past in a blur of stars, and the ground rushed toward his face.

DALIA'S FIRST THOUGHT was *Huh, how about that, there's another Antonio Reyes here and he's competing tonight.*

She wished Tony would hurry up and come back already so they could laugh about that together.

And then she saw the screen that showed the competitor in the chute ready to come out.

Tony's hat. Tony's shoulders. Tony's everything.

The resolution on the screen wasn't great, and he'd put on a different shirt since she'd last seen him, but she'd know him anywhere.

Ever since she'd learned the truth about spring break, she'd played through the hotel pool incident a hundred times over in her mind. She saw his fool self, twenty years old and convinced he was bulletproof, stoked on adrenaline, hungry for excitement and attention. Saw him diving—*diving*—off the balcony. Saw his open-eyed face hit the water with enough force to tear loose a membrane from the back of his eye.

And that wasn't even the worst of it. Sometimes she saw what *might* have happened—saw him off-balance, with his beer-dulled senses, saw him hitting the masonry edge of the pool instead of the water. Breaking his neck or cracking his skull.

And now…

Now he was on the back of an angry animal that weighed just under a ton. Which was bad enough for an able-bodied man with perfect vision, let alone one who was half-blind.

She heard herself whisper, "Wait, no."

And then the chute opened and there wasn't time to think anymore.

Dust Devil started fighting before even leaving the chute. One instant Tony was being driven toward the rails as the bull's hooves hit the ground in a juddering impact. Then the bull bucked, flinging Tony up and out, his raised left hand like the end of a whip. All his vertebrae, all the separate bones and muscles and ligaments in his body, were being alternately stretched and compacted at intervals of fractions of seconds.

That was all bad enough, but it was nothing compared with what the bull could do to Tony once he got him off his back, with his skull-crushing, rib-shattering hooves and blunt-tipped, cudgel-like horns.

It was starting now. The bull was shaking him loose. Tony lost his seat. Except for the hand gripping the rope, he was completely airborne now.

The bull bucked again. Tony lost his hold, flew through the air and slammed to the ground in a cloud of dust.

And still the bull bucked, not the least bit

appeased at having dislodged the irritating presence on his back. He was just plain mad.

And suddenly Tony was on his feet, moving fast toward the gate, not even limping. He used to spring up exactly that way after getting knocked down in football, bouncing like a rubber ball, like the ground wasn't good enough for him. Every cocky line of his posture said, plainer than words could have done, *Yeah, you knocked me down, but you didn't* keep *me down.*

He was gone, through the gate, safe. The bull was led away.

It was all over.

Dalia half fell forward, elbows on knees, face in hands. Waves of sickness pulsed through her in time to the rush of blood loud in her ears. The nausea passed, leaving her weak in the limbs.

Then the weakness passed, too, and for the first time she was able to think.

How did this even happen? Did Tony suddenly decide he wanted to ride a bull that night? No, that wasn't possible. He had to plan in advance to some degree, because he had to bring his own gear—rope, chaps, vest, spurs, gloves. Even a Western shirt to change into. He'd brought those things with him, and kept them—where? In the toolbox of his truck, maybe? Stowed away someplace, *hidden* from her.

*His little surprise.*

And before that, he had to fill out a Professional Bull Riders membership form and pay the fee.

Just how many days in advance had he started plotting this whole thing out?

And he didn't *tell* her?

No, of course he didn't tell her. Because if he had, she'd have told him it was a terrible idea. She'd have seen the crazy stunt as proof that he hadn't grown up and never would.

Which it was.

The truth had been there all along. All this afternoon and evening, all those hours when she'd been basking in his company, enjoying their banter, daring to imagine a *life* together, a *future*—he'd known he was going to do this foolish thing. All of yesterday, too, when she'd been looking forward to today, planning what she would wear, giddy with anticipation. Everything she thought the day meant—it had all been an illusion. A lie.

This whole day—what she'd allowed herself to think of as their first back-together date—had been doomed from the start.

Just like their relationship.

TONY ZIPPED HIS riggin bag shut and shouldered the strap. No need to wait around. No prize for him tonight; he hadn't quite made eight seconds.

He was elated anyway, full of that rush that came only with exertion, competition, risk. That feeling of being fully alive, with all his senses turned to maximum. It had been so long since he'd done anything that really tested him physically. Now he'd done it, and he was okay. Better than okay. A little sore, but all in one piece. Not beaten, not hurt. Just the good kind of sore that meant he'd done something demanding and come through it just fine.

All he wanted now was to get back to Dalia. That was the only thing he needed to make the feeling perfect.

And there she was, heading his way.

He stopped in his tracks a moment and

just watched her. Those long legs striding toward him in those boot-cut jeans. That strappy tank with the lace down the sides. That beautiful face with its unsmiling intensity.

"Are you out of your mind?" she asked.

Tony knew a rhetorical question when he heard one.

"Just crazy about you, baby."

He put his arm around her and pulled her to him. "Oh, man, that was such a rush. Did you see how the bull almost rammed my face against that pipe before we even made it out the chute? Wouldn't that be something, if I'd wiped out right then and there?"

"Yes, Tony, I saw it. I was right there in the stands and I saw the whole thing. And yes, it would have been *something* if you broke every bone in your face."

She wasn't hugging him back.

"Are you mad?" he asked.

"Brilliant deduction, Tony. Yes. I'm mad."

"Why?"

"Why? *Why?* Because you just risked your life for no good reason."

His arm fell back to his side.

When she spoke again, her voice was

low and shaking. “Do you know how many times over the past few days I’ve imagined the scene at the hotel pool? And every time it sickens me—not just because of what happened, but because of what could have happened. I have thanked God daily for sparing your life and protecting you from getting hurt worse than you did. Bad as it was, it could have been so much worse. And now here you are, years later, when you ought to know better, doing the exact same thing.”

“It is not the exact same thing!”

“How is it different?”

“Well, for one thing, I’m sober. For another thing, there wasn’t any point to balcony diving other than showing off.”

“Oh, and there *is* a point to bull riding?”

He raised his hands high.

“It’s rodeo! It’s what people like us, cattle-raising people, have been doing for hundreds of years to celebrate our way of life.”

“It isn’t *your* way of life. You’re a town boy and you always were. Visiting your grandparents’ ranch on weekends does not make you a cowboy. And riding a bull is not an actual useful skill. Nobody rides a bull as part of legitimate ranch work.”

"Maybe not, but they do have to show grit and determination and physical courage. Anyway, if it's so stupid, why is it okay for other people to do it? Why did we come here to sit with hundreds of other spectators if it's all such a waste of time?"

"It's different for the other competitors. They're not blind in one eye."

"Bull. It's the same risk for everyone. It's all muscle memory. I don't have to see—I just have to feel, get my rhythm right, hold on."

"Oh, yeah? And what if you'd detached the other retina? What if you'd lost what's left of your vision?"

He made a scoffing sound. "That would be such a freak occurrence that it's not even worth considering."

"It's not all that unlikely for someone who behaves as idiotically as you do."

*Boom.*

Tony stood there a solid second, unable to reply, like the breath had been knocked clean out of him. When he did speak, his voice sounded strange in his own ears, like it was coming from a long way off.

"And there it is. It's almost a relief to hear

you say it, after waiting all this time for the shoe to drop. Tony is an idiot. Tony is an idiot, everyone!"

"Stop trying to make me the bad guy. You're the one risking your life, trying to prove your manhood with an infantile stunt. You could have been killed, Tony."

"Yeah, well, guess what? People get hurt. People get killed. People with all sorts of jobs who aren't doing any kind of stunt. Ranching is one of the riskiest jobs in the nation, did you know that? Death by livestock, death by equipment—"

He stopped.

"Death by sunstroke. Like my father. That's what you were going to say, isn't it, Tony?"

"I didn't say it."

"Yeah, you're just a paragon of self-control."

"Right, well, you're the expert on that, aren't you?"

"On what?"

"Control. The truth is, you're a control freak, Dalia, and you always were. Even today, our first date after getting back together, you couldn't just enjoy being with me. No, you had to take me to school. Lecture me about my *monocular vision*—like I don't know what it's like to have just one working eye, after living that way for six years. Oh, no. I don't know anything, but one night of research and suddenly you're the expert. You were always the expert, about everything. You never let me forget I wasn't good enough or smart enough for you—not then, and not now. You talk about me being hurt, but you hurt me like nothing and no one else ever could. You make me feel small."

For a second, she was actually at a loss for words. She just stood there staring at him, wide-eyed.

Then she swallowed hard and drew herself up.

"Well, then I'll get out of your way so you can feel big again."

She turned and walked away.

DALIA'S HEART WAS POUNDING, her legs were shaking, and she felt sick to her stomach. Their beautiful day was ruined. Everything was ruined.

"Dalia, wait."

She stopped. Was he actually going to apologize? What could he possibly have to say to her now, after everything he'd already said?

But all he said was "Let me take you home." Calmly. Quietly.

She shut her eyes and suppressed a groan. She'd forgotten they'd come in his truck.

She turned around. "I'm not accepting a ride from a driver with limited peripheral vision and no depth perception."

It was a cheap shot, and she knew it, and also pretty silly since he'd driven her there in the first place, but Tony didn't even flinch. He didn't look angry anymore, just tired.

"What're you gonna do, then? Walk? Hitchhike?"

"Oh, I see. I don't get to risk *my* personal safety. Only you get to do that."

"Come on, Dalia. Don't be like that."

Don't *be* like that? Who did he think he was, acting like he was the adult in this situation?

"Just let me take you home, okay?" he said. "You don't have to talk to me or look at me. I just want you to be safe."

"I'll take an Uber."

Tony frowned, looking doubtful. "Do we have Uber in Limestone Springs?"

"Yes, Tony. We have Uber in Limestone Springs."

She heard the irritation and impatience in her own voice. Why was she being so nasty?

Tony backed off like she'd hit him. "Okay, okay. I just never heard of anyone using it around here. But if you're sure…"

"I'm sure. Now would you please just go?"

Still he held his ground. "I'd rather wait with you 'til it comes."

"And I'd rather not have to look at you anymore tonight."

He stood there a moment longer, sober-faced. Red dust from the arena still clung to his jeans in patches. As angry as she was, part of her wanted to go over and brush it off and tell him… Tell him what? That she was sorry? Why should she be sorry? He was the one in the wrong.

"Okay," he said.

He shifted his riggin bag on his shoulder, turned and walked away.

Once he was out of sight, she took out her phone, opened the ridesharing app and hoped fervently that they really did have Uber in Limestone Springs.

## *CHAPTER NINETEEN*

"WAIT A MINUTE, back up," Lauren said from Dalia's laptop screen. "Didn't you say Tony *drove* you to the fair? So how did you get back home? Did he drive you home after your big fight? Was it superawkward?"

Dalia sighed, a sigh that felt like it came from all the way down in her toes. "Yes. I mean no. I mean, yes, he did drive me to the fair, but no, he didn't drive me home."

She dropped her head into her hands. "Why did I let him drive me?" she said, almost wailing. "What was *wrong* with me? I already had my doubts about him driving at all with his vision, and I'd told him so. After all that, why would I still let him come for me and drive me there like some sort of *princess*, and put myself in the position of getting stranded?"

Lauren's jaw dropped. "Stranded? Seriously? He just *left* you there?"

"What? No. He wanted to take me home. I'd actually forgotten we came together. I was all set to storm off when he called me back and said he'd take me home. But I said no, I'd just take an Uber. So no, I wasn't stranded. But I could have been. It's the principle of the thing."

"Okay," said Lauren, in a way that meant she knew Dalia was leaving out a lot.

Dalia didn't want to repeat that part of the conversation because she suspected she hadn't exactly come off well in it. The things she'd said sounded childish and mean in her memory. Tony was the one who'd been calm and dignified and practical, putting her safety above his own feelings.

"It was one of those chatty Uber drivers, too," Dalia said. "Turned out to be a distant cousin through my mother *and* my father, if you can believe that. Showed me all these pics of his wife and little children. He seemed like a nice enough guy, but I did *not* feel like talking just then. Uber really ought to make the silent ride option available across the board and not just for premium users."

"Yeah," said Lauren. "So elitist of them."

Silence.

Then Dalia said, "You might as well go ahead and say it."

"Go ahead and say what?"

"You know what. You think I'm wrong, don't you? If you'd been in my place you wouldn't have been the least bit bothered by the bull-riding thing. You'd have thought it was sexy."

Lauren shrugged. "Wasn't it?"

"No! It was terrifying."

"What about that other time you saw him ride a bull, when he was eighteen?"

Another pause. Then, "Okay, yes. That time was amazing. But this? This was just plain irresponsible. Tony's already done permanent damage to himself with another crazy stunt. How could he take a risk like that again?"

"Well, the guy's already a firefighter."

"Yes, he is. And that's another risk he shouldn't be taking."

"It sounds like he's one of those personalities that have a high excitement quotient. Some of us are just that way. We need a lot of risk and physical challenge in our lives to feel alive."

"I know that. But he's physically impaired now. He can't go around living on the edge like an adrenaline junkie anymore."

"Whoa, hold on. Don't you think you're being kind of ableist here?"

"I'm being realistic. He has to understand that there are certain things he can't do anymore."

"But is this one of them? Is there a vision test for bull riding?"

Dalia opened her mouth and shut it again. Finally she said, "If there's not, there should be. Bull riding is dangerous enough for guys with perfect vision."

Lauren leaned forward on her elbows. "Okay, but here's the thing… Other rodeo guys are putting themselves at risk, too, right? And so are other firefighters. I mean, there could be a guy right beside him fighting a fire who also has some preexisting condition that puts him in greater jeopardy. Or there could be a perfectly healthy guy beside him who gets hurt, or killed, in spite of not having any kind of impairment at all."

"That's completely irrelevant."

"Why?"

"Because those other guys aren't Tony!"

Lauren sat back and smiled.

"Exactly. That's what the problem is. You're afraid."

"No, I'm not."

"Yes, you are. You've always been afraid of losing Tony—to other girls, or a wild partying lifestyle, or some sort of accident. That's why you get so angry with him, because anger is the bodyguard of fear."

Dalia opened her mouth and shut it again.

"Okay, you may have a point. In retrospect, I admit I could have played the whole bull-riding thing differently. But I didn't. Maybe Tony and I just bring out the worst in each other."

"Or maybe you're just not used to reacting on a purely emotional level. From what I've seen, other guys don't bring out much of anything in you, good or bad. You just don't care with them like you do with Tony."

Dang it. How was it possible for a ditzy idealist like Lauren to be so downright wise when it came to Dalia?

"I wish you were here," Dalia said.

"I'll come if you want me to."

"No, I couldn't ask you to leave Aspen in October to come to central Texas."

"I do want to come stay in Texas at some point, though. It's weird that I've never actually been to La Escarpa, when you think about how much I travel and how you came home with me so many times when we were in school."

"It isn't weird at all. I went to school where I did for a reason—I wanted to get away from this town, where half the people are related to me and everyone knows my business. I wanted to make it on my own, in a city where I knew no one and no one knew me or my family, using skills that have nothing to do with ranching. I'm glad I did it. But now that I have, and now that I've come home again...I don't feel the same about it anymore. All the Tony drama aside, I've *liked* being home. I belong here in a way that I don't anywhere else. And I've come to realize that no one ever does anything truly alone. Everyone has a family, a background, a history, a people. Mine are here. And I was starting to think I could have a future here, too."

"Whoa, seriously? That's huge. Have you told your mom?"

"No. All this was before things blew up with Tony."

"Well, what if Tony wasn't in the picture at all? Would you want to be there then?"

"I don't know. He *is* in the picture, and I can't take him out. I don't know what to do."

"You can always come to Aspen. Who knows, you might fall in love with the van life."

Dalia chuckled. "Oh, I doubt that. But thanks for the offer."

She looked out her front window. The curve of driveway that Tony's truck had come down the night before disappeared in a bend at a clump of oaks. But there was more history here than hers with Tony. Trucks had come and gone down that same driveway since before she was born, picking up cattle and taking them to market. Before that, cowboys on horseback had driven herds north to the Chisholm Trail. Somewhere out there in the pastures, a herd of curly-coated Angora goats used to browse, and get rounded up for shearing twice a year.

She thought of Alejandro Ramirez, who went away to fight for his country and never came back, and Romelia, who held on without him and kept the ranch alive.

"I've got to go," she told Lauren. "I need to talk to my mom."

DALIA'S MOM WAS on the sofa with her foot up, knitting something pale green and fuzzy. She gave an eager smile when Dalia came into the living room, and Dalia felt a pang of conscience. They hadn't talked much since last night, when Dalia had come inside after the Uber driver dropped her off and found her mom waiting up, with the same knitting project in her lap.

She'd taken one look at Dalia's face and said, "Oh, sweetie. What happened?"

And Dalia had said, "I can't right now, Mom. I'm sorry, I just can't."

Then she'd gone straight to her room, where she'd stayed almost the entire day, concentrating on work, avoiding both her mom and the construction crew. Tony hadn't sought her out, and now he and Alex and their guys were gone, and it was safe to come out.

Dalia was grateful to her mom for giving her the space she needed. She knew it must be driving her crazy, not knowing. She and Eliana always talked over all of Eliana's romantic relationships in minute detail—which, considering how many relationships Eliana had been in over the years, had to add up to thousands of conversation hours.

"Are you hungry?" her mom asked. "I thawed that sausage gumbo Teresa brought and started some brown rice in the rice cooker. It should be ready in half an hour."

"That sounds perfect. Thanks for doing that. I'm sorry. I'm supposed to be helping you. I should have seen to dinner instead of leaving it to you."

"Oh, that's all right. I got—one of the guys to do it before they left for the day."

"Good."

Dalia took a seat on the ottoman by the sofa and held out the bundle from Ray and Syndra. "I got you something last night."

Dalia's mom pounced on the Ziploc bag and opened it. "Ooh, what is this?"

"Angora roving—no, wait. Angora is the name of the goat, but the fiber is called mohair. So mohair roving, and yarn made with mohair fibers around a silk core. I thought you might like it."

Her mom rubbed the fibers expertly between her fingers. "I love it! I've never worked with mohair before, but I've always wanted to. It's supposed to have a lovely halo—that's, like, the aura of the yarn around the core. I'll have to find some project with open stitch work to show it off. Thank you, sweetie. Where'd it come from?"

"From this couple I met at the fair. It was so cool, Mom. I wish you could have been there. This man who raises the Angora goats used to work for Grandpa at La Escarpa years ago. He remembered Dad when he was a little boy."

"Did he? How wonderful! What did he say about your dad?"

"That he was an impeccable little cowboy and a hard worker. He said Dad used to have a pair of Lucchese boots when he was a boy?"

"Oh, yes, those boots! Martin was so proud of them. They must have been pretty pricey—a real extravagance for a growing boy. But the Ramirezes were ranching royalty, and nothing was too good for Martin. Most of the country kids I went to school with were not well off. They were always talking about how they wished they lived in town where they could ride their bikes to their friends' houses and go to the movie theater whenever they wanted. But not Martin. He was the lucky one, and he knew it. There was always something special about him, even when we were kids—not just the land and the boots and the family name, but Martin himself. I thought he was terribly good-looking, of course, but he was so quiet I didn't really know him—and he was a year older than me. As far as I could tell, he never even looked at me until I went out with Carlos."

They'd already strayed pretty far off topic from what Dalia had meant to talk about, but now that she had an opening, she decided to probe a little. "Yeah, what was *that* like? How did it even happen?"

"Well, Carlos was very good-looking, too. His boys look a lot like him, especially—well. But he was wild, you know. He invited me to a pasture party out at the Mastersons'."

"You went to a pasture party? With beer and everything?"

"Oh, honey, there was a lot more than beer, at least at this one. It was not a good scene. A far cry from the parties your brother used to have in the low acreage."

Dalia felt like the floor had just dropped away. "You knew about those?"

"Of course I did. I wasn't thrilled, but I figured it was better than him driving all over the county."

"Well, what did Poppy and Nana say about you going to the Mastersons'?"

"Nothing, because I didn't tell them. They never would have let me go out with Carlos Reyes. So I said I was going out with my friend Gretchen—you remember her, she used to have a booth at the Persimmon Festival. Sold those little persimmon jack-o'-lantern-looking things."

"You *lied* to Nana and Poppy?"

"Well, not exactly. Gretchen and I did go to the party together. I'd just arranged to meet Carlos there. I told Nana and Poppy I was going to spend the night at Gretchen's house after."

"Whoa! Whoa!"

"I remember I wore my fringed miniskirt, a cowl-necked sweater and shiny cuffed ankle boots with gold buckles and stacked heels."

"What were you thinking?"

"I was thinking Carlos was really hot!"

Dalia covered her ears. "Mom! Stop!"

"Calm down. The story ends happily. Well, so we got there. And Carlos looked amazing. He was a sharp dresser by late-seventies standards. But he'd already been drinking for a while, and doing some of the harder stuff, and he was a little worse for wear. Long story short, I realized I'd made a huge mistake. But by then, Gretchen had already taken off with a senior boy from Schraeder Lake, leaving me to fend for myself, with no way to get home except with a compromised driver—unless I walked to the nearest farmhouse to call my parents, which would have meant admitting I'd been doing something underhanded."

"What did you do?"

"Only thing I could do. I hoofed it."

"To the nearest farmhouse to make that phone call, I hope?"

"No, to Gretchen's house. It was only about five miles—all country roads, no highways."

"How did your shiny ankle boots with the stacked heels hold up?"

"Not great. I could feel the blisters forming on my toes. But I didn't have a lot of options, so I sucked it up and kept going. And just when I had myself convinced that things were going to be okay after all, a truck passed me and then pulled over. It was a pretty lonely road and I didn't have so much as a good-sized rock to defend myself with. But then the driver got out, and it was Martin Ramirez with his gorgeous boots with the Cuban heels and his felt hat and his perfect crisp shirt. And he said, 'Renée Casillas. What are you doing walking this road at this time of night?' Well, I didn't even know he knew my name. I was awestruck, I guess. With anyone else I would have tried to bluff my way through, but there was always something about Martin that made you stand up straight and tell the truth. So I did. And he didn't say anything about what an idiot I was to agree to meet up with Carlos at the party in the first place. He just said, 'Get in. I'll take you home.'"

"Oh, my gosh. What did you say?"

"I said, 'No, thank you. I've already been too quick to get into vehicles and situations with the wrong people tonight.' And he said,

'Yes, you have. But I'm the right people.' But I just shook my head. So he said, 'All right, walk if you want. I'll follow you and make sure you get there safe.'"

"Did he?"

"For about a quarter mile. That's as long as I lasted before I gave in and got into his truck. It was so *clean*. I'd never seen such a clean truck. I sat there, and Martin drove, and we didn't say another word to each other until he pulled up at the curb of my house. I didn't know if he just thought I was silly, or resented me for inconveniencing him, or maybe was just thinking about ranch chores he was going to do in the morning. But then he turned to me and said, 'Don't go out with that guy again. Go out with me instead.'"

Dalia could just hear him saying it, in that matter-of-fact but authoritative way of his. "And what did you say?"

"I said, 'Okay, but you'd better come in and meet my parents.' He looked mildly surprised, which for Martin was a huge emotional display. But he did it. He came inside, met my parents and actually made pleasant small talk with them. It was the most I'd ever seen him speak at one time. It was a revelation. I think I fell in love with him that night, listening to him talk about truck engines with my dad."

"What'd they say about you being home early?"

"Oh, they didn't mind. I just said Gretchen had taken off and left me stranded, which was true as far as it went. They never liked Gretchen, anyway. So then I had Martin's parents to meet, which I did the next day at church. He exerted himself again, and found me after the service and introduced me. And there was no looking back."

"I never heard any of this. I thought you two *met* at church."

"Well, we did. We just never got acquainted until the night of the party."

"But why am I just now hearing this story for the very first time?"

"I thought it best to stick with the official version while you kids were growing up. Your dad was always touchy where Carlos was concerned. They'd had other dealings, and he could never hear Carlos's name without making that face where his eyes narrowed and his lips got all thin."

"Yeah, I know that face," Dalia said. She

didn't blame her mother for wanting to avoid provoking it—or her father for holding a grudge against Carlos and mistrusting his son the way he did. Dalia's mom wasn't a suspicious person by nature, and for her to have realized she needed to get away from Carlos that night, his behavior must have been pretty bad. She suspected her mother was glossing over a lot in her retelling.

Beyond that, she felt a grim pride in Tony, for wanting to get her home safe last night. Tony never would have treated her the way his father treated her mother.

"Well, you got Dad out of the deal, anyway," she said.

"Yes, I did. Marrying him was like marrying a prince. We were so happy in our little house in town, and then on the ranch once your grandparents retired. Your dad just stepped right into being a full-time rancher—he'd been preparing for it all his life—but I had so much to learn! Your grandmother helped me a lot. And you kids were so small and loving every minute of it, running all over the property from dawn 'til dusk. Every day was an adventure."

"Maybe it's time you started a new adventure," Dalia said.

Her mom's eyes lost that far-off look and focused on Dalia. "What do you mean?"

"Well, this might seem kind of random, but what if you got some Angora goats and built up a herd? That couple I met, Ray and Syndra, they could help. You'd love them, Mom. You're already set up well out here for goats. You'd have to add some fencing and a pen and some new outbuildings, but there's plenty of space for all that, and the goats wouldn't compete with the cattle for food since they don't eat the same things. You could set up a rotation system with the pastures to keep parasites in check. These goats are so beautiful, Mom. Smaller than Boers, and so fluffy, and with such sweet dispositions. I know you'd love being around them, and having shearers out twice a year, and learning about the fiber and how to mill it and where to market it. You're so crazy about fiber arts already, and so knowledgeable about yarns. You could bring a real passion to the work."

Her mom smiled. "Oh, honey. That's sweet of you. But I think I'm done with agricultural adventures. The truth is, I'm tired of ranching. Tired of living out in the middle of nowhere by myself. It was different when your father was alive and when you kids were still at home. It really was an adventure then. But now…now it's just work. And I'm lonely."

It wasn't much of a revelation. It was more or less what Dalia had been suspecting for a while. Her sociable, fun-loving mother—of course she was lonely. She'd been cheerful enough since Dalia had been home, but that was because she was enjoying having company for a change. Not that Dalia was the best company, but she was better than nothing, and the builders had been around most days, as well, bringing noise and activity and plenty of things to think about and decisions to make.

"What if you weren't alone?" Dalia asked. "What if…what if I moved home?"

Her mom reached over and squeezed her hand. "It's good of you to offer. But I couldn't let you give up your life in the city like that. And honestly, at this point I'd prefer to live in town. I've been holding off for years now, because I'd have to rent out the property, and you know how that goes. Renters never take care of land the way owners do. I know, it's not like I've been doing such a great job maintaining the fencing and pastures myself, but I've done okay, and I haven't overgrazed. Once I'm gone, I shudder to think what'll become of the place. But I think this business with my foot has decided the matter. I can't go on doing this."

"But what about your beautiful new kitchen and reconfigured dining room? And that fancy recessed entry to the master bedroom?"

"All the better to rent the place out. The rebuild had to be done one way or another—I couldn't rent out a house with no kitchen and a big hole in the side, could I? I've enjoyed doing the rebuild, but it's also given me some ideas for how to update the little house in town for me to move into."

"That's where you want to live?"

"Oh, yes. I know it's not very big—it just about burst at the seams once you and Marcos came along—but it's exactly the right size for me. The lot is small, but I like that. Less lawn for me to take care of. It's got that big post oak tree in the backyard, and there's room to keep a few chickens. I'd be able to walk to church once my foot is all healed."

"It sounds like you've really thought this through."

"I have. I'm sorry about the ranch, but I do think it's time to let go. Maybe I should just sell the place."

"Sell La Escarpa? Mom, no!"

"I don't like the idea, but I've got to be practical. You have a life in the city. We all know your brother doesn't want to be a rancher, and your sister, well…"

Dalia couldn't argue with that. But the thought of someone else, some other family running La Escarpa, living in the house where only Ramirezes had ever lived—or maybe not even a family but some giant agribusiness taking over, or the place getting sold to developers down the line—it made her sick.

But what was the alternative? Guilt her mother into staying when she didn't want to? Or take over the whole thing herself? It would be one thing to run the ranch with her mom, even if Dalia managed the bulk of the work. But doing it solo… Was she really up to that? She could always hire out the heavy stuff, of course, but that added up fast, money-wise. Could she balance the money and make it all work?

The really maddening part was, if she'd only played things differently last night with Tony, this whole situation might be taking a completely different turn. She might be texting him right now, saying, Can you come over? There's something going on that you need to hear about.

And the long and short of it was, they'd have gotten married and run La Escarpa together.

It wasn't just possible. It was how things were supposed to be. Tony *belonged* to her, the same way the land did. She could see that now. But she'd ruined everything. She'd been wrong, dead wrong. She'd treated Tony like a child because she was afraid of losing him—and ended up pushing him away and losing him all the same.

Could she fix her mistake? Or was it too late?

# *CHAPTER TWENTY*

DALIA WALKED INTO Lalo's Kitchen, straight through to the counter in back, not too slow and not too fast, like she had a perfectly legitimate reason for being there, which she did.

"Order for Dalia," she said to the kid at the counter.

He looked familiar—not like he was in her graduating class, but like she ought to know who he was. Late teens or early twenties, green eyes, nice smile. Might be the Mahan boy, the son of her fifth-grade teacher.

The kid went off to get the food, and Dalia took a seat at the counter. Stage One, accomplished.

It was ridiculous that she was here looking for Tony when he worked every day at her house. But he'd been different these past few days—cold, grim and terribly efficient. No more joking around with his guys, no more singing along with his carefully crafted high-energy playlists coming out of his portable Bluetooth speaker. Everyone worked in silence. The crew was on edge, but the work was coming on fast. They had all the windows and doors installed and were about to start on the metal roof.

All of which was fine from a work standpoint…but inconvenient for Dalia now that she wanted to talk to Tony. There was a hard wall of reserve around him that she'd never encountered before, and she couldn't get past it. In short, she'd lost her nerve. She'd also lost one whole day in Austin, driving her mother to a follow-up with the orthopedic surgeon, plus a lot of hours handling urgent business for her clients.

She didn't want to text him or call him. She knew she came off cold in text, and anyway, she wanted to feel him out, get a sense of where he was emotionally. She had to talk to him in person—not at her mother's house or his apartment, but in a neutral social setting. And thanks to Alex, she knew exactly where Tony would be on a Thursday night.

Which was how she'd come to be here, stalking her ex.

She'd told her mom she was craving some of those fried cheese curds from Lalo's, which she'd first tasted when one of her mom's church friends had brought some over as part of their meal contribution. And if her mom suspected she had an ulterior motive, she hadn't let on.

She took a look around, while keeping her gaze away from the pass-through in the wall that led to Tito's Bar next door. This was her first time inside Lalo's Kitchen. The space used to be a lawyer's office, and she'd never been inside that, either, but whenever she'd walked by it, what little she could see through the windows looked dingy and depressing. Now the place was open and airy, with gorgeous hardwood floors and little tables, mostly four-tops, nicely spaced for privacy. The counter looked like a thick, wavy-edged plank taken from the center of an old mesquite, covered with a glassy-smooth clear finish.

Tony and Alex had done the renovation. Alex had mentioned it that day she'd seen him in town. They'd done a beautiful job.

What if Tony wasn't even there tonight? What if she'd come all this way, and was suffering all this turmoil, for nothing?

*Quit being a coward.*

Time for Stage Two: locate Tony. She took a deep breath, turned around and looked into Tito's Bar.

Long narrow bar tables and benches, all covered in worn reddish-orange paint, ran the length of the room. People sat in groups, some with drinks and food, some with just drinks.

And there was Tony, with his arm curled around a little notebook and his head bent low. She couldn't see his face, but she'd have known that thick black hair, those shoulders, those long outstretched legs anywhere. He used to look exactly like that in English class, writing notes to her.

A mic'd voice boomed out. "Okay, quizzers. As of the end of Round Two, our team scores are as follows. The Trivia Assassins, ten points. The Home Brew Hop Heads, fifteen points. The Royal Quizzers, ten points. The Dagobah System, five points. The Three Amigos, ten points. And now it's time for Round Three, Technology. Question sixteen—what does HTTPS stand for?"

The Royal Quizzers had to be Tony and Alex. *Reyes* meant *royal.* If things had gone differently a few nights earlier, Dalia might be over there with them right now, eating cheese curds and drinking a craft soda, wresting the notebook away from Tony and writing Hypertext Transfer Protocol Secure in it, instead of Tony and Alex looking blankly at each other as they were doing now. It might actually be fun. The place wasn't like a *bar* bar, and the people in it looked kind of nice.

She swallowed hard and turned away again.

*Keep it together. Just hold tight, wait for a break in the quizzing...and go over to him.*

Where was what's-his-name with her order, anyway? How long did it take to walk a bag of fried cheese curds from the kitchen to the counter?

To steady herself, she focused on the exposed brick wall opposite the pass-through. The words *Flemish bond* popped into her head, and suddenly she remembered being somewhere with her dad a long time ago, some city—San Antonio? Austin?—where he'd pointed out this same exact bricking pattern on an old downtown building. Stretchers and headers—long and short bricks—alternating both horizontally and vertically. It helped, concentrating on the pattern. The orderliness was soothing. She was pretty sure her dad had said there was some reason for the pattern beyond aesthetics, like it made the wall stronger. How had he even known all that about bricking patterns? Did Tony know it, too? He was a builder.

The bricks were all different shades of brown, like horse coats—dun, chestnut, sorrel, buckskin, bay. The rough rectangles looked worn but solid, like they'd been around a long time and would be for a long time to come.

In the dining room at La Escarpa, Tony and Alex and their crew had removed the plaster from what used to be an exterior wall—before the 1910 kitchen addition—taken it right down to the old limestone and left it exposed. Dalia had been doubtful of the idea, but once she saw it, she knew Tony was right. All his work on the house was exactly right. He'd taken it back to its roots in some ways, modernized it in others, blending everything into a harmonious whole. No one could have done as good a job with the rebuild as Tony.

A man took the bar stool next to her, blocking her view of the wall. He already had a beer in his hand, and he held it up like he was saluting her with it.

"Smile!" he said. "It can't be that bad."

He had big round blue eyes and a weak mouth curling up in a stupid grin. It *was* a stupid grin; there was no other way to describe it. When people said *Wipe that stupid grin off your face*, this was *exactly* the grin they meant.

"What did you say?" she asked.

He didn't hear the warning in her voice.

"I said, smile! Turn that frown upside down. You'd be a pretty girl if you'd smile, but if you're not careful—" he gave her a wink "—your face might freeze that way. Anyway, it takes more muscles to frown than it does to smile."

"Oh? Says who?"

The guy blinked a few times. Most women probably responded to all that tripe with a nervous laugh because they were taken off guard and didn't know what to say or do. Well, she was about to take this guy down on their behalf.

"Everyone," he said. "Everyone knows it."

"Everyone," she repeated.

"Yeah. Everyone. Don't tell me you've never heard it before."

"Oh, I've heard it. I've just never been given any convincing empirical data. Why is it better to exercise fewer facial muscles? What's wrong with exercising your face, anyway? You'd think that would be a good thing. What are the names of the muscles used in smiling and the muscles used in frowning? Who conducted the study that showed this?"

The guy made an aw-shucks kind of face. "I don't know why you have to be like that about it, darlin'. All I said was smile. I'm just trying to help make your life a little more pleasant. Everyone knows life is better when you smile."

"Do they?"

The aw-shucks face dissolved. "Sheesh. You really do need to lighten up."

"Really? Well, who am I? Do you know

my name? You don't? Then how do you know what I need? The truth is, you don't know me at all. You don't know what kind of day or week I've had. You don't know if my dog just died or I lost my job or my house burned down or I got a terminal diagnosis. It might be taking everything I've got just to function at all with any kind of look on my face. But, no, you're right. It's my facial expression that's the *real* problem here. All I have to do is change the position of my lips, and everything will be just dandy."

She bared her teeth at him in an aggressively exaggerated smile.

He drew back. "Okay, okay! You don't have to bite my head off."

He picked up his beer and walked away.

Dalia did feel a little guilty then. But why should *she* feel bad? He was the one who started the whole thing. She'd been sitting there minding her own business, trying to keep from falling apart, and *he'd* intruded on *her.* Was she supposed to take it, just because he came from a different generation that thought it was perfectly acceptable for men to give random flippant orders to women who were complete strangers to them?

"Here you go, ma'am."

The Mahan kid was back, with a brown paper bag folded over at the top. He set it on the counter, saw Dalia's face and took a step back.

"Um...sorry about the wait," he said.

She felt horrible then, for turning her full death glare on the kid. He didn't deserve that; he hadn't done anything wrong at all. Maybe she should apologize. But what could she say? *Sorry, I didn't mean to glare at you. I'm just tense because I'm about to try to make up with my ex-boyfriend and some stranger just told me to smile.*

Silently, she put her card in the cube. She left the kid a big tip.

Then she waited for the quizmaster to announce a break so she could make her next move.

Stage Three: go talk to Tony.

TONY PICKED UP his beer stein but set it down again before he could raise it to his lips. Suddenly it didn't seem worth the effort.

Nothing did, really.

He was all right as long as he was working, as long as he didn't allow himself any downtime. But he had to knock off at some point, and once he did, he crashed hard.

He hadn't wanted to come tonight, but he'd wanted even less to stay home alone. Maybe the social noise of Trivia Thursday would drown out the constant replay of all the things Dalia had said to him that awful night after the rodeo. So he got himself cleaned up, put on a smile, went to Tito's, ordered a beer and did his best to focus on some trivia.

But it all seemed so…trivial. His mind kept wandering, and Alex had to repeat the questions for him two or three times before he could even get them into his head.

What was his problem? There was something weary and worn down and discouraged inside him that hadn't been there before. It didn't used to be this hard to pretend. Maybe he was just getting old.

And then he looked up from randomly scribbling in the trivia notebook to see Dalia, actually there in the flesh at the counter of Lalo's Kitchen, not twelve feet away from him.

He felt like something had grabbed him by the throat and stolen the breath right out of his lungs. Bad enough he had to cope with seeing her day after day at her mother's house while trying to get his work done. But here? Here, at least, he ought to be safe from Dalia sightings. Dalia at a bar? No way.

Though technically she was in a restaurant and not a bar. Still, the businesses shared a pass-through, and customers freely moved from one to the other, ordering from both of them, paying at whichever cash register.

What weird fluke had brought his twice-ex-girlfriend to the one place in town where he happened to be? It wasn't fair. This was *his* turf. Maybe she was picking up a food order. Maybe her mom sent her.

He sat there, frozen and miserable, waiting for her to look around like a normal person would and see him sitting there four yards off in the bar. But she didn't do that. She just…stared at the wall.

Was she shunning him? She had to be. The wall wasn't *that* interesting—even an exposed Flemish bond brick wall like that one.

Then R. J. Nash sat down on the other side of her, blocking her view, smiling in that dumb way of his. He even saluted her with his beer. Tony rolled his eyes. R.J. was always trying to chat up the ladies. It would be sad if he wasn't so obnoxious. Well, this should be interesting.

R.J. made some opening remark, and Dalia said something back. Tony couldn't hear, but he saw them go back and forth for a bit. It didn't take long before R.J.'s smile sort of froze.

Then Dalia *really* lit into R.J. She didn't raise her voice or anything, but Tony could tell by the set of her back that things were getting pretty intense. R.J.'s smile disappeared. He said one last thing to Dalia—something snide, from the looks of him—and got up and walked away. Tony had never seen that happen before.

He felt a rush of pride. *You tell him, Dalia.*

Then Luke Mahan came back from the kitchen. He handed her a bag, then sort of stepped back, looking confused and a little hurt. Did Dalia snap at *Luke*? That was not okay. Luke was a nice kid.

Oh, why was he even watching her this way? What was wrong with him?

Alex shook him. "Hey. Hey! Are you listening? Do you know the answer to question seventeen?"

Tony didn't know the answer to that question, or to the next. The rest of the tech round went by without the Royal Quizzers getting a single answer. Tony wasn't even pretending to listen anymore. He filled the margins of his quiz notebook with spiral doodles and didn't lift his eyes from the page. At least he hadn't given Dalia the satisfaction of looking over and seeing him staring at her with all this hurt in him. She must be long gone by now, back to La Escarpa with her take-out order.

The quizmaster announced a five-minute break. Tony pushed his notebook and pencil away, straightened up—and saw Dalia standing right across the table from him, staring somberly at him and clutching her take-out bag.

Alex stood up. "I'm gonna go to the bar," he said.

He was on his way before he finished the sentence, leaving Tony and Dalia staring at each other in silence. Then Tony spoke.

"WHAT DO YOU WANT?"

There was a bite in Tony's voice that Dalia had never heard before, and his face looked hard.

"I— There's something I have to say to you," she said.

"Oh, yeah? Did you think of more things that are wrong with me? Why don't you make a list and stick it under my door? That way you don't have to look at me. That's what you said, isn't it? That you didn't want to look at me any longer than you had to?"

He ripped a page out of his quizzing notebook. "Here, I'll get you started with some of the things you said last time. *Idiotic. Infantile.* What else you got?"

His eyes were so cold. She'd seen him mad before, but not like this.

"Why are you being so combative?" she asked.

It was a dumb question, in light of how she'd treated him the last time they'd spoken, but she didn't know what else to say.

"Ooh, that's a good one." Tony wrote down *combative.*

This was going all wrong. "If you would just stop being so hostile, and listen to me—"

*"Hostile,"* Tony said, writing it down. "And *bad listener.* Also *not a real cowboy.* Oh, and let's not forget *unsafe driver with limited peripheral vision.*"

Dalia didn't know what to say. Was she really that critical and difficult a person? Was there anything she could possibly say now that wouldn't make things worse?

Well, yes. She could say *I'm sorry.*

Which, in retrospect, was probably what she should have led with.

"Tony, I—"

"Whatever it is, just don't. Please."

He didn't look cold anymore, just sad. "I can't do this anymore, Dalia. I'm keeping it together so far, but I am right on the edge, and I cannot afford to fall off. So whatever it is you think you have to say to me, just know that I've probably already said it to myself. I get it. I'm no good for you. Maybe I never was, or maybe things are too broken between us to ever be made right again. So please just walk away, and steer clear of me at the house, and let me finish my work, and after that we don't have to see each other anymore. Okay?"

Dalia's throat swelled, and her eyes stung.

*Things are too broken between us to ever be made right again.*

"Okay," she said, and walked away.

So much for Stage Three.

TONY DOWNED THE last of his beer and joined Alex at the bar.

Tito was there, polishing glasses with a soft white cloth, looking snazzy in his white shirt and black vest. Here was a man who took pride in his work.

"You okay?" Alex asked.

"Course I'm okay. Barkeep! Pour me some of that añejo tequila."

Tito nodded approvingly. "And for you?" he asked Alex.

Alex hesitated a second, then said, "Same."

It was a nice gesture. Tony knew Alex liked good tequila as much as he did, but the good stuff was not cheap, and Alex was a lot tighter with his dollars than Tony, so he didn't often indulge. It was a show of support, having a drink with his brother in his hour of need.

"Look, you don't have to worry," Tony told Alex. "I'm okay…more or less. And if

I was gonna get wasted, I'd do it on something cheaper than añejo."

Alex visibly relaxed. "Okay."

Tito took down the bottle and poured.

Tony picked up his glass. He swirled the golden liquid and watched the tears run slowly down the sides. Then he took a sip, swished it around his mouth for a few seconds and swallowed.

Tito chuckled.

"What's so funny?" Tony asked.

Tito pointed. "The two of you just sipped your tequila in exactly the same way, at exactly the same instant."

"How 'bout that?" said Tony, punching Alex on the shoulder. "I guess you are my brother after all."

"Yeah, who knew," said Alex.

"It makes me happy to see people drinking quality tequila, and drinking it the right way," said Tito.

"We get that from our dad," said Tony.

"No, we don't," said Alex. "I mean, yeah, we do, but only because he taught us. Not because there's, like, a tequila-sipping gene or something."

"How do you know there's not a tequila-sipping gene? I bet there is, and I bet you and me both have it."

"Actually," said Tito, "studies of identical twins separated at birth have indicated that there is a strong genetic component to a lot of weirdly specific nonphysical traits. Mannerisms, food preferences, stuff like that."

"There, see?" said Tony. "Tito agrees with me."

"Of course, that doesn't mean *all* of personality, or even physiology, is entirely due to heredity," Tito went on. "The nature-versus-nurture debate has been raging since ancient times, but modern scholarly consensus is that heredity and environment influence each other so inextricably that the dichotomy is meaningless."

"Ah, now you're just talking noise," said Tony.

Some other customers sat down at the end of the bar.

"If you gentlemen will excuse me," Tito said, and he glided over to wait on them.

"Too bad we can't get *him* on our trivia team," Alex said. "We'd kill it for sure."

"Seriously, though," said Tony. "What do *you* think?"

"What do I think about what?"

"Nature versus nurture. Which is more important?"

"Didn't you hear? Tito said it's a meaningless question."

"He has to say that. He can't take sides—he has to do his whole friendly-barkeep thing."

Alex took another sip of tequila. "Well, nature versus nurture isn't the whole story, is it? It can't be. What about hard work? That's the most important thing of all. Hard work can overcome a bad genetic package or make the most of a good one. It can help you rise above a not-so-good home life, too."

"But where does hard work come from?" said Tony. "Is it part of environment? 'Cause that's just another word for *nurture*. Or is it hardwired into your personality from birth? 'Cause that would make it part of nature. Which means it all comes down to the same thing."

"Mostly environment, I'd say. A solid work ethic comes from good home training. But there's more to it than just nature and nurture. There's got to be. They're both things that happen to you. There comes a point where you take a hard look at the hand you've been dealt and take charge. It's called growing up. I'm not saying the right attitude can overcome *anything*, but it can overcome a lot. We're not just at the mercy of all these forces beyond our control, whether it's genes or our personal history."

"Well, then that's a whole other thing, isn't it? A...whatever Tito called it—a dichotomy. Not just nature versus nurture, but fate versus free will."

Alex sighed. "I never thought I'd tell you this, brother, but you're overthinking."

"And what exactly *is* work, anyway? We've got to define our terms, right? Like, someone might say, 'I worked hard in football practice today,' but someone else might say, 'Well, *technically*, sports isn't work, it's play. Entertainment. You aren't really *working* unless you're producing something of value, like crops or livestock. Football isn't valuable, Tony. It's just a game.'"

"Well, I—"

Tony kept going. "And then the first someone might say, 'Oh, yeah? Who made you the authority on what words mean?'"

"Uh..."

"And the second someone might say, 'Don't take things so personally, Tony.' Well, you know what? It feels pretty personal to me."

Alex rubbed his chin. "Hmm. I feel like there are three people in this conversation. Or maybe just two, but I'm not one of them."

"Yeah, it used to be this whole thing between Dalia and me, during the first run of our relationship."

"I figured."

They sat in silence for a while. Then Tony said, "Okay, let's take you and me. We grew up in the same environment, but we turned out so different—tequila sipping aside. And that's got to be nature, right?"

"We didn't have the *exact* same environment. We had two major differences."

"Really? What were they?"

"Each other. By the time I was born, you were already there. You didn't have yourself for a big brother."

"Ohh, so that's what made the difference. I was like a cautionary tale to you. That's why you turned out better than me."

"What? No. Stop putting words in my mouth. I didn't turn out better, just different. Part of that is who we are, our basic personalities. Part of it is our history, which includes us interacting with each other. And part of it is what we choose to do with all that. You have to try. The world is full of people who have lots of abilities and opportunities but don't put them to good use. And there are just as many other people who don't have much but make the most of what they do have and succeed, anyway."

Tony swirled his tequila again. "Okay. But even if everyone's trying their hardest, someone still has to come out on top, right? Which means you might go all out and do your best and still fail, and then where are you? You didn't hold back, and you still weren't good enough. You just didn't have the stuff."

"But you can't live your life that way, keeping score. It doesn't work. Life's not a contest. There's always going to be someone better and there's always going to be someone worse, if you're looking for that, and the people who are better in some ways might be worse in others. You're never going to know enough of someone else's story to make the right judgment about it. And you're not responsible for any of that, anyway.

You've just got your own life, and you've got to make of that what you will."

"But—"

Alex turned, grabbed Tony by the shoulder and faced him head-on. "But nothing. Listen to me. It happened, okay? You took a dive off a hotel balcony and hurt your eye and ended your football career and your college career. But who's to say that's totally a bad thing? Life is about more than how much money you make and how famous you are. Would you really want to go back to being preaccident Tony? I'm not talking about the opportunities you had back then—I'm talking about the man you were. Think of everything you've learned, all the ways you've changed. You're humbler now. More compassionate. Preaccident Tony wouldn't be able to talk down belligerent drunks or comfort children the way you do in firefighting calls. He wouldn't be a volunteer firefighter at all. And who's to say that's not a truer calling for you? You're a builder now, too. Look at these two buildings that we renovated. We did that, you and me. Look at all the people who come here to eat and drink and hang out and relax. Maybe that was the goal all along, who you were meant to be. A guy who comforts people when they're hurt and rebuilds things when they break. Yeah, you might've gone on to have a long rewarding pro career if you'd never gotten hurt. But maybe not. You could've gotten hurt a lot worse in a game. You could've gotten mixed up in drugs and gone down the professional-athlete death spiral. You just don't know. And none of that matters because it isn't real. It's not out there like some alternate reality. This, here, today, is what you have. Good health overall. An honorable way to make a living that you're good at. People who care about you. A future. That's a lot. And you need to stop seeing it as second best."

Alex turned him loose and went back to his tequila.

*Things break. Sometimes they can be fixed, and sometimes they can't.*

And other times…

They can be made better than they were before.

Maybe.

"Hey, Tito," Tony said. "Close me out. I got something I need to do."

## *CHAPTER TWENTY-ONE*

THE WIND BLEW on Tony's face through the open truck window. He'd had barely three hours of sleep, but he'd done what he set out to do, and for the moment he was content. Over to the right side of the highway, the sky had that deep blue early-morning glow, with just a few stars that hadn't winked out. He had time. He'd get to La Escarpa before the crew, and work quietly by himself with nobody watching or getting in the way or asking questions. If he timed things right, he'd have everything ready before Dalia even made her first cup of tea, and he'd be alone with her just as the sun rose.

And then what? Would it work? Would it change her mind? Was there any hope for them, after all these years and everything that had happened?

He could still hear all the things she'd said to him, that night after the rodeo. She'd said she didn't want to have to look at him anymore, and since then, he'd done all he could to make sure she didn't have to. If the sight of his face was that sickening to her, well, then he'd keep it out of her sight.

Just like he'd kept out of her way after she'd sent his things back.

But he hadn't done all that for her sake, no matter what he'd told himself. He could see that now. It had been cowardly of him, hiding that way, pushing her into breaking up with him because he didn't have the guts to tell her the truth, and then burying himself under her rejection and letting his hurt and anger smolder underneath. Letting the gap between them get wider and wider with each year that went by.

But not this time. He wasn't going to go another six years without seeing or talking to her. He would own up to what he did and take the consequences. If he'd done that before—if he'd told the truth about the accident and thrown himself at her mercy—things might have been different. This time, he was going all in. She might not take him back, but if she didn't, at least he wouldn't have his own cowardice to blame.

The early-morning air felt good on his face. It had been a hot fall so far, getting up to ninety degrees most afternoons. A good rain might have cooled things off, at least for a while, but all the rain they'd had over the summer was long gone, and now the abnormally thick growth of a wet summer was drying out. Humongous thickets of sunflowers, some reaching as tall as eleven feet, lush and green just a few weeks ago, were withering into woody stalks as big around as the tailpipe on Tony's truck.

There was always a moment, whenever Tony was driving north on the highway, when the outlines of the trees on the horizon suddenly came into the shape that meant La Escarpa was just ahead. That mott of elms along the rise by the creek. That one half-dead cedar tree with the bare branches at the very top. That big ancient post oak with the rounded crown, head and shoulders above the rest. He'd been driving this highway for a decade now, and even through those years of not seeing Dalia, still he always had that special awareness every time he passed her home. He couldn't not notice.

This time, as he saw it, he saw something

else, over to the east. A warm, bright glow. But it wasn't the rising sun.

It was fire. In the grass beside the highway, in the ditch with the withering sunflowers and the dried grass and brush.

The wind was out of the south, as usual at this time of year when there wasn't a storm. There was no way to predict exactly what the fire would do, but most likely it would spread north and east…to La Escarpa.

Everything he knew about wildfire and how to fight it, and the layout and topography of La Escarpa—the position of the house and outbuildings, slope, fencing and where the cattle were currently being pastured—churned around in his mind.

He called Mad Dog. Then he did a U-turn and drove back the way he'd come.

DALIA HAD BEEN getting up at six in the morning for so many years now that she couldn't remember when she'd last slept in. Her morning routine was practiced and perfected to the point that she could go through the motions swiftly and smoothly without thinking. Regardless of what sort of upheaval might be going on in her life, personally or professionally, each day by a quarter to seven she was dressed and groomed with her bed made, ready to sit down with her first cup of tea.

Even the morning after the rodeo, with that lead weight of anger and disappointment inside her chest, she hadn't missed a beat in her routine.

It felt good to have something she could count on, a ritual she could perform with minimal mental energy. No matter how bad things might get, she was starting from a place of order and control.

She'd showered and dressed and had her work stuff ready to go in her room, all plotted out from last night, her bullet journal lying open beside her laptop and phone. All she needed now was that cup of tea.

With the kitchen still at loose ends, the electric kettle was camping in the living room, along with Dalia's tea things and her mother's coffee and French press. Dalia filled her latte mug with water, poured the water into the kettle and pushed the button down. The kettle began to hiss, softly at first and then louder. By the time its hard little click had sounded, she had the infuser filled with one slightly rounded teaspoonful of loose-leaf tea. She poured the steaming water over the tea leaves and set the mechanical timer. It started ticking away—a soothing sound.

By now, she could hear her mom moving around in her room.

"You want me to start some water for your coffee?" Dalia called out to her.

"Please," her mom answered.

She filled the kettle again and depressed the button.

Only then did she look out the big front-facing living room window.

She stood frozen for a moment, at first not understanding what she was seeing, and then not wanting to believe it.

"Hey, Mom?"

Her mom opened the door and came hobbling out. "Yes, sweetie?"

"I think we'd better call the fire department."

TONY DROVE SOUTH before turning left on Craddock Road and cutting across to Ybarra. Another left took him to the gate of the low acreage.

The gate was secured with a padlock, the

same one that'd been there since the days of Marcos's pasture parties, and the combination was Marcos's birthday. It was still fresh in Tony's mind from when he'd helped set up for the firefighter fundraiser.

The roadbed ended just a thousand feet or so past the gate, where the livestock trucks parked to load cattle, and where Marcos's friends used to set their tailgates down and open up their coolers. Beyond that, it was just cattle trails, too narrow for his truck.

Looked like he'd have to hoof it. He knew the way, but it'd be slow. A four-wheeler would be better, if one just happened to drop out of the sky right now, but even that would be a tight fit.

Then he saw something even better.

A beautiful sight.

A buckskin gelding, barely a football field's length away.

Buck was watching him, head high and alert, ears forward, like he remembered Tony and wasn't too impressed with him.

"I've ridden a bull," Tony said softly. "I can handle you."

Dalia's father used to have different calls for the stock. It was pretty cool, really. For cattle, he would plant his feet apart, throw his head back and let loose with a wild cry.

For Buck, he used a long, high, piercing whistle.

Buck flicked his tail, as if to say a punk like Tony could not possibly know how to whistle like that.

Tony raised both hands to his lips. For everyday cheering and crowd control, the one-handed circled-thumb-and-forefinger method was more than enough, but this situation called for the two-handed, middle-and-index-finger combo.

His whistle rang out across the low acreage and echoed back again.

And Buck came running.

Little puffs of dust kicked out behind his hooves. He covered the distance in a few seconds and came to a smooth stop. Tony bowed his head close to Buck's and ran a hand along his neck. Buck accepted this for a few seconds before whuffling and nudging Tony, like, *Dude, enough. Get on with it.*

He didn't have a lick of tack on him, but that couldn't be helped, and maybe it was all right. It'd been a while since Tony had ridden any horse, let alone his ex-girlfriend's horse that he had a not-so-great history with. Longer still since he'd ridden bareback. But once upon a time, he and Alex used to spend long summer twilights in the paddock at their grandparents' place, riding Suerte and Bizcocho—riding bareback, much of the time, because their grandfather thought it was a valuable exercise in horsemanship.

Tony used to be able to mount a bareback horse as easily as he could swing a leg over a bicycle, but that was a lot of years ago. Could he still?

He had to.

He grabbed a handful of mane just before the withers, gave a sort of skip, and let the momentum of his swinging leg carry his body up and over the horse's back. Partway up, he grabbed the withers with his other hand to pull his upper body into place.

He swung a little harder than necessary, and for a second there it looked like he'd keep right on swinging and come off Buck's other side. But he managed to correct, and then there he was, seated on that broad back exactly as he was supposed to be.

"All right, Buckleberry Finn," he said. "You've got a pretty good deal at La Escarpa. But if you want to keep it that way, if you want to have hay this winter and grass next spring, then we've got stuff to do."

No doubt all this amounted to only a bunch of *blah, blah, blah* in the ears of a horse, but Buck could feel the energy in the words. At least, that's what Tony hoped.

He clicked his tongue against the roof of his mouth, and they started.

There were two switchbacks leading down the scarp. One of them was pretty close to the house. The horse trail to his left would take him across the creek and then to the switchback, but first it made a big loop to the south and back again. What if he headed more or less straight west? There had to be cattle trails that way. Maybe not broad and clear like the horse trail, but if a cow could manage it, a horse could, too.

Buck was clearly not thrilled about leaving his nice familiar trail to plunge into a lot of scrub, but he went, and before long they met up with a decent cattle trail. It didn't used to be so brushy out here—Mr. Ramirez wouldn't like it. The mesquites were just tall enough that he couldn't see over them, even on horseback, and too densely spaced to pass between with any comfort or ease. The thin, thorny branches sprouted straight from the ground and scratched at his legs and Buck's sides.

*They ought to get a dozer back here and clear all this. Free up space for more hay or better grazing.*

He couldn't be sure he was heading the right way, but his gut told him he was. He hoped they didn't come across any rattlesnakes or feral hogs.

He kept going.

Then the way started opening up a little. The mesquites got bigger and farther apart, with limbs crossing overhead instead of three feet from the ground. Ahead, the horse trail Tony hadn't taken curved in from the left, joined another horse trail from the right, and disappeared into a thick tree line of oaks and elms maybe a quarter mile away. It meant Tony was right, and the crossing of the Serenidad Creek was straight ahead.

Maybe now they could make up some time. He urged Buck into a canter, and Buck obliged. No doubt he could see the horse trail, too, and was more than willing to leave the scrub behind.

Now that the way was clear and he knew he was going the right way, Tony started to enjoy the ride. It was a whole different sensation, riding bareback. A less secure seat, but also a better connection to the horse. Loose legs, open chest. He could feel the three smooth beats of the canter, over and over. Buck had a nice easy stride.

Tony's heart was light, weirdly enough. Once he crossed the creek and came out the tree line on the other side, he'd be able to see the fence. Maybe the cattle would be there already, away from the smoke and spreading flames. Then he could cut fence and they'd take it from there. He was no expert on wildland work, but he'd done enough to know that animals were pretty good at self-preservation if you helped them out a little.

He'd forgotten how much fun riding was. Why did he ever give it up?

An explosion of pain went off in his head. For a second it was like a fireworks show, and then everything turned black.

## *CHAPTER TWENTY-TWO*

DALIA SHUT OFF the propane at the tank behind the garage. She'd already put out all the pilot lights in the house.

From the other side of the fence, in the orchard, a voice called, "Here, chick chick chick! Come on, girls! Hurry up, now!"

"Mom! What are you doing out there?"

"I'm getting the chickens back in the coop!" her mom said, a bit tartly, as if this should be obvious.

"I could've done that."

"No, you couldn't. They're not used to you yet."

"Well, don't climb up the steps of the coop, anyway. The last thing we need is for you to fall and break your other foot. Let me shut them in."

"Okay, but hurry. And don't spook them."

Dalia went through the gate and shut the door behind the last chicken while her mom turned on the hydrant that watered the fruit trees with an underground irrigation system. That would wet the ground, though not the trees' foliage.

"Do we have sprinklers out here?" Dalia asked.

"No, but we should."

The machine shed stood on the other side of the orchard, just outside the back fence. That could be nasty in a fire, all those tanks and cans and bottles of gas and oil and chemical solvents, but it wasn't like there was anything that could be done about it now.

Next to the machine shed lay the former pumpkin patch, now shriveled into a mass of dried leaves and vines. Beyond that, the Sudan grass they'd used for the corn maze had been cut for hay but not baled, with the stalks and coarse leaves lying in raked golden-brown rows.

"Nice little fields of tinder we've got there," Dalia said, pointing. "At least the Bermuda grass is all put up in the feed barn."

"Which is worse, though, fire-wise?" her mom asked. "Rows of dried leaves and stalks lying on the ground, or combustible bales packed into a building?"

"Huh. Yeah, I don't know."

If the fire even reached the feed barn, it'd have to engulf the house first—assuming it moved steadily from south to north, which it seemed like it would, but who knew? It might circle around through the horse paddock and—

*The horse paddock.*

At present, there was no horse in the horse paddock. After the FFF, Dalia had noticed the grass in there was looking a little tired, so once the hay was in the barn, she'd turned Buck out into the hundred-acre hay parcel to feed on the tall stuff around the fence edges. The hay field made up the southernmost portion of the property, bordered by river and creek just outside its south and west fences, and by a road on the east. Which was all well enough, but she'd left the gate in the north fence open so Buck would have access to the creek for drinking. And *that* meant he could be just about anywhere in the hay field or the low pasture, in a total area of five hundred or so acres.

Where was he now? And where was the

fire? Would he make it to the creek? Would it protect him?

"I should go open the gate for the firefighters," she said.

"Do you think you should take the time?" her mom asked. "They do know the code."

"Yeah, but will the opener box even be working when they get there, or will the electronics be fried?"

"Oh, surely the fire's not *that* close yet."

Dalia didn't know. She couldn't see past the bend in the driveway, and she had no way of knowing how fast the fire was spreading or how far away it had been when she first saw the smoke.

Then her heart gave a sick lurch.

"The penned cattle," she said.

Before turning out Buck into the low acreage, she'd separated some steers from the rest of the herd and put them in the pen that ran alongside the scarp fence, between it and the driveway, in a short strip. From there they would be loaded up to go to market.

At least, that had been the plan. But if the fire reached them and they couldn't get away…

Her mother looked at her, eyes wide. Apparently she'd just remembered the same thing.

If only they'd waited one more day! Then the steers would be with the rest of the herd in the back hill pasture. They could cross the creek from there and continue to the upper corner of the pasture, where the fence could be cut from the road, if it came to that.

Instead, they were trapped.

She thought of the Bastrop fires. All that livestock, lost; all that property, destroyed. Years later, the land still hadn't recovered.

She could drive down to the pen, but that would mean going back to the house for her keys. Or she could try it on foot.

She started running.

Her mom called out something behind her, but she kept going. She rounded the bend in the driveway—

And saw a great cloud of smoke rolling up the scarp on her left.

She couldn't see the short end of the pen yet, but she knew the cattle must be pressed against it, desperate to get through—unless, of course, they'd been overcome already. But if they had, wouldn't she have heard them bellowing? For that matter, shouldn't they be bellowing now? The pen was just on her side of the scarp, and it wasn't very wide.

There wasn't time to reach them, but she kept running.

Then she heard the sound of sirens and saw the flash of lights through the smoke.

*Wait, what?*

That couldn't be right. There was no way they could have gotten here that soon. Her mom did say their response time was impressive, but this was ridiculous. Unless her perception of time was seriously messed up?

Well, who cared? They were here now.

An outrageously tricked out F450 emerged from the smoke and slowed to a stop beside her. One of the doors opened. The cab was crammed full of what looked like a lot of rugged, outdoorsy astronauts. Someone grabbed her arm and pulled her inside.

His face was covered by an apparatus—it looked like a protective clear shell over a breathing tube leading into a canister, topped with a hood and a helmet. All she could see of him was his freaky golden eyes. It was Alex.

He said something, but the words were too muffled to understand. Then he clicked a button on a device at his chest, and his voice, now weirdly amplified, came out of the device.

"Where's Tony?"

"How would I know?" said Dalia. "You just got here. You're the first batch I've seen."

He shook his head. "Tony was already out here. He's the one who first called in the fire."

*Oh. So that's how the department got here so fast.*

"Well, he didn't come to the house."

Even with only his eyes showing, Alex managed to express a lot. Exasperation, mostly, but also concern. "Dang it. The heck with tracking his phone—I ought to take him to the veterinarian and get him implanted with one of those GPS pet-tracking chips."

"When did he call it in?" Dalia asked. "How long has he been out here? Where'd he call from?"

By now the truck was pulling to a stop. Alex didn't answer her questions. He just said, "Look, *do not* do anything stupid. Okay? We've got enough work here as it is.

Do not make it worse. Do you understand me? Can I count on you?"

"Yeah. Sure."

She watched the firefighters get out of the truck in their bulky protective gear. She knew Alex was right. She had to stay put, let the firefighters handle things, not go out and try to do it herself and end up making more work for them. But this was her home, her heritage…her future. And on top of that, Tony was out there somewhere.

This was how Romelia felt, with her man gone, and the land she loved that she'd once thought the two of them would work together in danger.

And then…

She saw a figure through the smoke.

Not the ghost of a Revolutionary soldier and ranchero, but a real live, flesh-and-blood man in a graphic T-shirt and jeans.

Riding a horse. *Her* horse. Bareback.

*Tony.* He was cantering, and his seat was all it ought to be: tall in the body, with loose legs, open hips, open chest. When he reached her, he brought Buck to a halt with a subtle shift in body position and slid down.

His hair stood on end. The whites of his

eyes looked bright at first in his smoke-blackened face, but they were bloodshot, and blood covered one side of his face.

"Where's the herd?" he asked. His voice sounded rough with smoke.

"In the back hill pasture—except for some steers I put in the pen."

"The steers aren't in the pen anymore. I cut the fence at the scarp and they headed to the switchback lickety-split. They're in the low acreage now and on their way north. If we have to, we can cut the fence at Burr Oak Road and let 'em out there. The fire shouldn't cross the road."

Then he was gone again, on foot this time, so fast that she might have thought she'd imagined the whole thing, if not for Buck still standing there.

A big knot of dread and fear suddenly came untied inside her, leaving her weak-kneed. She held on to Buck, head whirling.

Romelia couldn't have been much more stunned by the appearance of Alejandro's ghost than Dalia was then.

THEY FELL FROM the sky, these perfectly formed leaves and grass blades made entirely out of ash. They came from the south, floating down out of a dirty haze as the wind kept pushing the smoke north. Whenever Tony touched one, it dissolved into grayish-black dust.

It was all over now, except for the cleanup and sitting on the structures just to be safe. Tony knew he ought to be done in, but his senses were dialed up and he felt fantastic, like after a game where he'd performed great and he'd won.

"Hey," he heard from behind him. Something caught in his chest at the sound of Dalia's voice.

He turned. "Hey, yourself," he said, trying to sound cool and calm, like he saved people's ranches every day.

She was looking at him funny. Not angry, but not quite Tony-I-love-you-I-need-you, either. More like his shirt was inside out.

He looked down at himself. His Texas graphic T-shirt had blood spilled all down one side.

"Oh, man! I really like this shirt. I need to go after it with some Oxi-stuff."

"I don't know how much that's going to

help. It has about a hundred little burn holes in it, too."

"Does it?" He pulled it out by the tail and studied it. "Huh, you're right. Really tiny ones. Well, dang."

"I think you might be focusing on the wrong thing here, Tony."

He wasn't looking at her, but he could hear the smile in her voice. He decided to play dumb.

"What do you mean?"

"I mean you've got a big gash on your forehead and there's blood all over your face."

She started to reach for him but seemed to change her mind partway through and pointed instead. He touched his head on the right and felt the swelling and the beginnings of a scab.

"Oh, right. I sorta got clobbered by a tree branch."

"It attacked you?"

"No—well, maybe. I didn't really see. But something definitely hit me, when I was riding the Buckster on the cattle trail. Probably I ran into it."

She nodded, like she was marking something off on a list. *Lack of peripheral vision on right side—check.*

"He was real good, Bucky was. Didn't run off or anything. I looked up afterward, like, instantly, and there he was, standing over me. I don't know how he even moved that fast."

"You mean the tree branch knocked you off the horse?"

"Yeah, but it wasn't bad."

"Oh, no. Just bad enough for you to black out and not come to until after Buck had time to turn around and saunter back over to where you were lying."

"Well, it couldn't have been too long. Otherwise..."

He saw the look on her face and finished up lamely, "Well, I'm alive, aren't I?"

"Seem to be. But I think we'll get you checked out, anyway."

Her voice was stern, but her face was another story. She actually took his arm and gently guided him, like he needed help, like he was hurt for real. It was sweet even though it wasn't necessary.

"Head injuries always look worse than

they are," he said. "It's because they bleed so much."

"Mmm, is that so? Well, sometimes they're worse than they look. Sometimes you can be walking around looking fine in the short term, when you're actually hurt—like when you smack the surface of a swimming pool with your face and your retina's getting ready to tear."

"Point taken."

SHE STEERED HIM over to where Mad Dog was set up, at the truck with the medical equipment. When Mad Dog saw Tony, his eyebrows shot up.

"What happened to you?"

Dalia answered for him. "He hit a tree branch while he was riding my horse and got knocked off."

"Actually, I'm not a hundred percent sure that's what happened," Tony said.

Mad Dog frowned. "You mean you don't remember?"

"I…didn't see it too well. But for sure something hit my head, and I did end up coming off the horse, so…yeah, that's probably what happened. But that was a long time ago. I've been running around doing lots of stuff since then."

"Oh, yeah, in that case you're fine for sure," said Alex. "It's not like a quarterback ever got right back up again after having his clock cleaned and went on playing for the rest of the half without anyone being the wiser that he had a screw or two loose."

"Have a seat," Mad Dog said, motioning to the camp chair. Tony sat, and Mad Dog started checking the wound.

"I don't understand about this horse," Alex said. "You say you found him in a pasture, got on and started riding?"

"Yeah, pretty much," Tony said.

"And he *let* you?"

"Letting had nothing to do with it," Tony said smugly. "With horses, it's all about your energy. You got to show them who's in charge."

He glanced at Dalia and smiled. She shook her head but smiled back.

After Mad Dog finished cleaning and dressing the wound, he said, "All right, bud. I want you to answer some questions for me. What is your full name?"

"Antonio Ignacio Reyes."

"And where are we?"

"La Escarpa."

"And who am I?"

Tony gave him a blank stare. "Seriously? I've never seen you before in my life."

The silence lasted three full stunned beats. Then Tony burst out laughing. "I'm just messing with you, man. I know who you are. You're the coach. No, you're Batman. No, wait! *I'm* Batman!"

"I'm going to put you in a neck brace right now if you don't cooperate," Mad Dog said.

"Okay, okay. Your name is Malcolm McClain, but everyone calls you Mad Dog, and I really don't know why, because you're, like, the most mild-mannered guy I know. And you're the fire chief."

He did fine at the motor tasks Mad Dog gave him. But when Mad Dog shined a penlight in Tony's eyes, his expression changed. "Okay, something's wrong. One of your pupils is not dilating."

"Oh, that's okay," said Tony. "I mean, it's not from hitting my head. That pupil already didn't work right."

"Oh? Why's that?"

"'Cause I have no vision in that eye."

Everyone within earshot—Wallace, Andy, Samantha—turned around. Suddenly Tony was the center of attention.

"I, uh, had an accident to my eye," Tony said. "And the long and short of it is, I now have a primary macula-off retinal detachment."

"When did this happen?" Andy asked.

"'Bout six years ago."

There was a brief pause, long enough for everyone to do the math, and then, almost in unison, they all gave a slight nod, as if to say, *Ah, that explains a lot.*

"So you can't see the big E anymore, huh?" asked Mad Dog.

"Nope. I'm down to 'no light perception' in that eye."

"Well, then. No wonder your pupil doesn't dilate."

"Did anyone else know about this?" asked Wallace.

"First I heard of it," said Samantha.

"Me, too," said Andy.

"Well...now you know," said Tony.

"I already knew," said Alex in an aren't-I-special voice.

"So did I," said Dalia.

Mad Dog put the penlight away. "All right, then. Take it easy the next couple days. Try to get plenty of sleep and avoid caffeine. And it'd be a good idea to get yourself checked out by a doctor. If you experience any dizziness or balance problems, nausea, mental confusion, anything like that, get medical attention right away. And maybe stay away from ladders and power tools for a while."

"You know I'm a builder, right?"

"What you are now, is on temporary leave," said Alex. "So you can sleep in and lounge around the apartment."

"Speaking of work," said Dalia, "how'd you come to be out here so early this morning? You and the crew don't generally show up until eight or so. If you were the one who called the fire in, you had to be way ahead of your usual time. What were you doing?"

Tony's eyes widened. He raised his hands to the sides of his head and groaned. "Oh, man. Oh, *man*. My timetable's all messed up."

He stood, took Dalia by the arms and looked into her face. "Look, Dalia, just—just wait here, okay? I'll be back. Actually, no. Go inside and wait there. And don't look out the windows. I gotta go get my truck. Will you do that for me? I'll tell you when you can come out. Okay?"

It was not okay at all. She could think of half a dozen questions right off the bat. But she swallowed them all down and said, "Okay."

He gave her a quick smile, and then he was off, calling, "Hey, can somebody gimme a ride?"

## *CHAPTER TWENTY-THREE*

SHE WENT AHEAD and drank that cup of tea, though by now it was stone cold. To sit inside and wait, in the aftermath of a fire at La Escarpa, when there was stock to check and fence to mend and cleanup to be done, and Tony being all mysterious with yet another surprise, went against every instinct she had. In fact, she wasn't sitting at all; she was pacing around the living room.

Just how long was this going to take? What was Tony *doing*? She could hear his voice out on the porch, and Alex's, too, but she couldn't make out the words, and she didn't peek. She'd drawn the living room shades first thing; the newly installed kitchen and dining room windows were already covered with brown paper in anticipation of painting. *Canyon Dawn*—that was the paint color her mom had chosen. Dalia loved how it looked against the exposed stone wall—pale and soft and restful. She loved the new cabinets, and the granite countertops from Marble Falls, and the reconfigured master bath and closet, and the old fireplace in the master bedroom left over from when the room used to be the detached kitchen, and the exterior with its walnut lintels and new masonry that blended perfectly with the old, just like Tony said they would.

The front door opened. Tony stood there, his face eager and excited.

Then he said, "Oh, sorry," and shut the door.

And knocked.

She chuckled and opened the door.

He'd taken the time to spiff up since she'd seen him last. Most of the smoke was wiped off his face, and his hair looked recently finger-combed. Some bright spirals of fresh sawdust were caught in the hairs of his forearms. He looked as formal and nervous as he had eight years ago when he'd picked her up for their first official date.

"Close your eyes," he said.

Marcos used to say that to her when they were little. *Open your hand and close your eyes and you will get a big surprise.* And, boy, was that the truth. Marcos had put a lot of surprising stuff in her innocently outstretched hand—grub worms, cicada shells, fuzzy caterpillars, grasshoppers—before she wised up and realized she didn't have to go along with it. Twenty years later, she was still suspicious of surprises. Clearly it was all Marcos's fault that she had trust issues.

She closed her eyes.

Tony took her hand, but he didn't put anything in it, just led her slowly, carefully, out the front door and along the porch to the left. It was actually pretty comical, how slow and careful he was.

At last he stopped.

"Okay. You can look."

She opened her eyes.

Hanging in the corner of the front porch, just off the new kitchen, was a new porch swing.

But no, not quite new. And not quite old.

She walked over. It was the exact shape and size of the old one, but the wood was a mix of finishes: peeling paint, weathered cedar, bright new lumber.

Then her breath caught.

Running along the top, right where Tony

used to rest his arm when they sat there together with her head on his shoulder, was a worn board with words carved into it.

*Tony loves Dalia.*

She put a hand to her mouth.

"The old swing got busted up pretty bad," Tony said. "Your mom actually said I should burn it. But there was a lot of good stuff there that I thought was worth saving. So I rebuilt it. I used the old pieces for templates and salvaged all the old wood I could—house siding, window trim, porch boards—and filled in the rest with new lumber. I think it looks all right."

She smiled at the false modesty. "It looks perfect, and you know it."

He smiled, too. "Yeah."

"When did you do all this?"

"Last night."

"Last *night*?"

"It wasn't *that* hard. I had all the materials in the garage me and Alex rent, under the apartment. I'd saved a lot of the weathered stuff to take to that Architectural Treasures place in town, but I just couldn't bring myself to hand it over. So once I got the idea, I had all the materials and tools right there, and I knew what I was doing. And when I'd finished, I caught a few hours of sleep, then loaded up the swing and headed out. I wanted to get here early, ahead of the crew, and get the swing put up, and see you alone, and...apologize. But then I saw the fire and things took a detour."

"That's why you were here so early? To do this?" She swallowed hard over a lump in her throat. "Tony, if you hadn't come...if you hadn't seen the fire when you did, and called it in, and acted so fast to move the stock..."

She couldn't finish, couldn't bear to think of what might have happened.

"That's true, isn't it?" he said. "I hadn't realized."

"Yes, you had."

He grinned. "Yeah. I had."

Then he said, "Did you, uh, did you see the board on top?"

She laughed, a little shakily. "Yes. Yes, I saw."

He leaned over toward the swing and swept a hand under the words in an exaggerated flourish.

"There's writing on it," he said. "See? *Tony loves Dalia.*"

"I see."

Why did she have to say it like that, all dry and flat? What was wrong with her that she always got so tongue-tied at times like this? She knew how cold it made her sound. But the truth was that sometimes she felt so much that none of the words she could think of were enough.

Tony put his hands in his pockets, looking nervous again. Probably she'd been giving him a full-on death glare.

"It's true," he said. "I know I've let you down a lot. But I love you, Dalia. I never stopped. Look, I…I want to explain about why I rode the bull."

"You don't have to—"

"Just listen, okay? I guess it started when we were at the FFF, and I was kinda down because I couldn't land the football as well as I used to, and—for other reasons, too. And then I rode Mr. Mendoza's mechanical bull. And it felt so good to perform well at something like that, it was like I was young again and my vision didn't matter and I could still do things. And it made me remember that other time, at the little rodeo, when you were there and you saw me ride, and...I wanted you to feel that way about me again."

How did he *do* that? He didn't second-guess; he just said what he felt and didn't worry how it would sound.

She wasn't like that, and she never would be. But maybe she didn't need words.

She took both his hands and kissed them. His fingers opened up and cupped her face.

And standing there with her head bowed and her eyes shut, feeling him but not looking at him, she found some words after all.

"I do feel that way about you, Tony. I always have. And as far as you wanting to feel young again—look, you're twenty-six, okay? You're not exactly over the hill. You're still an amazing athlete. And you're a firefighter, which I would think would be enough risk and excitement for anybody. But you're not me. You crave things like that. That's who you are. You like taking chances. And if you want to keep riding, I'll try not to be scared. That's why I got mad, because I was scared. I don't always think straight where you're concerned. I get so scared of losing you that I don't even know who I am sometimes. I shouldn't have said all those things to you that night."

"It's okay."

"It's not okay. Let me say this. I was wrong. I let my fear make me controlling and mean, just like you said. I want to stop that. I don't know how, but I've got to. I've got to let you be who you are. I know that. But you're going to have to be patient with me, okay?"

He ran his thumbs along her cheekbones. "Let's just be patient with each other."

She knew he was going to kiss her, but he took his time about it, moving so, so slowly. There was time to savor everything—the smell of smoke and sawdust, the light pressure of his hands on her face, the ends of his hair tickling her forehead. She could feel how his breathing sped up, and still he went slow, his lips just brushing hers.

And then she couldn't wait any longer. She slid her hands behind his head and drew him to her.

Applause burst out from somewhere, but she didn't care. Tony's arms gathered her up, holding her tight and turning her away a little, putting his back between her and the crowd, like he could shut out the world. The applause got louder, with cheers and whistles. Now Dalia was laughing, and she could feel Tony laughing, too. He pressed his lips to her forehead.

"You know, there's still plenty of work to be done out here," Alex's voice called.

"I'm officially off work," said Tony. "I'm concussed, remember? I'm supposed to be resting."

"Yeah, not sure that counts as resting."

Tony led Dalia over to the porch swing, settled into the corner and pulled her down next to him like he used to do.

"How's this?" he called.

"Better," said Alex.

Dalia leaned back against his chest. It felt so perfect and right, sitting here with him, with the front hill pasture spread out before them and the steeple of the old Baptist church shining white out of the trees across the highway.

"I'll go to Philadelphia if you want," he said.

The words seemed to come from nowhere, stirring Dalia out of a reverie about the shape of his hand as it rested against the porch swing's top board.

"What?" she asked.

"You know, to live. If you want. I know we talked about you maybe spending more time down here, and maybe moving here, but if you'd rather go back to the city, I'd be down for that."

He sounded brave and sacrificial, like he'd volunteered to go to a remote and desolate foreign land.

She smiled and nestled deeper against him. "I would love to see you in Philadelphia, with your Texas T-shirts and your boots. There's a lot there that I want to show you. But when you do come, it'll be to help me move back home."

She felt him straighten up behind her. "Seriously? You're doing it? You're coming home to stay?"

"Yes, I am. My mom wants to move to town, and I…I want to take over La Escarpa."

"Wow. Wow! I just… Wow. That's great news. You, uh, you need a good hired man?"

"Why? You know any?"

"Oh, yeah. I know this one guy, he can call

a horse out of a pasture and ride him bareback and get all the cattle to safety when the ranch is on fire. He can ride a bull, too, but he's retired from that. Well…semiretired. He doesn't have great peripheral vision or depth perception, but he knows this ranch real well, and he's got outrageous carpentry skills."

"Yeah? Sounds like I ought to bring that guy in for an interview."

"He's ready to start whenever you say."

She draped her arm over his along the back of the swing and laced their fingers together.

"Well, then you can tell him he's hired."

# *EPILOGUE*

*One and a half years later...*

TONY CLOSED THE grill and breathed deep of the meaty, smoky wave of scent that came wafting out. Just one minute more, and the two-inch rib eyes from La Escarpa Brahmas would be done to perfection.

He shut his eyes and stood still, listening. An insect was making a steady *tick-tick-tick*, and a woodpecker added a *rat-tat-tat* once in a while. The gobble of a wild turkey floated up from somewhere in the back hill pasture.

He moved the steaks to the platter and tented them with foil, added the potatoes and asparagus in their foil packets from the warming rack and covered the whole thing with a weighted mesh dome in case the barn cats made a dash for it while his back was turned. Calypso was already on high alert, rubbing his ankles like crazy. She was always superfriendly whenever he grilled.

He heard Dalia coming from a long way off, making plenty of noise so she wouldn't startle him. It was a genius system.

He turned his head a little and nodded so she'd know he'd heard her. She came the rest of the way quietly, slipping her arms around him from behind and laying her head against his back.

He covered her arms with his hands. "Hey, you."

"Hey, yourself. Something smells amazing. Are the steaks ready?"

"They're resting. We'll give 'em a few minutes more. How's the flan?"

"Chilled and ready to serve. You know, I love watching you grill. You're so artistic about it, the way you move around and squint at the meat and touch it with your finger and dab at it with the tongs. You look like a painter or a sculptor or something."

"I *am* an artist, aren't I?"

"Mmm-hmm. And a work of art yourself."

"Oh, yeah? Well, just think how good I'd look if I had my nice grill setup in between the two wings of the house, with the flagstones and the firepit and the stone benches and the grapevine trellis overhead. I haven't forgotten that, you know."

"Oh, I know. And I'm sure it'll look marvelous. But I think it's already pretty nice the way it is. And anyway, the Reyeses have enough going on without starting a new project, besides being too cash poor at present to buy the materials."

He grinned. "The Reyeses. That's us. You and me."

"I know it is."

They carried the food to the outdoor table, already set with turquoise plates and a glass bowl filled with clusters of little pink roses from the antique rosebush.

He took her hand. "Happy anniversary, Mrs. Reyes."

TONY HALF SAT, half lay in his Adirondack chair, long legs stretched out and crossed at the ankles, a cushion stuffed behind his head. One hand lightly caressed Dalia's arm; the other rested on his perfectly flat abs. Beyond them, the house's shadow crept past the yard fence into the pasture.

"Place looks pretty good, huh?" he asked.

"Sure does," she said. She liked hearing the pride of possession in his voice.

"It's nice how it all came full circle, isn't it?"

"How what came full circle?"

"This place. We're both of us descended from Alejandro Ramirez, and now here we are, reuniting the different branches of the family and all. It's kinda poetic."

"Antonio Reyes. Are you saying you married me for my property?"

"No way! I married you for your looks. I'd have followed you to Philadelphia if that's what it took, and you know it. But I'm glad things worked out the way they did. I never thought I'd end up a rancher, but it sure feels right."

"Do you miss living in town, though? The gym, the bar, Trivia Thursday, all that?"

He turned his sleepy-eyed face toward her and smiled. "Nah. I thought I might a little, all the noise and activity. But there's lots going on in the country, if you know to look for it. And as far as Trivia Thursday goes, it's not like I'd be playing anyhow, with my team all busted up. Alex doesn't have time for trivia anymore, or money for beer."

Alex and Tony's grandmother had died last spring, and almost overnight, their grandfather went from proud self-sufficiency to needing help with almost every aspect of ranch work and personal business. It would've been nice if Carlos had stepped up to help, but he went into a tailspin of gambling, hard living and brushes with the law that made everything worse. Tony helped all he could, but by then he was deep in wedding prep, besides laying down new fencing and putting up new outbuildings at La Escarpa, and most of the burden fell on Alex. After finishing their current contracts, the brothers agreed it'd be best to lay off new building-for-hire projects until things calmed down.

So Reyes Boys Construction was shelved for now. Alex kept working for Manny doing auto and tractor repair and got a second job at Architectural Treasures.

Then in October, their grandfather died, and once the dust was settled and the will was read, it turned out that in spite of everything he'd promised for years, in spite of basic decency and common sense, their grandfather had left everything, the ranch and the money, to their dad. It was a hard blow, especially to Alex. Right away he contested the will, which kept things tied up so Carlos couldn't take immediate possession and sell the place, but also meant the cattle still had to be looked after, which meant more work for Alex.

"Any news with the probate?" Dalia asked.

"Nope. Claudia doesn't seem real hopeful. Says it's more a stalling tactic than anything. The longer things drag out, the more chance there is for Dad to do the right thing and cut Alex in—or at least sell him the house and home pasture."

"No way could Alex afford that."

"I know, but he won't listen. He's all obsessed with earning and saving money now. The only thing he does for fun is that historical reenactor group, which sounds exhausting, like another job. If he met a good woman he might wise up and get his priorities straight, but how could we possibly arrange *that*?"

She gave him a sidelong glance.

"What are you plotting, Tony? You've got

that crafty look on your face. Are you thinking of matchmaking for your brother?"

"Who, me? I would never—"

"Yes, you would."

"Okay, yeah, I would. It's just, I was thinking, you know, now that your sister's back in the area..."

Dalia sat bolt upright. "Oh, no. No no no no no."

"What? Why no? I thought they looked real good together at the wedding."

"That is no basis for a relationship. Eliana's all wrong for Alex. Seriously, Tony, do not try this."

"Well, okay. I won't if you really don't want me to. But I thought it'd be nice. My brother, your sister."

"Are you kidding? That's the worst thing about it. It's bad enough she's cycled through so many romantic relationships in her life, from high school on. Her exes are *everywhere*. Do you have any idea how many men I have to avoid at the grocery store? It's a minefield. But *Alex*? I can't avoid him, he's family. If Eliana broke Alex's heart—well, it would break *my* heart, that's all."

"Aw, that's sweet. But maybe she wouldn't

break his heart. She's got to settle down sometime."

"Does she? Because I sure don't see any signs."

"Well, you gotta admit, she did a good job as maid of honor."

That was true. Dalia would've rather had Lauren—not that Lauren was such a practical person, either. But if Lauren was an attendant, she couldn't take pictures. And there really wasn't anyone else Dalia could ask.

"She did. She really rose to the occasion. I never knew she had it in her. When she gave that beautiful toast at the reception, I actually thought she'd grown up at last. But then that gaggle of adoring guys started swarming her, and it was back to business as usual. And now she's living just an hour away? I'm not sure how I'll like that."

"Don't write her off. I think she'll surprise you yet."

She smiled at him. "You're probably right."

She started stacking their dishes to take to the kitchen, but he took her hand and pulled her toward him. "Why don't you come over here for a while and share my chair? The dishes can wait."

He made room for her, and she slid into the chair alongside him. He still had scratches on his arms from the mesquite stump he'd taken out of the Angoras' pasture; she traced them with her fingertips.

Then she heard what sounded like a vehicle coming down their driveway.

"Who's coming? Are you expecting someone?"

Tony shot out of the chair like a clay pigeon from a target launcher. "It's nobody! I mean, it's just Alex."

"You invited your brother out for our first wedding anniversary?"

"No. He won't be here long. Don't look at him! And don't take the dishes to the kitchen yet. I'll handle Alex. You just sit back down and don't move. And close your eyes."

"Close my eyes? How long is this going to take?"

"Not long. Just do it, okay? Please."

"Oh, all right. I'm not about to say no to a good excuse to put my feet up and rest awhile, after the year we've had."

It really had been one thing after another,

and for more like a year and a half—first the kitchen rebuild at La Escarpa, then updating the little house in town for Dalia's mom to move into, then hurry, hurry, hurry to cull through a household's worth of stuff accumulated by seven generations of the same family living in the same house. Then off to Philadelphia to clear out her apartment and tie up loose ends, and back to Texas again to move into the house.

A visit to Ray and Syndra's place to see their herd and setup and pick their brains was followed by a cattle sale, right in the thick of wedding planning. Then the wedding itself, one gorgeous day in May, and a weekend honeymoon on the River Walk. Back home, they hit the ground running—prepping for the goats, buying breeding stock, building the shear shed and the kidding shed, making hay. Then came the firefighter fundraiser, and suddenly the Angoras' coats were a mass of long spiral curls, ready for shearing—the first shearing at La Escarpa in decades, and Dalia's first ever. No sooner were the shearers paid and the fleeces bagged, labeled and sent off to the mill than a breakneck holiday season commenced, followed by *another* shearing and their first kidding season.

She kept her eyes shut, but she could hear the Angoras chuckling and bleating to each other in their enclosure to the south, beyond the orchard and chicken yard. The babies were all weaned now, and the herd's coats were fluffing up again. She and Tony finally had a chance to catch their breath, but it wouldn't last long.

"Okay. I'm back."

She could hear the hushed excitement in his voice and the sound of Alex's truck engine fading away. She opened her eyes.

Tony stood just off the back corner of the house. Sitting beside him was a black-and-white, midsize dog with an alert, eager, intelligent face, perked ears and feathered front legs.

"This is High Ridge Durango, from High Ridge Kennel," Tony said. "He's one year old."

"He's ours?"

"He's yours. We just doubled the size of the goat herd with the kidding, and I figured it was time."

The dog watched her with keen eyes, his

sensitive ears flicking and quivering. She itched to pet him, hug him, roll around with him and give him belly rubs, but he was a working dog and she had to start their relationship off right.

"Durango, come."

He trotted over, closing the space smoothly, with minimum lifting of the feet, all essential in a border collie gait.

But one essential thing was missing.

"Where's his tail?" she asked—like it had been misplaced, like Tony had forgotten it somewhere, somehow. Which was exactly how it felt. A tail was a vital part of the overall border collie package—a long lovely plumy tail, hooked at the end like a shepherd's crook, held low when the dog was working, held high in play, sweeping from side to side in polite wags. All Durango had was a stump, barely enough to wag.

Tony put his hands in his pockets. "Um, yeah, about that. He's a good dog, good genetics and aptitude, but...he had an accident. Not that the breeders were negligent, but, you know, stuff happens. The kennel property backs up to a cattle ranch, and Durango slipped through the fence one day when he was a puppy, and a Hereford stepped on his tail. And the long and short of it is, they had to dock his tail. They said it shouldn't affect his performance, but it did affect his price. That's why he's full-grown and hadn't found a home yet. It's also how I was able to afford a dog from High Ridge. He's a bargain dog."

*A bargain dog.*

Well, that was a valid consideration. Between buying the Angora herd and putting up all the new fencing and outbuildings, the Reyeses weren't exactly flush with cash. But was that really the motive here? Dalia was the frugal one. Tony was extravagant, especially when it came to buying things for his wife. Maybe price wasn't the only reason he'd decided on this dog.

Tony shuffled his feet. "Is…is that okay?"

She sank her hands into the silky fur of Durango's ruff; she rubbed his throat, his ears. "It's perfect. He's perfect. You're perfect."

He grinned. "You're gonna have a great time teaching him, I know. He's had some preliminary training, but there's plenty left for him to learn, and he'll learn it from you, with our herd, on our ranch."

She took Durango through some commands. He obeyed perfectly, eagerly, never taking his eyes off her.

"Look at that," Tony said. "He knows he works for you even though he just met you. I told him so when I picked him out. I said, 'You're gonna be Dalia's dog. You know that, right?' And he looked at me and wagged his stump tail, like he did know."

"He'll work for you, too."

"Nah, not really. I'm just the hired man. You're the foreman."

She kissed him.

"Thank you. Now I have something for you, too."

"Is it a firepit?"

She reached behind the back cushion of her chair and took out a package not much bigger than a deck of cards. "What do you think?"

Durango settled down by Dalia's chair. She scratched behind his ears. Tony unwrapped the tissue paper to reveal a onesie with a Texas map.

He froze. His head was lowered so she couldn't see his face, just that ridiculously good head of hair. Then he looked up, eyes round.

"Is this…" He cleared his throat. "Just to be clear, is this a down-the-road kind of thing?"

"About eight months down the road."

"Are you serious? How is that possible?"

"Uh…"

"You know what I mean. We *just* started trying. And you said we had, like, a fifty-fifty chance of conceiving in the first year without birth control. That's what you said."

"Well, I don't know what to tell you. I conceived."

She was getting a little concerned. He looked so stunned.

Then he made a dive at her, gathered her up in a clumsy hug and said, "Good job!"

"Thanks! I can't take all the credit."

"Man, we got to get in gear. So much to do and just eight months to do it. I'm gonna get the Reyes family cradle from my grandparents' house. They never actually gave it to my dad, because it's a family heirloom from Spain and they were afraid he'd sell it for cash. But me and Alex both slept in it whenever we visited, when we were babies."

Dalia took the dishes inside while Tony cleaned the grill. Then they took their usual evening walk around the place, stopping to put the chickens in their coop for the night. Durango went along. He left the chickens alone—turned his head away like he was deliberately shunning them—and eyed the goats with professional interest. Tomorrow Dalia would start working with him.

The heat of the day had gone, leaving a lovely twilit coolness. It felt natural to come back to the house by way of the front porch. Calypso was curled up in the porch swing, fast asleep. She was getting a little old for the rigors of barn cat life. Dalia might just make a house cat of her soon. A skinny gray tabby watched Calypso from the porch rail, as if he'd like to join her on the swing but didn't think he'd be welcome. He was a new arrival at La Escarpa and hadn't quite found his place yet.

*But I have*, Dalia thought.

* * * * *

## COMING NEXT MONTH FROM

# HARLEQUIN HEARTWARMING

Available March 9, 2021

### #367 SECOND CHANCE COWBOY

*Heroes of Shelter Creek* • by Claire McEwen

Veterinarian Emily Fielding needs help with her practice, but she refuses to hire Wes Marlow, who left town and broke her heart years ago. Can Wes win back her love if he convinces her he's home to stay?

### #368 THE DOCTOR AND THE MATCHMAKER

*Veterans' Road* • by Cheryl Harper

Naval surgeon Wade McNally has a plan: date the perfect woman and build a perfect family. But charmingly unpredictable Brisa Montero catches his eye, and she's always been great at ruining plans...

### #369 THE SOLDIER'S UNEXPECTED FAMILY

by Tanya Agler

When Aidan Murphy shows up to take guardianship of his nephew, he doesn't expect to find that Natalie Harrison has already accepted the position! And neither of them has any intention of quitting the job.

### #370 A WYOMING HERO

*Eclipse Ridge Ranch* • by Mary Anne Wilson

For Quinn Lake, following tech CEO Seth Reagan to a ranch was purely business, but a case of mistaken identity gives her a reason to stay—and after learning to love again, Quinn can't imagine leaving.